HITLER'S FINGER

The Sam Harris Series

Book 2

PJ SKINNER

First edition

ISBN 978-1-9996427-0-9

Cover design by Self Publishing Lab

Berlin April 1945

The two officers shared a cigarette and stared into the ruins of the Third Reich. The broken silhouettes of bombed buildings and piles of rubble stood out against the iron-grey sky. It had been a cold hard spring and the two men struggled to hide from the north wind which blew through the gaps in the houses. Monotonous shelling pounded the suburbs, increasing in intensity as the guns approached the centre of Berlin.

Dr Kurt Becker flinched when a deafening explosion shook the ground, shifting on his feet and looking around for cover. *Too late to back out now*. He took a deep drag on his cigarette and passed it to his companion, an SS sergeant, a veteran of the Winter War. Both men wore battered greatcoats pulled tight over their black uniforms, and black leather boots, still polished out of habit. Clearing his throat, Becker spat on the ground and ground it in with his heel. He forced himself to speak.

'The Führer is going to kill himself.'

A coughing fit broke the shocked silence that followed this revelation, as the other man choked on the strong smoke from the cheap tobacco. Handing back the cigarette, he shook his head in denial.

'Don't be absurd. That's blasphemy. What if someone heard you? Anyway, why would he do that?'

'Reichsfuhrer Himmler offered a surrender to the Western Allies without consulting the Führer. Betrayal by one of his closest colleagues, combined with the fact that the Russians are less than a kilometre away, has made him lose heart.'

'I hadn't realised quite how close they were. No wonder he's a broken man.'

'He suffered a nervous collapse last week. I had to pump him full of drugs to get him back on his feet again.'

'What are we going to do?'

'There's nothing we can do. We're powerless to stop him. The war is over. He doesn't want to fall into Russian hands.'

'Christ, imagine what they would do to him. It doesn't bear thinking about.'

'Look what they did to Mussolini and his wife. The Führer was horrified. They will desecrate his body too.'

'Why doesn't he flee? He still has time to escape.'

'Where could he go without being captured? Anyway, he refuses to leave the bunker. We should plan for the future.'

'What future? Haven't you just told me that there's no future?'

'I've an idea, but it sounds a little crazy. You'll have to trust me.'

'We live in crazy times. What are you going to do?'

'Dr Haase, Hitler's personal physician, is away so,

as his deputy, I will inspect the Führer's body to confirm he's dead before they burn it. Can you prevent anyone from entering?'

'Why?'

'I need one of his fingers.'

CHAPTER I

London, September 1988

The telephone rang just as Simon insinuated his hand between Sam's thighs. She avoided the consequences of pushing it away when the ringing of the telephone shattered the silence with its shrill insistence.

'Really?' he said, whipping his hand away in fury. 'Who on earth would ring at this time of night? It's a bloody liberty.'

A rhetorical question. Only one person they knew rang with no regard for the time difference.

'Don't worry. I'll get it in the kitchen.'

She slipped out of bed and into her dressing gown, pulling the cord tight around her waist, guilty for the relief which flooded her body at escaping Simon's attentions. The tiled hall was cold under her feet and she shivered. She fumbled for the door handle to the kitchen in the dark hall for several seconds before encircling the cool ceramic globe in her grasp. She entered, shutting the door behind her, uncertain whether she needed to keep her conversation private or to let her companion sleep. The phone stopped ringing as she reached for the receiver.

She put the kettle on and waited for it to boil, leaning against the counter and reading the postcards on the fridge door. Steam escaped from the spout and flooded the cold air. As she poured the bubbling water over the tea leaves, the telephone began to ring again. Through the kitchen door she could hear Simon swearing.

'Hello?'

'Sam? It's me, Gloria. Are you awake?'

Gloria's husky voice crackled down the line. Sam smiled at the question.

'I am now. Is this a social call? It's three o'clock in the morning here.'

'Alfredo's missing.'

'Missing? In what sense?'

As an inveterate alcoholic, Alfredo was notorious for going AWOL from his life. *Why was this any different?*

'Disappeared. He left for the mountains to search for some Nazis with a gringo journalist and they didn't come back.'

Sam ignored the reference to the Nazis as being an exaggeration planted to excuse the hour.

'But didn't you stop seeing him?'

'We're back together. We couldn't bear to be apart.'

Sam thought of Simon waiting in her bed. Who was she to judge?

'And your father? What has he said about this?'

'I haven't told him. He'd be angry if he knew I was seeing Alfredo again and wouldn't give me any more money. That's why I phoned you. You're my only true friend. I need your help to find them.'

Gloria was being sincere about their friendship. The two women had formed a close bond following their first brush with adventure in the jungles of Sierramar. They were both fearless under their different facades and shared a Derring-Do and a sense of the ridiculous

5

that led to a similar outlook on life. And Sam was bored. She had just finished reviewing an interminable and over-worthy feasibility study of a coal mine in a safe jurisdiction with good logistics that never used one word where six or seven would do. Eight hundred pages of excruciating Germanic efficiency.

A sensible person would have stayed in London and searched for more work but she needed adventure. People made too many comments suggesting she ought to settle down now *that phase* of her life had finished. As if she had been partying and drinking instead of working at a respectable career.

Now she had the ideal excuse for an escape. Alfredo had probably gone off on a bender somewhere and would surface looking exhausted and sheepish, but what if something had happened to him? It was tempting to find out.

'Sam? Are you still there?'

'Yes, I'm still here. So, what'll I bring you from London, besides tea?'

'You're coming?'

'Yes, I'll come. I fancy an adventure. Can you guarantee that?'

'Oh yes, you can count on it.'

'Okay, I'll try to find a cheap flight. I'll ring you when I have the schedule.'

'Thank you.'

'Hey, what are friends for?'

'Is Simon with you?'

'Goodnight, Gloria.'

Sam hung up before Gloria launched into an unsubtle interrogation about her sex life. It would keep. She wouldn't explain her ill-advised decision to take Simon back at that hour of the morning. Or at any hour. It was like putting on a pair of shoes that had blistered her feet the last time she wore them. The pain they had caused her the last time she walked in them forgotten until she tried them again. She still wanted him despite his failings. It was an itch that needed to be scratched.

***

When she arrived back from her first trip to Sierramar six months ago, Simon waited for her at the airport like an overeager puppy, trying to carry her bags and asking inane questions. She had no idea how he had found out about her flight, but later her sister Hannah confessed to having given him the details, worn down by a barrage of requests. Tired after her long flight, she smelt of smoke and sweat and needed a shower. She was not in the mood to meet a lovesick swain, especially one who had broken her heart and hadn't appeared for months. She fobbed off his apologies and pleas for a reunion with conciliatory phrases about considering her options.

Yet there he was – larger than life and twice as canine – panting and fawning over her. It would have been funny if it wasn't so awful. She was flattered that he made a fuss of her in front of other people, a new phenomenon. In the past, his own glamour so absorbed him, he barely acknowledged her presence. Now she had become the star in a scene from a corny film and she revelled in it. Giving in to the thrill of being the leading lady, she let him kiss her, unperturbed by the flash of triumph she saw in his eyes.

And the first few weeks had been nice, being with an improved version of Simon, attentive and considerate, complimenting her often. Sam, seduced by the warm glow that came with having a plus one instead of excuses, enjoyed the approving glances from people who wanted her to settle down and live a normal life and stop *'gallivanting around the world as if she were Indiana Jones'*.

But his new behaviour wore off after a few months and he returned to his old ways taking her for granted. Sam noticed that he showed no interest in hearing about her adventures in Sierramar. Her life without him was an irrelevance. A growing resentment fomented a rebellion in her head. Being Mrs to his Mr was anathema to her growing feelings of independence. She didn't want to fade into a partnership where he held the spotlight firmly on himself. *She loved the sex but was that enough?* Determined to force him into considering her as his equal no matter how close to the edge that might take them, she had to try. If he wouldn't accept her as a full partner, he should forget it.

Only one problem interfered with this grand plan. She had missed her period and experienced the queasy panic of the possibly pregnant. Her doubts about Simon's staying power meant that she hadn't told him yet. He loved her more when he couldn't have her. *Would his feelings change if he had to share her? What sort of father would he be?* A question that seemed so rhetorical that she didn't want an answer.

And what about her? Did she love him or only her idea of him? His Simon-ness obsessed her, the arrogant handsome presence and the wicked charm. He chose her over conventional options which always amazed her. An inveterate tomboy who couldn't stomach girly behaviour, she was difficult to love. But he did. She loved him because he saw through her defences and wanted what she hid inside. But what if she told him she might be pregnant? Would a fat woman with stretch marks still interest him? She couldn't deal with this now. Gloria was a good no-nonsense sounding board. A trip to Sierramar would sort out her thoughts.

The cross voice of her abandoned boyfriend broke the silence.

'Sam? What the hell is going on out there? Are you coming back to bed or not?'

'Coming.'

She shuffled down the corridor trailing the cord of her dressing gown in the dust that lined the border between the skirting board and the tiles and entered the bedroom. Simon sat up in bed with the table light illuminating the tufts of his hair and making him look like an indignant owl.

'What the hell was that about? Why were you speaking in Spanish? Don't tell me. It was that Gloria woman again, wasn't it? Bloody foreigners.'

'Yes, it was. She's not a foreigner, she's my good friend so don't be obnoxious. She's in trouble, and she needs my help.'

'There's a surprise! The woman is a magnet for bad luck.'

Sam bridled but defending Gloria was pointless. Her name was mud for Simon. He blamed her for Sam staying on in Sierramar after her first job with Mike Morton.

'Well, it's not her. It's Alfredo Vargas. He's gone missing.'

'For God's sake. Isn't he the alcoholic? What can you do about a missing drunk who is thousands of miles away?'

Sam hesitated. Simon let out a hoarse disbelieving laugh.

'You're not going?'

'Um, I might.'

'Don't be silly, darling. That part of your life is over. You can't go. What about me?'

'Well, I only said I'd consider it. Let's sleep on it, okay? I'm so tired. I can't think straight.'

Muttering to himself, Simon moved over to let her into the bed. He switched off the light and reached for her. She flinched at his touch. He muttered something rude and turned his back on her.

***

'You're going back to Sierramar? That's nice, darling. Will you stay with Gloria?' Her mother, Matilda Harris, passed her a big cup of tea. 'Coffee cake? Go on, you know you want to.'

'A tiny piece. Whoa! That's not small,' said Sam.

'I can't let it get stale.'

'The squander bug is watching,' said Bill Harris.

'Daddy, the war is over.'

'Will you be going to the jungle?' he said.

'It depends on Alfredo.'

'Just in case you are, I have something for you. I got it from one of my clients.'

'Honestly, sweetheart. Sam doesn't want that thing.'

'What thing?'

Bill Harris rummaged in a box in the scullery. 'Ah, here it is.' He held a box with an alarming picture of a snake and some bolts of lightning shooting into it. He took out a black plastic module with two short metal prongs at the end.

'It looks like something from *Star Trek*. Can I use it to beam back to England?' said Sam.

'It's a stun gun for snake bites. If you get bitten by a viper, you stick this on the bite and press this button.' He squeezed the red button on the side of the module. A crackling sound like a fly getting electrocuted in a Greek restaurant came out of it and blue sparks flew from the prongs.

'I'm not using that. It's lethal.'

'But it might work. And if you are far from a hospital, it might save your life.'

'Take it, darling, you can never tell when you might need it,' said Matilda.

'I'll put in in my bag now,' said Sam, who didn't want to disappoint her father. 'Thanks, Daddy. It's brilliant.'

'You'll need batteries,' her mother said.

***

It wasn't easy organising a trip to Sierramar without arousing Simon's suspicion. He was prone to fits of jealousy as he couldn't help projecting his own behaviour onto her. If she tried to hide something, she always assumed that she might be seeing someone else, something so far from her mind as to require intergalactic travel. She carried on as normal and packed her suitcases while he worked, replacing them in the hall cupboard whenever he came over to her place. Her decision to go to Sierramar remained secret until he saw the supermarket bag full of tea and chocolate hidden in the wardrobe. By then she had bought the ticket which was non-refundable, from one of the bucket shops on the Tottenham Court Road.

'It was so cheap,' she crowed.

'I can't believe you lied about going to Sierramar,' he said.

'I didn't lie. I was ever so slightly economical with the truth but I never said I wouldn't go.'

'But you are going. And without me. A man can only take so much.'

He looked crestfallen, but he was a good actor.

'Oh, you'll be fine. You won't even notice I'm

gone.'

'How can you say that?'

'It'll do us good. Absence makes the heart grow fonder.'

She didn't feel as brave as she sounded but a reminder of how much he missed her would be productive when she broached the subject of her pregnancy. Oh God, how had she been so unlucky? She was so careful to take the pill each morning without fail. Bloody hormones. *And what was she supposed to do with a baby? Strap it across her back and carry on up the Amazon?* What a disaster. She considered telling her sister Hannah but the information would get back to her mother. Hannah was as leaky as a sieve. Anyway, she had had a pointless fight with her about Simon. She had gone to see her to say goodbye and things hadn't gone to plan. Hannah had been in a foul humour because she had broken up with her latest boyfriend and he wouldn't stop ringing her.

'He's like a stalker,' said Hannah. 'He won't leave me alone.'

'You should listen to him. Sometimes closure is a good thing,' said Sam, who had never liked him anyway, but got a certain enjoyment from annoying her sister.

'What? Like you and Simon? Ha! Do you imagine I'm as wimpy as you?'

'That's not fair, I wanted to give him another chance. We still love each other,' said Sam.

'You call that love, what he did to you?'

'That's in the past now. We talked it over and we are trying again. What's wrong with that?'

'You are so naïve. What makes you think Simon will be faithful this time? Has anything changed?'

'It's none of your business. Anyway, I've seen you together. You get on, in fact I'd say you fancy him yourself the way you gaze at him.'

'Don't be ridiculous.' Hannah blushed and Sam knew she had touched a nerve. Not that she blamed her. All the girls fancied Simon. 'Anyway, I'm sorry. I'm not cross with you. I'm cross with the stalker.'

'I'm sorry you're having a rotten time. Listen, I have to go now. Simon will be home soon and he's not happy that I'm off on my travels again.'

'You are not making it easy for him, home alone again.'

'I have to trust him. I can't spend my life wondering if he's strayed again. He has to police himself or he'll never grow up. I'm not prepared to go out with an adolescent anymore.'

'Okay, I suppose he's no worse than my disaster of a boyfriend. Have a good time with Gloria.'

'I will. Look after our parents for me.'

They hugged each other on parting, despite the argument, one in a long line on the same subject. Hannah disapproved of her being back with Simon, and for good reason, but so did her parents. Everyone did, and they were right, but now a complication she hadn't expected had intervened. She needed to get away, as far away as possible to give her thinking room. Gloria would know what to do.

CHAPTER II

Calderon August 1988

Alfredo Vargas had been working in his study when the telephone rang. Despite the loud and persistent nature of the tone, he failed to locate it in the sea of documents and open books layered on his desk like a giant piece of filo pastry. He put his ear to the pile and felt in the dust with his hand for the vibration that would give its position away. Finding the handset, he untangled the cord from a dead pot plant.

Whoever wanted to talk to him was persistent and determined. Most people gave up sooner. He held it to his ear with some trepidation. Perhaps it was someone to whom he owed money? Or his mother demanding an update?

'Hello, can I speak to Alfredo Vargas please?'

American accented Spanish. Nasal and whiny with a touch of Brooklyn.

'Who's speaking please?'

'Ah, you speak English. My name is Saul Rosen. I'm a journalist.' Alfredo noticed that English was not his mother tongue either. It appeared to be a weird mix of Brooklyn and some European accent. French?

'I still don't know who you are. What do you want?'

'I'm looking for Alfredo Vargas, the historian. I've

got a proposition for him.'

'What sort of proposition? I'm busy right now.'

'Are you Dr Vargas? That's a piece of luck. You've no idea how difficult it is to get hold of you.'

Alfredo made concerted efforts to avoid most human contact, which he found mundane and trying, so he knew how tricky it was to get hold of him.

'How did you get my number?'

'From Dr Gallagher in New York.'

'Ah, Dick Gallagher, that explains it. You've got work for me? What does it involve?'

'I need help with an assignment in Sierramar. It's confidential and may even be dangerous. I want you to research something for me.'

'What's the subject of this investigation?'

He tried to control his excitement. Alfredo was self-sufficient in funds, being the product of a wealthy family with money to burn, but he needed something to engage his mind. His drinking had spiralled out of control again despite the efforts of his girlfriend, Gloria. He wanted to make her proud and to get her father to accept their relationship but being underemployed only made drink more appealing.

'I'm working as a consultant for the Simon Wiesenthal Centre doing research into Nazi war criminals who fled to South America after the second world war. The War Crimes Commission is keen on finding and arresting them. I've been following several lines of inquiry that lead to Sierramar.'

'Sierramar? Are you positive?'

They had captured several notorious war criminals in Argentina, Chile and Brazil but he had never heard of any in his country. Sierramar was one of the few democracies in South America without a fascist regime in its past.

'Yes. It's not something I expected either. I guess as a historian you would expect to be aware of it, but that's the point. The Sierramar government colluded with the Germans to let war criminals escape justice. They hushed up the collaboration and hid the evidence.'

'So how can I help?'

'I thought you would have access to the files in the National Archives which might back this story up. They are unlikely to let an American access them, but I presume that you wouldn't experience any problem getting the information I need.'

'I go there often. Let me help you with this. It seems straight forward enough. How much would you pay me?'

'I can offer you one hundred dollars a day with an upfront payment of five hundred. Does that suit you?'

'That sounds about right,' said Alfredo, covering his surprise at the generous offer, most gringos had money. 'Do you have a pen with you?'

'Yes.'

'Okay, my fax number is 02687865. You must put the country code for Sierramar in front of it and you may need to eliminate the zero. Why don't you fax me a proposal and I will get back to you with my decision and my bank details, in due course.'

'I'll do that today.'

'Excellent.'

'Thank you, Dr Vargas.'

'Alfredo, please. Can I call you Saul?'

'Sure. Okay, goodbye for now.'

Alfredo hung up the receiver and sat back in his large leather armchair. Saul seemed willing to pay over the odds for some simple research but he would not look a gift horse in the mouth. It seemed like a proper job. He was dying to tell Gloria. *How difficult could it be?*

***

Ecstasy overcame Saul. He couldn't believe his luck in finding Alfredo, who seemed to be the perfect candidate for the job. He owed Dick Gallagher a bottle of whisky. There was no need to tell anyone the real reason he was researching the Nazi presence in Sierramar. It appeared unlikely that Alfredo would come up with anything concrete if he had never even heard of his government's collaboration with the Third Reich. *Were the incriminating documents sitting on the shelves of the National Archives, waiting to be discovered?*

It had taken years for him to follow the trail of Dr Kurt Becker from Brussels to Calderon. It might be a long time before Alfredo would come up with anything of substance. He could wait. Revenge is a dish best served cold, and this had mould on it. He folded the piece of paper with Alfredo's number and put it in a zipped compartment of his wallet. Then he went into his study and looked for a document to use as a template for Alfredo's contract. Money was no object in this case. His search approached a climax and he hoped it would finish with a bang.

***

Alfredo was almost as excited. He loved a new project and was impatient to get started. He found it impossible to wait for Saul to formalise their relationship before starting his research. The suggestion that there were Nazi war criminals hiding in Sierramar had mystified him. It challenged his status as a historian. At thirty-five years' old, his colleagues

17

considered him to be one of the most knowledgeable men in his field, but his studies tended to the esoteric side and he had concentrated on the study of the Valdivia and Inca cultures of South America.

The Second World War wasn't worthy of his interest; it took place only yesterday, for heaven's sake. Hardly history. He couldn't imagine his little country with its mountains, beaches and jungles being anything other than a democratic paradise. Despite the revolutions and fascist regimes that plagued the rest of Latin America, Sierramar had never had a civil war or a dictator. It had dodgy governments, with the usual bribery and corruption that accompanied real poverty, but the suggestion that it harboured Nazi fugitives shocked him. And yet, the story rang true.

Intrigued, he racked his brains for clues. There were people of German descent in Calderon, many of them his age, who hung out with the wealthy local families similar to his. He had met their mothers, but he couldn't remember their fathers. It had never occurred to him before because he didn't place much importance on family relationships. The history of the German community in Calderon was a mystery to him but he now determined to trace its origins. He started at the source of most of his local gossip, Gloria, his girlfriend and daughter of the nouveaux-riche Hernan Sanchez, a government contractor.

'Hello?'

'Hi, mi amour, what's up?'

'Do you want to meet me for lunch today? It's short notice but I need to see you.'

'I can be at the Banana Verde in an hour.'

'Great, I'll wait for you outside.'

He drove into the centre of town, buying a newspaper from the street vendor who breastfed her child at the traffic light in a cloud of exhaust fumes. Various little children sat on the divider in the middle of the road, under a tree with shrivelled leaves poisoned by lead particles, their dirty faces pictures of boredom and misery. He tried not to notice and refused his change with a wave of the hand. Calderon was a prosperous town but the indigenous population formed a large part of the begging and jobless in the capital. There seemed to be a family at every junction.

He sat on a bench outside the restaurant and read his newspaper in the shade of an ugly tower block. Some dusty birds pecked at the dry earth in the flower bed which held only painted stones and lumps of chewing gum. Gloria arrived half an hour later than promised, doing what looked like a handbrake turn into a parking spot, leaving a fresh arc of rubber in the road. She jumped out of the car in her skin-tight jeans and cowboy boots, her bright shirt straining at the buttons. Her hair had been painted in the multi-coloured stripes that passed for highlights in Calderon. She sucked on a cigarette and glancing around, her eyes screwed up against the bright rays of the noon-day sun.

'Ah, mi amour! There you are. Let's go inside.'

'How are you, darling? You look wonderful. I love your hair.'

'Thank you, it's all the rage.'

She did a flirtatious twirl in front of him and his heart skipped in his chest. He was a man besotted. Until they got together, he had considered Gloria so out of his league he had never dared to talk to her.

They pushed through the door into the cool interior and the manager showed them to the best table as befitted the daughter of Hernan Sanchez. A waiter gave them menus.

'Do you want to hear the specials?' he said.

'No, thank you. Can you bring me some potato soup with an extra portion of avocado, please? Alfredo?'

'Raise the dead soup please, although it would be a miracle if it worked this time.'

'Can you bring us a jug of fresh lemonade, too, please?'

'Certainly, Senorita Sanchez.'

The waiter withdrew leaving them in the relative privacy of their corner table.

'What's so important that you couldn't tell me on the phone?' said Gloria, 'and why do you look so exhausted? Have you been drinking?'

'Drinking? Oh, not really, that is, not much, only thinking amounts.'

'Thinking amounts? Thinking about what?'

'I've got a job.'

Gloria's jaw dropped so far that he could see her fillings.

'A job? You?'

She blurted out 'How wonderful!' before an embarrassing silence occurred. Alfredo didn't notice because she leaned forward resting her bosom on the table, a manoeuvre which distracted him.

'Yes, it's wonderful,' he said.

'Oi, concentrate. So, what's the job?'

'A journalist called Saul Rosen has rung me from New York. He asked me to research the German community in Calderon. My social contacts aren't as good as yours, and I'm not convinced this isn't a red herring so I wanted to pick your brains. I don't want to waste my time if there's nothing to find. I need your advice before I get started with searching in the National Archives.'

'How mysterious you are today. I'd love to help you if I can. Tell me all about it.'

'Okay, but I need you to please listen and not comment or fly off the handle until I finish. It's not an easy subject and its implications may upset you.'

Gloria lit a cigarette.

'Okay, I promise to listen first and shout later.'

'Well, believe it or not, this journalist claims he's found evidence that some important Nazi war criminals are hiding in Sierramar. He wants me to research the story to see if we can verify it. His research indicates that our government are aware of their presence and colluded with the Third Reich.'

Gloria looked as if she wanted to interject but Alfredo held his hand up to stop her. 'It's only natural that you'll defend our country to the death rather than accept this but please consider the possibility first. I have been doing a lot of thinking and it rings true in some aspects. I wish it didn't.'

'Hence the drinking.'

'Yes, I'm sorry. It helped soften the blow when it became clear there was some substance to the story. There are lots of wealthy German families in Calderon. Where did they came from and where did they get their wealth? The older men have disappeared or never arrived here. Why do so many families have a matriarch but no patriarch?'

He paused. Gloria looked as if she was struggling to contain an outburst. She lit another cigarette and smoked it, tapping it hard on the ash tray. The soup arrived. They both attacked their bowls without speaking. Gloria's brow furrowed in concentration. She pushed back her empty bowl and gulped down a glass of lemonade.

'You're right,' she said at last. 'There's been something odd happening in the German community in Calderon.'

Alfredo let out the breath he had been holding as surreptitiously as he could. Gloria paused, shutting her eyes as if to focus on her recollection of a half-remembered episode.

'There were some weird goings on among my German friends at school,' she said. 'Two were sisters who had blonde hair, but with dark eyebrows. We know what that means.'

And here she looked at Alfredo for affirmation but he was flummoxed.

'Ay, but men are so stupid sometimes. It means they dyed their hair. Blonde women have blonde eyebrows.' She sighed.

'So? How is that weird?'

'One of these sisters was in my class, and she became a friend of mine, so we used to have sleepovers. Sometimes we had a glass of wine stolen from my father's drinks cabinet. One night, she had too much wine and I asked her why she dyed her hair blonde. She was only fourteen then.'

'What did she tell you?'

'When the girls were little, they both had blonde hair and their father doted on them. Their hair began to turn brown as they got older and their father got furious because he wanted them to appear more Aryan. He told them that the Aryans were the master race and they would enslave or eliminate others when the Fourth Reich came into being. He had a violent temper so their mother protected them from his rages by dyeing their hair.'

'What happened to him?'

'I don't know. I remember that he often left them alone for weeks without telling them where he went. He disappeared for good with several of his friends when we were about eighteen. Rumours circled that they had left the country for Argentina.'

Alfredo was transfixed.

'Oh God,' he said, 'I'd no idea that Nazi fugitives came here. I must find out more.'

'Be careful. If the government helped the Third Reich to hide some of their war criminals from justice, they won't be happy to be exposed as collaborators. They'd be in their late sixties and seventies now so a lot of them are still alive.'

But Alfredo was no longer listening.

CHAPTER III

Berlin, April 1945

Dr Becker removed the severed finger from his pocket and unwrapped it from the greased proof paper in which he had concealed it. Dropping it into sterilised saline in a glass vial, he sealed it with hot wax. Then he put the vial into a metal tube and screwed on the top. With trembling hands, he placed the tube into a large canister of dry ice. Its removal from the corpse had been straightforward despite his trepidation. No-one wanted to enter the room while the smell of almonds hung in the air.

Death had been instantaneous. Hitler's head was on the coffee table with blood dripping from his right temple. The automatic, a Walther PPK, was lying on the floor below the dead hand that had dropped it. Becker strode over to the body. The state of the Führer's hands shocked him. Drug abuse had blackened the nails on the end of his thin, grey fingers. They were not the hands of a well man. No wonder the Führer stayed hidden in the bunker for so long.

The finger came away without a struggle. The enormity of the sacrilege was hard to ignore but Becker kept telling himself that he was doing this for posterity. He wrapped the body in a blanket and went for help.

Staff removed it from the bunker for cremation with that of his mistress, Eva Braun. Nobody noticed that the Führer's left hand was missing a finger.

He found it easy to get permission to leave Berlin with the impending arrival of the Russians and the consequent breakdown of normal procedure. Nobody cared any more. People were trying to get away and many were taking what they could and abandoning Berlin. He requisitioned a truck and half a dozen young soldiers, who looked as if they hadn't started shaving yet, for a *mission of utmost national importance*, a phrase guaranteed to make people jump to attention and ask few questions.

The soldiers agreed at once, grateful to get out of Berlin and head for the relative safety of the coast with no questions asked. He packed his own trunks full of booty from the sacked Jewish houses in Belgium. Gold chains and watches, delicate porcelain wrapped in mink coats, portraits of plump eighteenth-century matrons. Confident he could buy anything he wanted in South America, he left most of his clothes behind. It would also make him less easy to spot when he started his new life in Sierramar.

Directing his driver to follow the truck, they started off down the road. His identification papers as a member of the Führer's household got him through the checkpoints with no delays. No one dared to question his right to travel wherever he wanted. Despite the chaos of troops and civilians streaming in both directions on the main roads, they made good progress and arrived at the Port of Hamburg with plenty of time to catch the tramp liner to Sierramar before it left.

Becker and a group of thirty other SS and Gestapo officers hired the steamer under a neutral flag for making their escape from Europe when they realised they had lost the war. Dockworkers ignorant of the valuable cargo they handled loaded everything from cars to containers of furniture and paintings looted from conquered towns, and crates of gold bars, diamonds and jewellery aboard the liner. The cranes lifted the pallets from the dockside and lowered them into the bowels of the ship while the passengers waited on the shore and confirmed that their belongings went on board. Most of the men had brought their families with them. They stood on the quay drinking coffee in their fur coats as if waiting to go on a cruise.

Kurt Becker walked to the back of the lorry with a member of the steamer's crew and flung open the door.

'Okay lads, it's your lucky day. You have arrived in Hamburg and if you wish, you may board the liner to South America and start a new life.'

There was no answer. It was dark in the lorry and when his eyes adjusted, he saw the soldiers slumped on the floor of the container in a way that suggested death rather than sleep. He jumped up onto the running board and into the lorry. He shook one of them by the shoulder. The young man's face rolled towards Becker, his fixed eyeballs staring into space. He poked one of the others with his toe but he didn't respond.

'They're dead. What on earth happened to them? What have you got in here?' asked the crewman.

'I don't understand what happened. The container was airtight but there was plenty of air for the journey.'

Then it hit him. The dry ice had evaporated, giving off carbon dioxide which flooded the container and suffocated the young men. He felt sickened. The finger was cursed. He made the crew man pick up the canister and wrap it in sacking. They left the bodies in the truck, just more casualties of war. Then they went up the gangway to talk to the captain.

'Good evening, captain. I need to keep something frozen while we're on board. Have you got somewhere that I can store it?'

'I don't know what it is, captain, but they were all dead,' said the crewman. 'Don't let him put it on board.'

'The soldiers suffocated. It was a terrible tragedy, but it has nothing to do with the canister,' retorted Becker.

'What are you talking about? What's so bloody precious?' asked the captain.

'Some samples for my medical practice. I brought them here packed in dry ice and it evaporated on the way. The soldiers who hitched a lift in the back of the truck have suffocated. I never realised that might happen, I swear. You have my word there is nothing dangerous in the canister, but I can't leave it behind.'

'As long as it's safe, you can lock it in the auxiliary meat fridge for the journey,'

'That'll be fine. I'll keep the key.'

The captain shrugged. He was making a fortune taking this ship to South America. If he got there without incident, he would never have to work again. He didn't care what was in the canister.

'Right you are, Dr Becker. Ensign, show him the fridge.'

***

It took a month to sail to Sierramar through sometimes stormy seas. Kurt Becker checked the fridge daily for signs of tampering but it remained sealed. The senior German officers on board held meetings about their plans for Sierramar and swore each other to secrecy. The news from Germany got worse and more difficult to receive. By the time the liner got to the port of

Guayama, the war seemed far away, not only in distance.

They gazed at palm trees from the deck and bright coloured pastel buildings in the residential part of the city. Buses and cars crawled along the congested boardwalk. The steamer docked in the port in the northern part of the city which was dirty and battered by time and neglect. Large customs sheds lined the wharf and ancient cranes like a flock of skinny birds stalked the rails. Dockers swarmed towards the ship followed by stray dogs hoping for a windfall. The sun pierced the thick humid air cloaking them in heat and sweat.

The German Consul was waiting as they came down the gangway, unsteady on their legs after a month at sea. It was like landing in paradise compared to war-torn Europe. Even the oppressive heat and filthy port did not put them off. The Consul carried a stack of passports containing fresh identities for their new lives. People surrounded him shaking his hand, wanting to be the first to escape their past as if a new name would wipe away the memories of the things they had done and justified to themselves on that long journey. They had invented heroic back stories of suffering and sacrifice to ensure that no one questioned their choice to leave it behind and start again. Kurt Becker had not asked for a new name. He kept his identity because he wanted to work as a doctor and needed to use his certificates. Anyway, the people who knew what he had done had perished in the gas chambers. There was no one left to accuse him.

'Who'd come to this shit hole at the end of the earth to find me now?' he said, wrinkling his nose at the smell of the port and slapping his arm. 'Even the mosquitos are macho.'

Most of the officers had already decided that they wanted to live in Calderon in the Andes where the climate was more similar to that of Germany and they could do dairy farming. Their children would go to the German school and be with other Aryans rather than mixing with the mestizos. The snow-capped volcanoes were too steep and dangerous for skiing but the sight of them would ease homesickness in those pining for the Alps.

After they got their passports, they waited on the quay for their belongings, negotiating with the dockers to get them carried to the waiting lorries organised by the Consul. He hadn't done this out of the goodness of his heart. The salary the Consul received in Sierramar did not keep him in the style to which he wished to become accustomed and he determined to make the most of this windfall. He had also negotiated the rental of houses in Calderon to get them started and was taking a cut from the proceeds. Despite this, the ideals of the Reich mattered to him and he felt the humiliation of the surrender deep in his bones. Helping these men get settled and escape the clutches of the do-gooders on the allied side who wanted to bring them to justice gave him some solace.

***

Becker had had his work cut out transporting the finger to Calderon without it thawing. The captain wanted to get rid of it as soon as they landed in port, so the Consul let him use the fridge in the embassy where they stuffed it into the ice compartment. The Consul solved the conundrum of how to get the finger to Calderon. He requisitioned an ambulance that had arrived from the United States and had not yet cleared customs. A healthy bribe to his contacts in the port ensured they would delay the importation paperwork until he arranged for the return of the ambulance to the customs shed after its journey to Calderon. The ambulance contained a fridge for blood products and was perfect for transporting the canister up into the Andes.

Dr Becker travelled on the ambulance to forestall any unforeseen problems on the way. It took three days to get to Calderon. Once there, he packed and stored the finger in the ice compartment of the Frigidaire in his new home. He installed a generator and a back-up for the fridge to keep it on in the case of power cuts or breakdown. He also ordered a new standalone freezer from the USA which took months to arrive. Guests to his house were unaware that the ice for their drinks had lain beside a frozen relic of their Führer.

***

Once the group got established in Calderon, they held a monthly meeting and planned to build a German village up in the mountains where they could get ready for the next phase of the Reich.

'We need a cover story for this village,' said Rolf Hermann.

'My view is that we should build something similar to the alpine villages back home, somewhere for tourists. That will give us a legitimate reason to employ Germans and keep the locals out,' said Hans Schmidt.

'We could make cheese and dairy products and sell them to finance the upkeep of the laboratory,' said his brother Franz.

'And who will run these enterprises?' said Rolf

'We must take turns or divide the work. Once our wives and children settle in Calderon, we can sort that out,' said Franz Rauf.

'I've got to run the laboratory,' said Kurt Becker,

'that will be a full-time job.'

'Solidarity is the most important thing here. We will figure this out,' said Boris Klein. 'The important matter is the perpetuation of the Reich. Without us there will be no future.'

The Schmidt brothers set out for the region of Lago Verde, a village in the Andes to the south of Calderon, to find a site for the village. They arrived after taking a bus on a narrow road skirted by cliffs. The village had cobble streets and low adobe houses with straw roofs. The local people were tenant farmers who shared their houses with their livestock to prevent theft. It surprised them to find the tall blond strangers in their midst inquiring about the purchase of suitable land for a settlement. The men introduced themselves to the mayor who also ran the local inn.

'Gentlemen, how can I help you?'

'We are looking for about one hundred hectares of land on which to build a new village and establish some dairy farming.'

'I can help you with that. There is a flat area in the valley across the peat bog, up on a rise. There is plenty of water and wood for construction, so you won't have to bring it in.'

'That sounds interesting.'

'Even better, Lago Verde is due to get both electricity and telephone lines soon and a timely bribe could make them stretch the wires to the new village.'

'So, can we talk to the owner to arrange a visit?'

'You're talking to him.'

'Ah, and the bribe?'

'Ditto.'

***

'How's construction of San Blas going?' said Holger

Ponce, the clerk at the Ministry of Public Works.

'Slow. It's difficult to walk stuff in from Lago Verde. It will take us fifty years at this rate. We need to build a road to the site,' said Rolf Hermann.

'I can get you permission for the road from the Minister. A well-placed bribe will help to speed it up.'

'No problem, just say how much. We'll need a contractor. I presume you can suggest someone suitable?'

'I know just the man,' said Holger.

'Does he sympathise?'

'He is a budding fascist. Right up your alley.'

'What's his name?'

'Hernan Sanchez. I'll set up an introduction and you can go from there. Don't let his age put you off. He's dynamic and gets things done. It'll be more expensive than some contractors but it's worth it for the efficiency. Besides that, he has good government contacts we can tap into.'

'Set up the meeting.'

CHAPTER IV

Alfredo, August 1988

The National Archives were stored in a concrete carbuncle on top of a hill in the centre of Calderon's political district surrounded by government buildings. Known as the blister, the architect designed it with a marble façade, but the budget for the polished stone went towards the purchase of an art deco house in Miami for the Minister of Education. The entrance to the building sat at the top of a featureless flight of steps that suggested a gulag rather than a place of learning. Immune to the ugliness after using it for years, Alfredo's focus on the mission ahead was such that he tripped and fell hard onto the flagstones that surrounded the door.

'Are you injured, Dr Vargas?' asked the security guard.

'No damage done, thank you,' said Alfredo, conscious of the sharp gaze of a fellow academic on him as he staggered to his feet.

'Fucking drunkard.' The loud comment, intended to wound, floated over his head as he brushed the concrete dust off his trousers.

'I prefer borderline alcoholic,' he said. Despite his comeback, humiliated washed over him. He often drank too much, but he never came to the Blister unless he was sober. The terror of missing something important kept him sharp. His academic reputation was precious to him, despite his casual exterior. His bruised knee throbbed, but he avoided limping as he showed his pass at the door. He didn't want anyone to see he had hurt himself in case they sensed his weakness and imagined him vulnerable to their criticism. *They were just jealous.*

Out of habit, he headed for the section of the archives that contained the research on the Valdivia cultures. After standing beside the files for several minutes without moving, a tap on his shoulder startled him out of his reverie. He turned to see a slim young man with a pudding bowl haircut and a name badge which said 'Kleber Perez, Library assistant'.

'Dr Vargas, isn't it? Can I help you?'

'Oh, thank you, that would be great. I need to see any archives concerning the German community in Sierramar during the 20th century, specifically any mention of families who arrived here after 1940. I don't know where to start, to be honest. This is not my area of expertise.'

The young man fixed him with a piercing stare. Concern or anger flashed across his features but he recovered his aplomb. Alfredo wondered if he had imagined it. Perhaps the young man had heard about his drinking.

'You will need to follow me. We are in the wrong place to start a search for modern history. The card indexes are on the other side of the building.'

'Excellent. Much appreciated. Lead on.'

They walked out into the atrium and crossed to the other side into an identical room with a long bureau of reference cards at the entrance and filled with high, dusty bookshelves in a half circle, which moved open and closed on rails for easier access. The young man picked his way through the box with the speed of a card sharp, selecting several references and removing them from the boxes. He presented them to Alfredo.

'There you go Doctor, that should get you started. Tell me if you need anything else.'

'Thank you, Kleber.'

Alfredo sat on one of the hard, wooden benches opposite the indexes and reviewed the cards that Kleber gave him. The young man was an idiot. If Alfredo had wanted to learn about German cooking and traditional clothing, he would not be in the National Archive. Young people these days, what sort of education were they getting? He limped over to the cabinets and replaced the cards. But into which category did Nazis in Sierramar fall? *Politics? Foreign relations? Fantasy?* Being methodical would get results. He picked up the first card box and moved over to a table. One by one he removed the cards and examined the summaries and then replaced them in the box. He went through three boxes and found a grand total of two references to German immigrants, both stored upside down. Not encouraging but Alfredo was used to dead ends.

He went to the stacks to locate the papers. Neither document occupied its slot in the filing boxes, but the lending cards stapled on the boxes showed that the same person had taken them both out, a certain Armando Bronca. Alfredo smiled. This was a joke name in Spanish meaning 'starting a fight', a nickname used by Ramon Vega, one of his friends from university days. Alfredo had not seen him for several years following an altercation in a bar which had nothing to do with Ramon and a direct result of

Alfredo's alcohol intake. He hoped that time had healed the wounds caused by his sarcastic tongue, sharpened by too much drink.

***

Ramon Vega lived in the valley parallel to that of Calderon in a farmhouse surrounded by modern houses where there used to be pasture. Alfredo drove down the winding road fringed by eucalyptus trees, avoiding the potholes and the chickens. Built in the time of the Spanish occupation, Ramon's house had settled with time as the foundations had dried out. The walls leaned inwards and the roof bowed. A riot of bougainvillea and climbing hibiscus crawled over the white building and invaded the crevices in the windows. The door hung open and dust danced in the bright sunlight penetrating the dark interior. Alfredo stepped into the entrance, keeping one nervous hand on the door.

'Hello? Is anyone at home?'

He heard creaking floorboards complaining as Ramon approached. A large silhouette filled the hall.

'Alfredo? Is that you?'

'Yes, it's me. Punch me now so we can be friends again.'

'You stupid sod!'

The deep voice caught in the massive throat. Moving rapidly for such a large man, Ramon launched himself at Alfredo. At the last moment, Alfredo realised that his friend's arms were open and his hands were reaching and not bunched into fists. He relaxed and let the tidal wave of affection that was Ramon Vega flow over him. Tears ran down his cheeks but he didn't know to whom they belonged. Why had he waited so long to apologise? What an idiot. He should have realised it would be like old times.

When the two men had unwrapped themselves from their fitful embrace, Alfredo followed Ramon into a sitting room lined with books. Shelving covered the walls and many groaned with the weight of double rows of books of every shape and size. Alfredo sank into a comfortable armchair from which he knew it would be hard to extricate himself. Ramon sat opposite in its twin leaning forward with his elbows on his thighs.

'Marta! Bring us some fresh coffee, please. And some empanadas.'

A squeak of assent emitted from the kitchen.

'What do you want, old friend? It must be important for you to brave my wrath after such a long time.'

'I am sorry, so sorry. I have been such an idiot. I have an urgent matter to discuss but our friendship is more important and I am a fool.'

'Come on, don't upset me again. Let's pretend it never happened. Spill the beans. Start at the beginning and leave nothing out.'

Alfredo told Ramon about the call he had received from Saul Rosen, leaving out the bit about the generous payment, and the strange story of Gloria's school friends and their dyed hair, and then about the missing documents in the library. Ramon remained perched on the edge of his seat washing down cheese empanadas in a sea of milky coffee. His brow furrowed deeper and deeper until he resembled a worried bulldog.

'So that's it. You can point me in the right direction as the trail is cold and I don't know where to start.'

'How extraordinary,' said Ramon. He stood up and moved to the door which he opened to look up and down the hall. He shut it again and turned around shaking his head. 'What a coincidence. I can't believe it.'

'Believe what? I don't understand.'

'Saul is not alone in doing research on Nazis in Sierramar. This subject has been my sole focus for eighteen months after a chance discovery in the archives. I found a whole box of documents in the basement under the wrong section which I guessed someone had put there by mistake. But it didn't take me long to realise I'd stumbled upon a cover-up.'

'The only filing cards I found on the subject were stored upside down. I found your note when looking for the relevant documents in the file boxes.'

'I still have them. There is no point putting them back. They'll disappear too. Like the fugitives that came here in 1945.'

'What do you mean disappeared?'

'Some of them have died, but the others melted away and I am trying to trace them. There's a hard core of about six of them left. I have been concentrating on collaboration and I haven't searched for them yet.'

'They must be the people we want.'

'Exactly. Anyway, I've almost finished a report on the government collaboration with the Third Reich that I hoped to have published.'

'Hoped? Are you having trouble finding a publisher?'

'I'm having trouble with a lot more than that. There are prominent people in Sierramar who want to prevent this document seeing the light of day. You wouldn't believe the people involved. It goes right to the top and most of the main protagonists are still alive.'

'Jesus, that's terrible. You should be careful that they don't find out what you are doing.'

'I kept my studies a secret until now but I fear that I am being watched. It's a feeling I can't shake off.'

'What are you going to do?'

'I'm leaving the country for a while and will try to get the report published in the United States. Once it's in the public domain, there isn't anything they can do to stop the information getting out.'

'When are you going?'

'Next week, so it's lucky you caught me here. I'll tell you what. Why don't you borrow the document for a few days and photocopy any relevant pages?'

'That's a hell of a responsibility. Are you confident it's a good idea?'

'I'm more worried about keeping it here. They would steal it if they got the chance. It's an isolated house and easy to burgle. I would feel better if I knew you had it safe. People are aware we aren't on speaking terms. They won't suspect you of having it.'

'So, when do you want it back?'

'You can give me it when I pass by your house on my way to the airport. Ring me if you have questions before I go.'

'Okay, I'll take it.'

'It's the sole copy. Don't lose it or take it to the bar with you. It could get you killed if someone knows you have it.'

Alfredo ignored the pointed reference. 'I'll guard it with my life.'

'I'm sorry but you have to go now. I'm expecting a visitor and my guest is shy.'

Ramon winked and Alfredo realised that he was still taking part in extracurricular activities with other people's wives despite his perilous personal situation.

'I'm going, don't get caught.'

'Don't be silly. Who'd suspect me of being a secret lothario?'

He had a point. Despite his big brown eyes and a mop of unruly black hair, he was as wide as he was tall and looked like a genial toad, not the kind of man who seduced other men's wives, although it wasn't the irate husbands that worried Alfredo. He took the document and stuffed it in the poacher's pocket of his jacket.

Waving goodbye, he stepped back out into the sunshine and headed for his car. He drove back up to his house, pondering on the coincidence that had led him back to Ramon after that stupid argument. He couldn't even remember what it had been about. Again, he regretted his addiction and what it had cost him. It was unfortunate he could stop drinking for months and then, when he thought he'd got free, the tendrils of addiction would enfold and seduce him with the power of a siren.

***

Kleber Perez watched Alfredo leaving Ramon's house. Alfredo wasn't carrying anything, but he was wearing a jacket that could conceal a multitude of secrets. This was the worst possible outcome. *How could a drunk like Dr Vargas put together a few nebulous clues and come up with the jackpot?* There must have been a connection between them in the past. *How else would Alfredo have known Armando Bronca was a nickname?*

Kleber thumped his fist on the handle bar of his moped. He should have changed the name on the files when he had the chance. In his experience, most rich people knew each other, so it wasn't surprising that Alfredo knew Ramon and recognised the nickname. He jumped on his bike and made for the nearest public telephone in a local shop opposite the police station. He had to join a queue for the phone and he sat quivering with indignation in the corner until it was his turn.

'It's me. I have bad news about Ramon Vega. He has a new accomplice.'

'Wasn't he was working alone?'

'He was. I haven't seen him talk to anyone for months.'

'Jesus! This is a disaster. We have to get rid of him before he talks to anyone else.'

'I can do it.'

'Okay, but make it look like an accident. We can't leave any clues.'

'Leave it with me.'

***

On reaching his house, Alfredo locked the doors and made a pot of strong coffee. He was dying for a drink but alcohol would not help him navigate the noxious pages. The house contained no alcohol, as he had drained the bottles the week before, on a binge that lasted two days. Instead he poured out a mug of coffee and added three teaspoons of sugar to give him a boost. Clearing the papers from his favourite armchair, which was a cavernous affair made of soft brown leather, he sank into its shiny embrace with the document and read.

The report was dynamite. *Could it be that Ramon had been writing a novel and was pulling his leg?* The more he read, the less believable it seemed. It was profoundly disturbing. The collaboration between the Nazis and the Sierramar government during the second world war took his breath away in its extent. The government of Nazi Germany had even presented Sierramar with a decoration for helping them out. No wonder certain people didn't want it published. Hot shame swamped him as he read about the Jews being expelled from the country in 1943 and their businesses being taken over by locals.

It didn't get any better. He leafed through photographs of people dressed as Nazis posing in front of government buildings. Not everyone looked Germanic, some appeared to be local. Worse still he recognised some of them, including Gloria's father, Hernan Sanchez, who looked about nineteen. Their arrogance horrified and bewildered him. *What would Gloria think if she found out about her father? Why hadn't he come across this information before?* He couldn't understand how this awful episode had remained secret. Now he knew why Ramon had decided to flee the country. The document was nothing short of explosive. The protagonists on the Sierramar side were well-known politicians. They would kill to get hold of it. He had to tell Saul Rosen.

He booked a call to New York with the operator. While waiting for the phone to ring, he pondered the contents of the report. Historical mysteries like the burial place of Alexander the Great and the whereabouts of the lost City of Atlantis often perplexed him. But hundreds of years had passed since those events, blurring truth and fiction until they were indistinguishable. What he didn't understand was how Sierramarians had kept something in the recent past so secret. Powerful people must have buried the references to their shameful collaboration, and those involved must have expunged any trace of their cooperation. It was strange and worrying. The telephone rang beside his ear making him jump.

'I've got your connection in New York, sir.'

'Thank you. Saul? It's Alfredo Vargas.'

'Hey, Alfredo, how are you? I suppose you realise that it's two in the morning?'

'Is it? I'm sorry to wake you. I lost track of time.

The thing is, I've discovered some important information pertaining to your research.'

'Wow, already? We haven't even signed a contract yet.'

'It couldn't wait. I hope that's okay with you. If you're a friend of Dick Gallagher, you must be trustworthy.'

'He is choosy. I had to go through a tough vetting process involving lots of alcohol.' He guffawed. 'So, what have you uncovered?'

'It turns out you were right. There's a whole can of worms down here involving our German friends. By an extraordinary coincidence, a trusted friend of mine has been doing research on this subject and he has discovered that there's a clandestine group of Nazi officers still hiding in Sierramar.'

'Outstanding! Just as I suspected. You've hit the mother lode. I'm surprised.'

'Yes, well that makes two of us. My friend has lent me his research and the collaboration between the Nazis and the Sierramar government was nothing short of appalling.'

'That's thrilling news. What are you planning to do next?'

'I want to investigate this group's existence in the present day. Are they still alive? Where are they hiding?'

Saul did not hesitate. 'Man, that's exciting. I'll come with you. Don't worry, you'll get paid. Contract or no contract.'

'You're coming?' Alfredo hesitated. He liked to work alone, but it was too late now, Saul had decided.

'As soon as I can get organised. I'll let you have my flight times in the next day or two.'

'I look forward to meeting you in person.'

'How do I find you in Calderon?'

'I'll pick you up at the airport. Meanwhile, I'll make a copy of the research for you.'

'I can't wait. See you soon.'

'Goodnight, Saul, and sorry for waking you.'

'No apology necessary. I won't sleep tonight but for once I don't care.'

***

Saul put down the phone and leant forward in the wooden hall chair, grasping his knees and resting his forehead on them. He took a deep breath and let it out. It caught in his throat. Finally, after years of searching, a bit of luck. He wasn't sure how he felt. Relieved? Ecstatic? He stood up and walked towards his bedroom, stumbling as his toe caught on his pyjama bottoms and almost falling headlong through the door. A sudden onrush of tears blinded him and he reached for his handkerchief on the bedside table. Removing his glasses, he sat on his bed in the dark, weeping his heart out. It was as if he had been lost his entire life and had found a map home. The threads were coming together. The final act was approaching.

He opened the slim drawer of the bedside table and took out a gun which he had bought in the local gunsmiths. A Glock. It was chunky and workmanlike and, according to the salesman, deadly. He had tested it in the firing room of the store, aiming at the human targets hanging in the back room. The recoil had thrilled him almost more than the holes he made in the paper tracings. He could shoot it at a real human being. Those evil men would pay. He didn't care what happened after that. It was in the lap of the gods.

CHAPTER V

Sam and Gloria, Calderon, September 1988

Sam's flight arrived at Calderon airport in the middle of a terrifying thunderstorm. Landing at almost three thousand metres above sea level was always a challenge due to the thin air, but now the sky was alive with streaks of lightening. Rain was sheeting down the windows of the aircraft making it hard to make out the runway and it was being buffeted from side to side by ferocious cross winds which whipped around the sides of the volcano overlooking the airport. The pilot had to abort the first landing as they overshot the runway. The engines roared as the plane gained height again through the sodden air pushing the passengers back against their seats.

'Okay, ladies and gents, it's raining and windy which makes it difficult to land. We'll go around and try again. If we don't get a quiet slot, we will have to fly to Guayama instead. Fingers crossed and here we go again.'

A hush on board was broken only by the rattling of rosary beads as they tried to land for the second time.

Even the air hostesses were gripping the edges of their seats. The aircraft landed with a big bounce and the tyres squealed as they fought for grip on the wet surface. One of the overhead lockers sprang open and someone's duty free cigarettes fell to the floor. Relieved cheering augmented the customary round of applause for the safe landing. Even Sam joined in with the clapping to shake loose the iron grip of the priest sitting beside her who had abandoned hope of being saved by higher forces during the landing and gone for human contact instead.

'Thanks be to God,' he said.

'Thanks be to the pilots,' replied Sam. Credit where credit's due, she thought. It was God that caused the storm so she wasn't too clear why he deserved any for trying to kill them. She was also angry at having to sit in the smoking section of the aircraft which she hated. An hour in the immigration and customs queues had not improved her crabby mood. She watched with envy as the local people filed past the immigration desks, chatting and waving their passports while she stood in a long queue of tourists being attended by only one desk. The search through her luggage in customs frustrated her even more. A man who appeared to be in a trance, picked up each individual piece of clothing and dangled it in the air as if expecting something to fly out. By the time she emerged outside into the shiny wet streets of Calderon, she was at the end of her tether and desperate for a cup of tea.

Gloria had not yet arrived. She had the habit of waiting for the plane to fly over her house before leaving for the airport. She was later than usual though, and Sam fretted. They didn't have a Plan B. If Gloria didn't turn up soon, she would have to change money at the horrible airport rates and take a taxi with the ensuing arguing about whether she should pay local or tourist prices. She could negotiate in Spanish after her first trip to Calderon, and that always had the effect of reducing the tourist premium, but she was stubborn. The longer she stood there, the more the taxi drivers besieged her, hoping that she would break and take one of them into town.

Then Sam spotted Gloria's jeep swinging into the airport road. Ignoring the do-not-enter signs, Gloria drove into the taxi lane and screeched to a halt right beside her. The taxi drivers swung away from Sam to protest at this sacrilege but one glare from the driver was enough to quell the rebellion. A bedraggled Gloria leapt out of the car and ran around to embrace her, smelling of smoke and patchouli.

'Hello, *gringa*. Sorry I'm late. Did you wait long? How was your trip?'

'Hello, Gloria. It's lovely to see you. How are you?'

'Oh, I'm fine. The usual.'

'Thank you for picking me up. What kept you anyway? I've been here over an hour.'

'Ah, but it's not my fault, Sam. The government changed the clocks and I keep forgetting what the time is.'

This piece of Glorified logic made Sam dizzy. She hugged her friend again and got into the car, holding on to her seat as it shot off into the traffic. Some things never change and Gloria still drove like Fangio. It began to rain again and the large volcano on the western side of the city poked out of a blanket of bright green conifers that draped over its sides like a cashmere shawl. The black rocks near the summit were free of snow for once and stood out against the clouds. Its brooding presence lent a sense of foreboding to the gloomy afternoon. She shook herself and turned to chat to Gloria.

***

'She should have arrived by now,' said Sam's father looking at his watch.

'I hope she rings us soon,' replied her mother.

'Give her a chance, she's only just landed.'

'You know how nervous I get. It's a long way to Sierramar.'

'Yes, but she's got Gloria to look after her. What can go wrong?'

They both laughed.

'Gloria is a treasure. Do you realise that she is Sam's first female friend? Most girls don't appreciate Sam's tomboy traits. I am so glad she has someone in whom to confide. Especially now she's back with Simon.'

'Hmmm, the slimy one. It's a pity she won't give up on that relationship. I think it's toxic for both.'

'A break might make her reconsider it.'

'It will be a welcome one for her. That feasibility study she reviewed was turgid in the extreme. I had to read some of it and I fell asleep twice.'

'I'll have to put up with the catty remarks about her lifestyle at the golf club again.'

'You ignore them, sweetheart. Sam is brave and adventurous and we should be proud of her.'

'Oh, I'm proud. I hate pretending to agree with them, not that I have any choice if I want to remain a member.'

'They pick on her because she's different. Hannah isn't married but they don't make comments about her. That reminds me. We haven't spoken to her in ages. Do you want to ring her, or shall I?'

***

Simon was not impressed to be deserted again. He stalked her flat, sniffing the pyjamas that Sam had dropped on the floor when she left to go to the airport. She would explode if she found out he had let himself in while she travelled. This was her territory, filled with balsa painted parrots and rugs with weird Incan insect and animal designs. It smelt of cooking and coffee. She had moved in after coming back from Sierramar and filled it with furniture from junk shops and cast offs from relatives. Coloured throws and big velvet curtains salvaged from a theatre covered the chairs. The big metal radiators were off and he shivered.

Why couldn't Sam be like other girls? He didn't understand why she had to go waltzing off to Sierramar to search for a drunk with his nutty girlfriend. Why wasn't he enough for her? Lots of other women were interested. He could have anyone he wanted. And that was the irritating thing. He wanted Sam more than other women. He missed her physical presence, the way she could pick up large pieces of luggage and chuck them on the bed with no visible strain. The way she fiddled with her fine hair and failed to put it in a neat bun no matter how much she tried. The way her shoulders looked when she emerged from the shower in a towel. He missed her cooking and her random pronouncements on government policy. She was different and he hated how much he wanted her.

After wandering around opening drawers and poking about in her stuff, he decided to visit her sister Hannah hoping she might offer sympathy and a plan to get Sam to come back. Hannah lived two streets away in a flat on the ground floor of a similar house. She opened the door abruptly when he knocked and looked as if she would shout at him until she realised who it was.

'Simon? What are you doing here? Is something wrong?'

She went bright red with embarrassment and confusion. Her uncanny resemblance to Sam struck him dumb. Hannah had the same light brown hair but wore it longer, and it fell on her shoulders in soft curls so different to Sam's curtain of ruler straight locks. She had a similar face and body to her sibling but they, too, had softer edges which camouflaged the harder edge to her character. Out of his depth, he stuttered.

'Um, are you busy? I wanted to talk about Sam.'

'Jesus, do you think I'm your agony aunt? I've got my own problems right now. I don't understand why you are here.'

'Please, I want your advice. No one knows her the way you do.'

'I can't talk now. Come back another time.'

'But I can come back?'

'If you must. Now go away.'

CHAPTER VI

Calderon, July 1988

Alfredo was eating breakfast when he heard the news. He had finished his second cup of coffee and was contemplating a third, when the telephone rang.

'Alfredo, is that you?'

Gloria's voice. Upset.

'Yes, sugar plum, is anything the matter? You sound strange.'

'I have terrible news for you.'

'Are you ill? Do you want me to come over?'

'No, sweetheart, I'm fine. It's Ramon.'

'Ramon? I saw him yesterday. He was in fine form.'

'His sister rang me to tell me his house burnt down last night, and he is missing, presumed dead.'

'A fire? This can't be a coincidence.'

'Why? A horrible thing has happened, but it has nothing to do with your visit.'

'I'll explain later. We must find out how it happened. Can you drive me to his house please?'

'I'll collect you in about twenty minutes.'

Alfredo hung up the phone and sat on a chair, his

head in his hands. He had palpitations and dread infiltrated his being. *This was not an accident. Could the fire be related to his visit? Had he caused the death of his friend?* The idea horrified him.

By the time Gloria pulled up to the house, Alfredo was already outside pacing the pavement in the bright sunlight, his eyes screwed up in concentration. He got into the car without greeting her.

'Seatbelt.' Alfredo tugged at his and then gave up. She didn't insist. 'He may be alive. Perhaps it's a mistake,' said Gloria

'Maybe.'

Conversation dried up and Gloria drove with more caution than usual in case any fire engines were coming back up the winding road. By the time they pulled up to the little farmhouse, it had burnt to the ground and the blackened stone walls and some stumps of hardwood furniture was all that remained. Piles of smouldering books with wet leather covers lay on the gravel outside the front door. The firemen still watered the remains of the structure, and the police were searching the ruins in a way that suggested they did not expect to find anything. Gloria and Alfredo got out of the car and approached them.

'Who's in charge here?' said Gloria.

'Me,' said one.

'What happened?'

'Well, madam, the house burned down.' He smirked.

'I'll thank you to have more respect officer. I am Gloria Sanchez, daughter of Hernan, and the house belonged to a friend of mine.'

'Sorry, madam. I didn't recognise you. I apologise.'

'What can you tell me about the fire?'

'It appears to be a case of arson. We found petrol

cans thrown on the ground at the back of the house. Someone set fire to the woodpile against the back wall and the flames spread to the roof. The amount of paper in the house didn't help much. They created an inferno.'

'And Mr Vega?'

'We found two corpses in the house. One in the maid's bedroom and one in the principal bedroom, both still in bed. They must have suffocated in their sleep.'

'Have you identified the owner of the house?'

'We can't be sure yet. The body has been burnt to a cinder.'

'How can I get the latest information on the case?'

'My name is Inspector Torres. I work in the police station on the road to the valley. Here is my card, or drop in any time and I'll fill you in.'

'Thank you. I'd appreciate that.'

She turned to offer words of encouragement to Alfredo but he had gone back to the car where he sat motionless in the front seat staring at the remains of the house.

'These people are maniacs,' he remarked as she got in.

'I'm so sorry. You were friends a long time.'

'Take me home, please.'

***

Alfredo sat in his armchair and picked at the stitching in one arm where hung loose. With his other hand, he swirled the ice cube around in his glass. Some cold whisky splashed on his hand, waking him from his reverie. Fear stalked the room. The state television channels had reported the inferno as an accident, but Inspector Torres had blamed arson.

The death of Ramon could not be a coincidence. *Had anyone been watching the house when he visited his friend? Did they realise he had the document? Was he next?* He tried to be rational. Would someone kill to stop the information about the Nazi unit in Sierramar from getting out? It seemed *unlikely, but what if they would?* He didn't need to finish reading the report to understand how incendiary its contents were. He should hide the document somewhere no one would dare look for it and he knew just the place. Putting on his coat, he hurried down the street, looking over his shoulder all the time.

The local shop had a photocopier, so he ducked into its claustrophobic interior. He made himself a copy of the whole document so that Saul could read it when he arrived in Calderon. The photocopying took almost an hour, but he didn't worry about being disturbed because the shopkeeper was kept busy by a constant stream of customers buying cigarettes and cans of cola. He returned to his house and collected his car. He stuffed the original document into his waistcoat and put the copy into the pocket at the back of the driver's seat amongst a load of old maps and leaflets, reasoning that no one would search inside a location in plain site. Then he drove to Gloria's apartment building.

Gloria opened the door and smiled.

'Hallo, I wasn't expecting to see you this evening. Are you okay? I know how fond you were of Ramon. This must be a nasty shock.'

'Still stunned, to tell you the truth. I suppose it hasn't sunk in yet.'

'So how can I help?'

'I need a favour.'

'Come in and sit down, honey. I'll help if I can.'

Alfredo followed her down the corridor to the

sitting room and perched on the edge of an armchair as if he might leave again. Gloria sat on the arm of the same chair and ran her fingers through his hair.

'What's up?' she asked

'I'm worried the fire may be related to my visit to Ramon yesterday.'

'I though it odd you went to see him. You told me ages ago that you two weren't talking.'

'We weren't, but when I searched the National Archive for information, I discovered that Ramon had borrowed literature related to the arrival of Germans in Sierramar. The coincidence struck me as extraordinary, but it was the only lead I had, so I decided I'd better swallow my pride. I went to his house and apologised for being an idiot. Luckily, he forgave me.'

'That was brave. He's a hot-head. I'm surprised he didn't punch your lights out.'

'We've been friends for ever. I guess he missed me. Anyway, he has been writing a detailed report about the relationship between the Nazis and the Sierramar government for the eighteen months.'

'Now that is a coincidence!'

'He had planned to take his report to Miami to publish before someone could stop him. He suspected that someone was watching him and he thought they might steal the report, so he gave it to me for safekeeping. He was going to collect it from me on his way to the airport.'

'You still have it? Isn't that dangerous?'

'Yes, I've still got it. There are certain people in Calderon who want to destroy any evidence of the collaboration with Nazi Germany.'

'So how can I help?'

'He must have been killed because of the report. I

need to hide the research before anyone realises that I have it.'

'Jesus, Alfredo! That's all I need. I can't hide the document here. My appartment's the first place that people will look.'

'Oh no, I don't want you to hide the report in your flat. I thought you could conceal it in your father's house. No one would ever look there.'

'My father's house? Are you mad?'

Her father's involvement with the fugitives should remain a secret. It was not for Alfredo to tell her something so personal. Hernan Sanchez would have to do it when the story came out, which was the inevitable result. So, he was economical with the truth.

'It's not as mad as it sounds. He's friends with many of these collaborators. They'd never suspect him of harbouring the document, and he won't be aware he has it. Hide it in his house without telling him.'

Gloria walked over to the sideboard and poured herself a large whisky. She had her back to him and he waited for her to turn around.

'Want one?'

'Yes, please.'

She poured another whisky, putting the cubes of ice in his glass one by one. He felt like the world had gone into slow motion. 'So where is the document?'

'I thought you'd never ask. I've kept a copy to study, but the original is here in my waistcoat.'

'Hmm.' She fixed him with a stare and raised her eyebrow in a way that made him instantly erect. 'Maybe I'd better remove it then?'

'Be careful. I'm armed and dangerous.'

'Oh, I hope so. You'll pay for this.'

***

Gloria's father was thrilled when she announced that she was inviting herself to lunch the next day. Hernan Sanchez did not see enough of his daughter and often wished she would move back in with him. This would cause massive arguments about her social life and his opinions about the company she was keeping, so it was unlikely to happen soon. He hoped that she would calm down enough for them to get on better but he was a realist and accepted she wasn't ready yet.

'Hello, Papi, it's me.'

Gloria breezed in trailing cigarette smoke and gave her father a big hug.

'Hello, darling. You look lovely as always.'

'Thank you. So do you.'

Ritual greeting over, they both sat at the dining table while Hernan's maid served them a bowl of soup. They ate in silence. Gloria wondered how to hide the document without her father spotting her.

'I've got to go to the bathroom, Papi. I'll be back in a minute.'

'Okay, sweetheart, I'll get Rosa to serve the main course.'

Instead of heading for the guest bathroom, Gloria flounced off towards the ensuite bathroom taking her bag with her. Her high heels clattered into the bathroom and out of the other side into his bedroom.

The chest of drawers that belonged to her mother was still on her side of the bed. Her father almost never opened it unless he was being nostalgic and trying to sniff the clothes for a residual smell of his wife. She opened one of the heavy drawers which slid out revealing her mother's expensive undergarments still waiting for their long dead owner to put on again. She moved the clothes aside, took the document out of her bag and slipped it between the silken folds of an ivory petticoat, taking care to disguise its shape by putting a chemise on top.

Admiring her handiwork, she stepped back feeling emotional. '*Gracias, Mami,*' she said and re-joined her father at lunch. She had a habit of wearing her mother's jewellery and then returning it to the box that her father was familiar with so he wouldn't think anything of her going into his room. Besides, she never took it for good in case her mother turned up one day and needed it. He loved her for that, amongst other things.

'Okay, darling? Let's eat then.'

***

'It's done. The house burnt to the ground.'

'Is he dead?'

'I watched while it burned and no one came out. The police found two bodies, one in the maid's room, one in the main bedroom.'

'But did they identify him yet?'

'They won't tell me, but who else would it be?'

'You've done well. I need you to confirm that Dr Vargas hasn't got a copy of the report.'

'Okay. I'll check the house next time he leaves.'

'Be careful. Don't let anyone notice you.'

CHAPTER VII

Calderon September 1988

Calderon was free of traffic so they made good time to Gloria's flat, stopping on the way to buy fresh bread at the baker's. Gloria screeched to a halt in the basement garage and jumped out of the car. Sam, thanking the fates she had survived another hair-raising trip in the Gloria-mobil, dragged her bags out of the boot and they took one each to the elevator, straining to lift them off the ground.

'Did you bring your furniture with you?' asked Gloria.

'No, but I brought jars of mint jelly and chutney for anyone who carries my bag.'

'Suitcases should have wheels.'

'Someone might invent them. Let's have a cup of tea and you can tell me about Alfredo.'

Soon they were sitting in the kitchen sipping cups of scalding hot tea.

'How have you been?' asked Sam, 'and your father?'

'Oh, we're both fine. Trying to get along as usual.

And you?'

'Same here. We're well. No dramas.'

'That's good. How about Simon?'

'I'm more interested in Alfredo. Have you found out what happened yet? How long has he been missing?'

'Two weeks or more. I'm worried about him,' said Gloria.

'Has he been drinking?'

'No more than usual and less than before. I'm convinced his disappearance relates to something a lot more sinister than drink.'

'You'd better start at the beginning.'

'Well, it started when a journalist from New York rang Alfredo and asked him if he could research Nazi fugitives in Sierramar.'

'Nazi's in Sierramar? Didn't they go to Argentina or Brazil or something?'

'That's what we thought but Alfredo discovered that there may be a group of them here in Calderon. There was no information in the National Archive but he found evidence that his friend Ramon had been researching the same thing. So, he went to Ramon's house and it turned out that Ramon wrote a report which showed that the national government were complicit in welcoming the fugitive officers to Sierramar and helping them start new lives. Ramon had planned to go to Miami to publish his research but his house burned down that night, and he died in the fire.'

'Oh my God, that's awful. Did the research burn too?'

'No, Ramon had lent the report to Alfredo to photocopy.'

'Was the fire deliberate?'

'The police suspect arson but they haven't found the culprits yet. Alfredo was nervous because he thought someone had seen him visiting Ramon.'

'Why did he think that?'

'Someone tried to burgle his house not long afterwards while Alfredo was picking Saul up from the airport. He's the journalist who went missing with Alfredo.'

'Did the burglar get the report?'

'Alfredo didn't leave it in the house.'

'Where is it now?'

'It's hidden in my father's house. I put it in a drawer under some of my mother's clothing when he wasn't looking. It is safer that way.'

'When did you last see Alfredo?'

'He left with Saul to look for the fugitives in the mountains over two weeks ago. I haven't heard from him since.'

'Did you report him missing to the police?'

'Sam, don't be so English! That's the last place I'd go.'

'Don't exaggerate. They're not that bad. Where were Alfredo and Saul going?'

'That's the problem. I've no idea. They left suddenly, and I didn't get a chance to ask him. He left a message with my maid saying he'd be back in a few days but I haven't heard from him since. We need to start from scratch.'

'What do we know so far?'

'Well, they were searching for German men who came to Sierramar after World War II. Those men must be over sixty-five years old if they came here about forty-five years ago.'

'How did they get here?'

'There were no flights in those days so they came in

by boat to Guayama and then travelled to Calderon along the old road.'

'Don't all foreigners register with the migration office when they arrive in Sierramar? I did. Perhaps they had to do that then also?'

'That's not a bad idea. There might be a record of their arrival in the archives. If we discover who came here, we can use their names to locate them. Someone in migration might check the records for us. I think my father has a contact who works there. I will ask him.'

'Okay but tell him I am looking for a relative or something. We don't want him getting suspicious.'

***

Sam woke up with a start during the night. She glanced in alarm at her surroundings struggling to work out where she was and what was going on. The Viteri painting with its multicoloured balloons told her she was in Gloria's flat. The glass in the windows rattled and her bed shook as if to throw her off. She realised that it was a tremor. They were part of life in Calderon, which sat on the slopes of a volcano that periodically came to life and dusted the city with several inches of volcanic ash, but she had never experienced one before. Unsure if it was terrifying or fascinating, she sat up in bed and watched the lampshade swinging from the flex on the ceiling. She felt as if she were inside a Christmas present being rattled by a diffident child. Gloria appeared at the door to her bedroom.

'Don't be afraid. It was a minor tremor. We don't need to leave the building. It's safer indoors anyway, as a piece of concrete can land on your head in the street.'

'Hmm, I don't fancy that. It gave me a fright though. I don't think I can go to sleep again right away.

My heart is thundering in my rib cage. Do you want a cup of tea?'

'Good plan. I'll put on some water. See you in the kitchen.'

Sam shuffled into the kitchen in a pair of tiny slippers provided by Gloria who seemed unaware that her friend had penguin-sized feet. Sam's large feet were a source of chagrin due to her inheriting a shoe fetish from her mother that rivalled Imelda Marcos; one unrequited due to the lack of women's shoes in her size. Humming, Gloria poured water into a bright yellow teapot. It was typical of her to be so unaffected by what seemed like disturbing events. She had a sangfroid about her that singled her out.

'Can you get the milk from the fridge, please?' asked Gloria. 'Or should I say milkshake?'

'Hilarious. It wasn't that strong.'

'So, are you going to tell me about Simon or not?'

Straight to the point as usual, Gloria had no sympathy for Sam's barriers. She did not distinguish between what might be private and what she discussed in technicolour detail. There was nothing sacred for Gloria's inquiring mind. Sooner or later they must talk about him. No time like the present as the latest episode had the potential to produce an earthquake in Sam's existence if the clues were pointing in the right direction.

'What about him?'

'Come on. I'm not stupid. You've got that face on, as if someone killed your cat. Something's wrong. Did you break up with him again?'

'No, I didn't. We are happy together.'

Gloria raised an eyebrow so high it was in danger of disappearing into her highlights.

'Really?'

Sam blushed. Gloria's disbelief seared through her pores.

'Well, um, relationships and all that.'

'Is he sleeping around again?'

'No, well, I don't think so, although it's difficult to tell. That's not the problem.'

There was a pause as she sipped her tea and took a deep breath.

'It's like pulling teeth, gringa. Out with it.'

'I think I might be pregnant.'

A teaspoon fell on the floor as Gloria's hand flew to her mouth. They both jumped. The neon light in the kitchen flickered making them both look even more shocked.

'Holy shit and all the saints,' said Gloria. She rummaged in her dressing gown pocket for her cigarettes. Withdrawing one from the packet with shaking fingers, she clicked the lighter without success. Sam leaned across the table and grabbed the lighter. It worked first time and soon Gloria was sucking on the cigarette as she regained her composure.

'What will you do, Sam?'

'Do? What do you mean?'

'If you are pregnant? Will you keep it?'

Good question and one that Sam had asked herself many times. What did anyone do when they were going out with a man who couldn't keep his hands off other women and then they discovered that they were pregnant, or might be? Raw panic bubbled under her sternum and she stared at her cup of tea.

'That's not something I've considered yet,' she mumbled, 'I won't know how I feel unless it's confirmed. My first instinct is to get an abortion before anyone finds out. It's wicked, but I can't do the whole baby thing right now.'

She looked up from her tea expecting to see Gloria glowering at her with disapproval. Instead her friend's face had gone white, and she held on to the edge of the table as if on a roller coaster. Pain or fear showed in her eyes. Sam waved her hand as if to dismiss the topic.

'I may not even be pregnant. Ignore me.'

But it was too late. Gloria did not respond. She shut her eyes as if visualising something far away and Sam wondered what on earth she had triggered with her premature panic attack. She waited for Gloria to speak. After what seemed an age, her friend opened her eyes again and spoke so softly that Sam struggled to hear her.

'I had an abortion,' said Gloria, 'after getting pregnant when I was nineteen. I was so innocent that when the nuns told me I couldn't get pregnant before I married, I took it literally.'

She forced out a laugh but the painful sound stabbed Sam like a knife.

'I didn't even realise I was pregnant until my mother noticed me putting on weight and took me to the doctor. When they told me I would have a baby, it shocked me to the core, but I wasn't as horrified as my mother. It would have been a terrible scandal had anyone found out. Single mothers were beyond the pale. My parents were not prepared to go through the disgrace.'

'What happened?'

'They shut me in my room for days, forbidden to see or talk to anyone, and then my mother announced that we would travel Miami. She said it was to buy baby clothes. I didn't understand what she had planned until we pulled into the doorway of the clinic. I had no choice.'

'How awful for you. It must have been hard to forgive your mother.'

'She had colluded with my father to get me an abortion which devastated me, but I understood. She was already ill, dying, from cancer and she didn't want to leave me alone with a baby.'

'But why didn't they discuss it with you? Didn't you have a right to decide, too?'

'They were ashamed because in those days, nice girls didn't get pregnant. They tried to protect me, I guess. When I got back to Calderon, the father of the baby had disappeared.'

'Did he run away?'

'I never found out what happened to him. He may have returned to Peru. I was afraid to ask my father, because I suspected he had something to do with it.'

She faltered. Fat tears leaked from her eyes, splashing on the Formica table top and she wept, wailing with grief. Senor Sanchez had a reputation. He was not a man to be crossed. Sam could imagine his rage when he discovered that someone had deflowered his daughter and left her pregnant.

'I'm so sorry, Gloria. I didn't know.'

'That's why I don't have children. I can't anymore. Something went wrong.'

Her bravado had evaporated. Sam now understood why Gloria wasn't married in the land of the teenage engagements. She had always presumed that Gloria had chosen to be single, like her. Poor Gloria, there were no fairy tale weddings for the barren in Sierramar, no matter how rich you were. Speechless with sorrow for the hidden pain trapped behind Gloria's glossy façade, now leaking out in the form of bitter tears, Sam put her arms around her friend and held her as she mourned.

***

The contact provided by Hernan Sanchez waited at the door to the Migration building. He was short and plump with a bad wig resembling a random piece of cat skin perched at an angle on his head. He beamed at them, a smile of such radiance it almost made him handsome.

'What did you tell your father?' said Sam to Gloria as they approached him.

'I said we wanted to check if any of your relatives had settled in Sierramar.'

'We could do that, too.'

'No, we couldn't. This is urgent. Senor Salazar?'

'Yes, Senorita Sanchez, it's a pleasure to meet you. And your friend?'

'I'm Sam. Hello, Senor Salazar, nice to meet you, too.'

'So, how can I help you ladies?'

'We need to look in the archives. My friend is German, and she is trying to find out if any relatives came to Sierramar after 1938.'

'You mean because of the war in Europe?'

'Yes, it would have been around that time,' said Sam.

'Follow me.'

They registered at the security desk leaving their ID cards with the guard and got into a rusty lift which plummeted deep into the earth at a disconcerting speed. The doors slid open at level B4 and they stepped into a gloomy basement with some old-fashioned microfiche viewers on a bench.

'Wait here, please,' said Senor Salazar. Apart from the bench running down one wall of the room, parallel rows of shelving containing boxes with numbered labels on them filled the space. He walked past the entrances to several rows of shelving before disappearing into one. After about five minutes he re-emerged pushing a trolley which had boxes on both the bottom and top trays.

'Here we are. If you can't find them in here, they don't exist. These are the records for residential immigrants into Sierramar from Germany for 1938 to 1946.'

'Thank you. This is fantastic.'

Senor Salazar beamed again and stood there waiting. Sam opened one box. It contained sheets of see-through plastic that appeared to have minute writing on them. She had no idea what to do.

'Um, I'm sorry, I don't know how to read these.'

'Ah, but you need to use the screens.'

'Please can you show me how to do it?'

'It would be my pleasure, Miss Sam.'

Mr Salazar selected a box and took the first sheet out of it. He sat at one screen and switched it on. A glass plate on the bench under the screen became illuminated. He lifted the plate and put the plastic sheet upside down on another plate below it. Sam was about to point this out but Gloria stopped her. He lowered the top plate onto the plastic sheet. The image appeared on the screen in a magnified form and they could see that it recorded the immigration of one Frau Magda Glaub from Cologne.

'Wow, that's great,' said Sam.

'I recommend you do this in order,' said Senor Salazar, 'work through the box from back to front and you shouldn't miss any records. Good luck in your search. When you finish, can you please log out at the security desk?'

'We will. Thank you,' said Sam. 'Gloria, we need to avoid repetition here to save time. I'll do the boxes on the top tray if you take those on the bottom. Let's pile the boxes which we finish checking over here on the bench and then we can load up the trolley again when we finish. We should make notes about any German men from twenty to forty-five years old who arrived from 1938 to 1946.'

Gloria, who hated being told what to do, rolled her eyes to heaven at Sam's British obsession with efficiency. However, this would not be a quick task if they weren't organised and she hated basements.

'Good idea,' she said.

They sat down at the microfiche screens, side by side at first, but then Sam moved down one machine to give herself more room. The work was straightforward from then on. The forms all had a similar template and gave the same information; name, date of birth, profession, origin. As they worked, Gloria gave out the odd exclamation and waved a microfiche in the air.

'I know him,' she said, 'he lives in the valley.'

After a couple of hours, Sam finished the last box, and she had a list of about twenty names.

'Well, I'm finished. What about you?'

'I'm on the last box. Give me a minute. I think these are women but I want to be positive.'

Sam made a table in her notebook with crude columns with the same headings as the report cards. She transferred the information from her list and then copied Gloria's data too. When they had finished, the table contained thirty-six names.

'So?' she asked Gloria, 'do you recognise anyone?'

'Most of them. I'm shocked. You should choose one to be your long-lost-relative.'

'There's a doctor, Dr Kurt Becker. I shall pretend that his sister is my grandmother. That will make it less obvious than using a real person.'

'Good idea. We should contact some of these people and pretend we are looking for her, or her brother.'

'Is there anyone that stands out?'

'Boris Klein. His daughters were at the same school as me. He made them dye their hair blonde so they would be more Aryan.'

'Holy crap! Do you know where they live?'

'I've got their phone number.'

CHAPTER VIII

Saul and Alfredo August 1988
Saul Rosen wasted no time in getting a flight to Calderon and travelled south from New York within the week. He had not slept or bathed and had only eaten scraps from the fridge before catching his flight. The chaotic apartment he left behind wore an air of neglect that suggested a deep depression or worse.

He had forced himself to pack a bag with items suitable for hiking and general tourist activities but he had none of the usual essentials like shorts or sun screen. He packed the Glock and bullets in his suitcase wrapped in his underwear. Old photographs of men in uniform went into his carry-on bag along with his single ticket and passport. He was feeling light-headed and struggled to act normally. His behaviour concerned his neighbours but in true big city style they left him alone.

'Poor man. I heard he was in a concentration camp. He'll never recover you know.'

***

Alfredo drove to the airport to collect him, feeling rejuvenated by his anticipation of the adventure and history generated by Saul's quest to find the fugitive Nazis. He would get revenge for his friend Ramon, whatever it took. Leaving the car in the official carpark, he strode across to the arrivals hall to find that they had delayed the flight by thirty minutes and that most of the passengers were still queueing in immigration. He bought himself a bitter coffee and a super sweet biscuit at a stall in the foyer. The muscles in his face tightened as he forced the coffee down his throat. Large groups of excited people were jostling to get to the barriers forcing him backwards. Some of them were holding helium balloons and other party paraphernalia. It was traditional for the whole extended family to welcome someone home from a trip abroad.

By the time, Saul emerged from the customs area, Alfredo was hopping from foot to foot in expectation. Saul was recognisable with his big nose and journalist's leather satchel. He was a tall man and stooped despite only being in his late fifties. Alfredo stepped forward to shake his hand and noticed that his shirt was pungent with sweat and in miscellaneous stains covered his trousers. He wrinkled his nose and tried to hide his disgust.

'Welcome to Sierramar. I'm Alfredo Vargas. I'm so glad you are here.'

'Thank you. That's a hell of a landing. I'll need clean shorts.'

'Oh, yes, I should have warned you,' replied Alfredo, who was not impressed by this smelly New Yorker. It was tempting to tell Saul that a shower would be a good idea, too, but he realised that personal hygiene often went by the wayside when people got obsessed. His own had improved from necessity after he met Gloria who was fanatical about it. So, he gave Saul the benefit of the doubt and wound down the windows in the car for the journey home.

It was a bright windy day in Calderon and the traffic had not yet built up enough to block the roads. They drove through the modern part of the town which seemed to impress Saul.

'I thought Calderon would be full of colonial streets with tiled roofs and stone roadways.'

'Oh, it has them, too. I live in the modern part of town. The old town is to the south. We can have a look around. They have lots of beautiful churches, covered in gold leaf.'

'Oh, I'm not one for churches. I prefer libraries.'

'We have those, too.'

'Don't worry, I wasn't expecting naked Indians with loin cloths.'

'That's a relief.'

***

They soon pulled into the garage at the side of Alfredo's house and pushing through the kitchen door with Saul's luggage. A door slammed.

'I didn't realise that you lived with someone,' said Saul.

'I don't,' said Alfredo, 'and the maid already went home.' He ran into the hall and out of the back door which was swinging open. A slim man with a pudding bowl haircut escaped through the back garden and jumped over the hedge. There was no hope of catching him. Alfredo turned to re-enter the house and stopped in horror. On the grass to his left lay the body of his dog, surrounded by dark fluid seeping into the earth. His throat had been cut and the gaping hole was already attracting ants. He gasped and turned away.

These people were dangerous. He struggled to control his emotions. Saul came to the door.

'Did you see who it was?' he said.

'I didn't, although I may have talked to him in the National Archive. I have an idea what he wanted.'

Saul was staring in horror at the damp body on the grass.

'Oh my God, he killed your dog. I'm so sorry. How devastating.'

'He wasn't much of a dog, more of a food disposal unit. He didn't like me unless I was eating.'

'Still, it's a shock. The bastard!'

'There's nothing we can do now. Leave the body here. I'll deal with it later. Shall we go in?'

The two men walked back inside the house trying not to smell the metallic odour that permeated the garden. Alfredo opened the door to the sitting room, and they went in. The room was carpeted with papers, some had been moved but otherwise the room remained as he had left it. He guessed that they had disturbed the thief before he had finished.

'Oh no, he's trashed the place,' said Saul, 'do you think he found the report?'

'I doubt it, my study always looks this way,' said Alfredo, 'even I can't find anything, so I doubt he did.'

'I apologise. If it's any consolation, my office also looks like a bomb site.'

Alfredo guffawed, but it worried him. Someone had seen him visit Ramon. But who? Whoever it was suspected he had the report on the Nazis in Sierramar and had sent Kleber to steal it. Or Kleber had been spying on him? Whatever the explanation, someone was concerned about the possibility that any information from Ramon's report might get released. It was lucky he took the copy with him in the poacher's pocket of his jacket. He patted it for reassurance.

'I know he didn't find the document because I've got it right here. We can discuss the latest events with a cup of coffee. Let me show you your room and so on.'

'Yes, that would be great. Do you think I might take a shower? I'm desperate to take off these dirty clothes.'

'Go straight up the stairs and it's on the right in your room. I'll put a towel on your bed for you. See you in a minute.'

While Saul was in the shower, Alfredo put the kettle on and laid the table. He took food out of the fridge and sliced some bread. Then he remembered that he had not left a towel for his guest. Grabbing one from the linen cupboard he dashed up the stairs and into the guest bedroom. He hung the towel on the hook on the outside of the bathroom door and turned to leave. Saul's clothes were lying on the floor in a heap. His suitcase was open and most of the contents had also found their way to the floor. There was a large pistol in the middle of the bed. It looked so incongruous that it shocked him. He didn't have time to examine it as he heard the water in the shower stop flowing as Saul shut it off.

'Your towel is hanging on the door,' he shouted as he left the room.

***

Kleber pushed open the door of the men's toilet with his elbows and went straight to the basins. To his disgust, there was no soap in the dispensers. He turned on the hot tap with his fingertips and put his hands into the flow of water. Gasping, he withdrew them again. Bloodied water dripped into the sink and swirled down the plug hole. Another man, who came out of one cubicle, took one look at the stain in the sink and left. Kleber turned on the cold tap as well and inserted his fingers into the stream. The blood was dry and difficult to remove from beneath his fingernails. He retched as he remembered how difficult it was to slit the throat through the fur with the dog wriggling and wagging its tail. At least people had the good grace to scream or faint.

He waited for the Minister to emerge from the government building where he worked, hanging back until he spotted him. Holger Ponce gesticulated at him, his face red with impatience.

'Did you get the report?'

'No sir, I couldn't see it anywhere. The place is like a rubbish tip. Anyway, I had to leave in a hurry when Dr Vargas arrived.'

'Vargas disturbed you? Is that why there's blood on your sleeve?'

'I had to kill the dog. It wouldn't stop barking.'

'Did you leave the body where he would find it? We need to scare him off.'

'Of course.'

'So, we still don't know whether he has the document.'

'No, but...'

'But what?'

'He collected an American visitor from the airport. I saw the name on a piece of paper. It said 'Saul Rosen, Simon Wiesenthal Centre. Collect at airport' and it had today's date.'

'The Simon Wiesenthal Centre? He sounds like a Nazi hunter. He may be trouble. Christ, I must warn Kurt. Thank you, Kleber. Keep an eye on Dr Vargas and his friend.'

***

Saul Rosen looked ten years younger after his shower. He had changed into a pair of corduroy trousers and a checked shirt, and his face was clean shaven, taking years off his age. He didn't seem sure where to place his limbs when he sat down at the kitchen table. Alfredo had made a big pot of tea and raided the bread bin for some muffins and rolls. A plate of cheese and ham sat in the middle of the table and a bowl of fresh figs from the garden completed the feast.

'Wow. You are quite the caterer,' said Saul.

'I eat well. I made tea but there's coffee if you prefer.'

'Tea is fine, thanks. So, where are we with this thing? I need to talk to your friend Ramon as soon as possible.'

Alfredo blanched. 'Ramon? Oh, crap! I haven't told you. Ramon is dead. He died in a fire in his house along with his books and research.'

'Dead? When? How?'

'The police say it was an arson attack. They found two bodies in his house but they haven't confirmed that one of them was Ramon yet. They are being secretive. Mind you it was a couple of days ago, and they aren't the quickest.'

'That's terrible news. I'm so sorry. Do you think it might be related to his research?'

'It must have been. I'm sorry. I should have told you right away but I've been upset and distracted. You shouldn't have come. It could be dangerous to carry on with this.'

'Are you kidding me? This could be the biggest scoop of my career. Your friend did not die in vain. We will chase down those sons of bitches and make them pay.'

Saul Rosen was standing now, his arm stretched out

as if he was shooting at someone. The metamorphosis startled Alfredo and he remembered the gun lying on the bed. Mild mannered journalist Saul Rosen had an alter-ego hidden under his clothes.

'Okay, you need to calm down. I couldn't help noticing the gun in your room. You can't take that with you. The police will put you in prison if they find it.'

'You weren't supposed to see it. I wasn't planning on using it. I heard Sierramar is dangerous.'

This explanation did not convince Alfredo, but he didn't want to start off on the wrong foot. He would broach the subject again on another occasion.

'The one positive in this situation is that Ramon gave me his report to read, so it survived the fire,' he said. 'I have hidden the report where they won't ever think of looking and made a copy which I have here if you want to read it.'

'I'm a little tired right now but I'd love to read it later. Can you give me more details on the contents? I want to know what we are up against.'

'More tea? Or would you prefer a whisky?'

'Have you got a bourbon?'

'Jack Daniels?'

'Perfect. On the rocks, please.'

'Let's move to the study. The chairs are more comfortable in there.'

They crossed the hall into the study.

'Can I have the corner chair, please?' asked Saul. A haunted look flashed across his face and vanished. The leather armchairs were identical but the corner chair was Alfredo's favourite. He was about to demure but he caught the look on Saul's face and decided that he didn't care where he sat. He gestured at it. His guest sat down and the tension flowed out of his body as fast as it had appeared.

Once they had settled into the leather armchairs, Alfredo gathered himself.

'As a patriot,' he said, 'this has been a painful revelation for me. I wasn't aware that Nazis had penetrated so far into Sierramar society. I knew that the United States intervened on the side of Peru in the conflict of 1941which had caused a marked antipathy against the allies and sympathy for the Axis countries. However, the details of that era had passed me by. I was always more interested in the Inca and pre-Inca cultures. It has been an immense shock to realise that the government legislated against the Jewish population during the war. They had been arriving since the 18th century to set up businesses in Sierramar. People organised protests against the Jews in Calderon and Guayama.'

'I hadn't come across this information in my research,' said Saul. 'I don't find it that surprising in the circumstances. It was happening in many countries.'

'But you, of all people, must find this horrifying.'

'Of all people, do you mean as a Jew?'

'Well, yes, I noticed your surname and made an assumption about your origin.'

'No offence taken. I am not a real Jew, only a historical offshoot.'

Alfredo didn't believe this either but there wasn't time for a discussion of Saul's genealogy.

'Good, where was I? Oh yes, there is a long history of contact, both cultural and trade related, between Germany and Sierramar. In the run-up to the second world war this relationship became ever more important. Sierramar sent raw materials to Germany and received manufactured goods in return without any cash changing hands. Ramon saw a copy of a letter in the archives that Hitler sent to the government in 1937 offering close cooperation with Sierramar. This arrangement carried on throughout most of the war. In 1945 Sierramar's government received a request for help from the German government for refugees from the Third Reich who were fleeing prosecution by the Allies.'

'Which they agreed to provide?'

'Yes, the German government arranged for a boat to sail from Hamburg with a cargo of fugitive Gestapo and SS officers. This boat docked in Guayama and the Consul welcomed the passengers with cheering crowds of local people. Many of the arrivals were war criminals being hunted by the Allies, including people who had worked at Auschwitz and Buchenwald doing experiments on Jews and other nationalities and murdering them in gas chambers.'

'That's appalling. I didn't know the collaboration went that far. No wonder they murdered Ramon. There must be many people in Sierramar who took part in this and are still alive. They have to be desperate to keep this a secret. We need to act fast.'

'I hoped you would take the report back to New York with you and publish it posthumously for Ramon.'

'I'd be delighted, but we can't stop there. I have the names of several members of the Gestapo who disappeared at the end of the war. I'd been searching for any trace of them for months and then I discovered that they may have been hiding in Sierramar. I guess they came on a boat from Hamburg. We have to find these bastards and get proof of their existence. Will you help me?'

'I will. The pride of Sierramar is at stake.'

'Where do we start?'

'First you need a good night's sleep.'

CHAPTER IX

Sam and Gloria September 1988

As soon as they got back to the apartment, Gloria searched for the piece of paper with the Klein sisters' number on it. This was no easy task. She had an address book, which Sam had given to her, but she had written nothing in it. Instead, she had put scraps of paper, with addresses scrawled on them, in between the pages. Sam shook it and all the papers fell out onto the table.

'But why haven't you copied the addresses into the book?' said Sam.

'It's so nice I didn't want to ruin it by crossing out addresses when people moved,' said Gloria.

'That explanation makes no sense.'

'It does to me.'

Sam rolled her eyes.

By laying the bits of paper out on the table and ironing them one by one, they found the address they were looking for.

'Here it is,' said Gloria, 'easy to find.'

'Define easy,' said Sam, planning on finding an

afternoon when Gloria was out to transfer the addresses into the book.

Gloria shrugged and picked up the telephone to dial the number. It rang several times before anyone answered.

'Good morning. Who's speaking?'

'Good morning. It's Gloria, Gloria Sanchez. Is that Heidi?'

'Gloria! Heavens, it's been a long time since we heard from you.'

'Yes, likewise. I have a friend from Europe staying with me and I thought it would be nice for her to meet you both. Some of her relatives settled here in the 1940s. Perhaps you have met them?'

'I doubt it. We are busy.'

Gloria ignored her. 'Well, in that case we'll pop in for coffee tomorrow. Does eleven o'clock suit you?'

'Can you make it the next day? We are busy tomorrow.'

'That will be fine. See you then.'

Gloria picked up the grudging nature of Heidi's tone but she didn't care. There were few families powerful or foolish enough to turn down a request from the daughter of Hernan Sanchez.

'They are eccentric,' said Gloria, 'so don't expect a lot of small talk.'

'That's okay. This situation doesn't call for much chit-chat,' replied Sam, subdued after Gloria's revelation about her aborted pregnancy and, although desperate for her advice about Simon, didn't want to approach the subject again without upsetting them both. 'What shall we do today?'

'There is another name on the list that rings a bell,' said Gloria. 'The record shows that Henrik Stern came here in 1939. He used to live around here with his wife.

They were reclusive and didn't come out often. He died a few years ago, but his widow stayed in the apartment. I'll send the maid to the building to see if the guard can confirm they are still living there.'

Gloria dispatched the maid who returned to report that Gerda Stern still lived in apartment 4B with her two sausage dogs.

'No time like the present,' said Gloria. 'Come on Sam, we will drop in for a visit.'

'1939 sounds early for a Nazi fugitive. They are more likely to be fugitives from the Nazis that early in the war.'

'I need to find Alfredo. This lady might help. She's German and should know the others. What have we got to lose?'

'Not all Germans were Nazis. I suppose it's worth a try but we should check out her background first.'

'I can't wait. Alfredo may be in danger. Are you coming?'

They soon completed the short walk to the Sterns' apartment building and asked the security guard to buzz them up. He recognised Gloria and did not bother to ask for permission from the maid. Going up in the lift, Sam chewed her nails and wondered what they should say. Gloria was humming and fiddling with her hair. They stood outside the door. Gloria knocked. There was the sound of shuffling feet and the door opened. Inside was a shrunken old lady in clothes that looked far too big for her.

'Yes?'

'Hello, Mrs Stern, it's Gloria Sanchez, and this is Sam Harris. We are doing research about German immigration to Sierramar. Do you mind if we come in?'

Mrs Stern hesitated. It seemed to Sam that she

looked panicked but Gloria did not wait for an answer. She strode into the gloomy apartment and made herself at home in the sitting room.

'I don't think I can help you,' quavered Mrs Stern. 'What do you want?'

'We are looking for Sam's maternal grandmother. She arrived in Sierramar after the war in Europe. She may have been travelling with her brother, a Dr Kurt Becker. A group of Germans came with him by boat to Guayama. I wondered if your husband was one of them?'

'By boat? No, he wasn't. He had nothing to do with them.'

'But he was German? Didn't you socialise with them?'

Mrs Stern had a funny look on her face, a mixture of fury and misery.

'No, we didn't. It's time you left now. I have no information for you,' she blurted out.

'But it seems so unlikely that you didn't meet any of them.'

'You don't understand what you are talking about.'

'Gloria, Mrs Stern has already given us her answer.'

'Please, Mrs Stern. We are looking for someone who has disappeared, my fiancé. His disappearance is somehow related to this group of people. Don't you know anything that might help us?'

Perhaps it was the doubt in her voice which triggered Mrs Stern's reaction.

'Get out of my house. Get out. How dare you come here asking questions about my husband? You understand nothing about us.'

She stood up puce with fury. Gloria had no choice but to leave. Sam tried to apologise. 'I'm so sorry to have upset you. Gloria's boyfriend has disappeared on a trip to find them and bring them to justice. She is worried. We didn't mean to insinuate that it could involve your husband. Please forgive us.'

But the little woman pointed to the door without saying anything. The two friends took the elevator down to the ground floor without speaking.

'That was awful,' said Gloria. 'Why was she so angry?'

Sam didn't answer. She had not been in favour of visiting Mrs Stern with no background information and she was cross with Gloria for barging in to see her. There was only one reason for the Sterns to avoid other Germans.

'That's why I didn't want to go. The date of their arrival suggests that they were Jewish refugees. No wonder Mrs Stern became hysterical. We should never have gone to see her without checking,' said Sam.

They walked back to the apartment and had a subdued lunch. Gloria was quiet. Sam ignored her, punishing her for the misery of Mrs Stern which hung over them like a dark mist.

CHAPTER X

Alfredo and Saul August 1988

The two men breakfasted early.

'I'm confident,' said Alfredo, munching on his toast, 'that none of the passengers who landed on the boat from Germany will have been using their real names. Have you any information about the new identities they were using?'

'I discovered that one officer had changed his name to Rolf Hermann.'

'Rolf Hermann? Wow! I was at school with his sons. We used to play football at their hacienda.'

Saul shook his head and sighed. 'Hidden in plain sight. I guess that no one here cared who they were. The war was far away from Sierramar. Are they still living there?'

'They make cheese and have done for many years. We had some of it yesterday for supper. Hermann may not be running it but the family still own the farm.'

'Is it far away?'

'About an hour's drive. We can go there today if you like. We need a convincing story if we're asking questions about his past.'

'Say I'm a tourist looking for some lost cousins.'

'We must change your name.'

'Yes, that's a given. How about Frank Hermann?'

'No, it must be the original surname to make sense. What was it?'

'Kaufmann. His name was Helmut Kaufmann. He was a lieutenant in the Gestapo.'

'Perfect. Frank Kaufmann it is then. Okay, so get sorted out and we'll set off in about ten minutes. Bring your camera. You need to look as if you are a gringo tourist.'

***

The road to the hacienda was the typical mix of potholes and cobblestones, throwing the two men from side to side in the ancient jeep. They drove past damp hillsides with a myriad of tiny fields in many shades of green as if verdant quilts had been laid over sleeping giants. Scruffy black pigs with ears that flopped over their eyes snuffled in the mud beside the road giving them the appearance of shy teenagers hiding behind their fringes. In the fields, sheep with long coats bleated as the car passed by, hoping for some feed. The air was so moist that drops of condensation hung from their coats.

'Wow, that's pretty countryside you've got there,' said Saul. 'Reminds me of Ireland.'

Alfredo had underestimated the distance and the state of the road and they didn't pull up to the farmhouse until midday. The cobbled farmyard was deserted except for two large Alsatian dogs who growled and crouched for attack when Alfredo tried to get out of the car.

'Hmm, this is tricky,' he said.

'Someone will come and rescue us. It's lunchtime.'

They sat in the car for almost an hour. When either of them attempted to get out, one of the large dogs would throw themselves at the door barking and snarling. They would have left but Saul spotted a curtain twitching in one window.

'There's someone in there,' he said. 'Let's wait them out.'

The front door opened and an old woman appeared. She clapped her hands together causing the dogs to slink off behind the farmhouse. The two men got down from the jeep and walked over to the door.

'Good morning, madam, we are looking for Rolf Hermann. Is this the right place?'

'Oh, it's the right place but you are too late. Rolf died two years ago, of a heart attack.'

'I'm sorry to hear that. My condolences.'

'He was a pig. Why did you want him?'

'My name is Frank Kaufmann. I thought he might be a relative of mine.'

'And what made you think that?'

'My mother told me he was her husband's cousin.'

'She was mistaken. My husband didn't have cousins. His father was an only child.'

She wanted them to leave. It was written all over her face.

'Was your husband's nickname Freddy?'

Her sour and dismissive demeanour changed, and, like the sun coming out from behind a cloud, a shy smile crept across her face.

'Yes, that was him. Before he turned into a pig.' She looked sad.

'I would love to see a photograph if you have one,' said Saul in a quiet voice.

She peered at him through eyes misty with age.

'I'm sorry I didn't answer the door earlier. I live alone and I don't open the door to strangers. I have photographs of him as a young man. Would you like to see the album?'

They followed the old woman into a house that would have been more at home in Bavaria. Wooden floors and net curtains and solid German furniture filled the rooms.

'Can I offer you gentlemen a tea?'

'That would be nice. Thank you.'

She showed them into the sitting room and disappeared into a kitchen behind the stairs. There was a fireplace with a couple of sofas facing each other across a solid wooden coffee table. The two men sat down on one of them and waited for her to return. Both men glanced around the room for clues to the origins of the family but there were no framed photographs. It was sterile.

Mrs Hermann came in with a tray holding cups of hot water and a plate of tea bags. Alfredo took one and watched in dismay as the tea bag floated without brewing.

'Now, Mr Kaufmann, what can I tell you about your cousin?' she asked.

'Well, I understand that he came to Sierramar at the end of the war. Did he come alone?'

'He came with five other officers from his regiment. They were young men who wanted to start a new life after the horrors of the war. A steamer brought them with about fifty other families to Guayama from where most of them moved up to Calderon.'

'Do you have a photograph of him at that age? I want to see if he resembles me.'

Mrs Hermann avoided his eyes but she got up and took a leather-bound album out of a bookcase which she hugged close to her but did not offer to Saul.

'You must understand,' she said, 'that they were different times. These men had lost the war, but they'd not lost hope of a revival of the Reich. They were determined to maintain our traditions.'

Saul nodded and stretched out his hands to take the album.

'I understand. My mother has not lost hope that one day Germany will be great again. They brought me up to believe too. I don't find it shocking.'

She handed it to him. He opened the cover and a photograph of a handsome young man in a Gestapo uniform slipped onto the floor. He picked it up, put it back in its binding and turned the pages. Alfredo looked over his shoulder controlling his breathing and pretending to have little interest. There was a photograph of six young men in Gestapo uniform posing outside a wooden building with a tin roof.

'Wow, so which one is Rolf?'

She pointed at a slim young man smoking a cigarette.

'And who are the others? Is this the group that came to Sierramar? Are any of them still alive?'

His excitement showed, and she looked at him with suspicion.

'I mean, they could tell me more about Freddy.'

'Let me see the photo. As far as I remember the fat one was Franz Rauf. He died young of a heart attack. The two men beside him are the Schmidt brothers. The man on the right-hand side of Frank is Kurt Becker and the one on the left, I am not sure, but I think he died last year of a stroke.'

'I was in the same school as the Schmidt brothers' children,' said Alfredo. 'They were nice lads, good at football. They left in sixth grade. I didn't see them again.'

Mrs Hermann ignored him.

'What happened to the Schmidt brothers and Kurt Becker? Are they still in Sierramar?' asked Saul.

'I believe Dr Becker retired to the mountains for his health. He was running a clinic somewhere in San Blas de Lago Verde. I don't know where the Schmidt brothers are. They upped and left without a word. They may have left Sierramar.'

Saul leafed his way through the album.

'That's a nice photo. Was that taken when you arrived in Calderon?'

'Yes, we had just arrived here. That's us in the cow shed.'

'How did you meet your husband?'

'We met at a rally in Berlin. He was so handsome in his uniform. I couldn't resist him.'

The photographs showed Rolf Kaufmann getting middle aged and then elderly, a nasty scowl becoming a permanent fixture on his face. Evil radiated from him.

The door to the sitting room opened and a young man stepped through into the light. Alfredo glanced backwards at him and did a double take. It was the boy from the library. What was his name? Kleber something? He could feel his gaze boring into the back of his head. He put his hat back on and tugged Saul's sleeve to signal that they should leave.

'Well, we had better go Mrs Hermann. It's been a real pleasure to meet you and to hear about Rolf,' said Saul, who had taken the hint.

'You're leaving already? I hoped you might stay for supper.'

'We need to get back to town before it gets dark. The lights on the jeep are not working.'

'Okay well, Kleber, can you see the gentlemen out, please?'

'Yes, madam. Will you follow me?'

Saul and Alfredo shook Mrs Hermann's hand. Alfredo removed his hat and replaced it in one swift movement. He walked behind Saul trying to keep him between himself and Kleber. They got to the front door and hurried towards the car. A sudden gust of wind blew Alfredo's hat clean off. He dashed across the yard, standing on it to stop it blowing away. As he stood up, he caught Kleber's eye.

'Dr Vargas?' said Kleber, 'what are you doing here?'

'Kleber? I could ask you the same question. I'm following up my research on German culture with my friend Frank Kaufmann. He is a cousin of Mrs Hermann's late husband.'

Kleber had a look on his face that suggested a violent disgust. He was staring at Saul.

'You are lying. There were no Jews in Mr Hermann's family. You should be ashamed of yourself taking advantage of an old woman. Now get out of here and take your nasty friend with you,' he said.

He whistled, and the dogs came running from the back of the house, barking and snarling. They went straight for the visitors, who ran to the safety of the car. They made it unscathed. The dogs were jumping up at the doors, scratching the paint. Kleber shouted from the door.

'Stay away from here and stop interfering in things you don't understand. I'm giving you fair warning. Stop looking or end up with your friend Ramon.'

He spun on his heel and went back into the house. There was no sign of Mrs Hermann who had melted back into the shadows. The two men sat panting in the car.

'These people are psychos,' said Alfredo.

'Who is he?' said Saul.

'He works in the National Archives. He must be the one who followed me to Ramon's place. I thought I recognised him in my house the other day. Look what he did to the dog. He's a dangerous man.'

'How did he know I was Jewish?'

'Because you stick out like a sore thumb. I guess Mrs Hermann must be lonely and blind to be fooled by us. We should get out of here.'

They pulled out of the yard with the dogs still barking and throwing themselves against the doors.

***

Lunch was waiting for them when they got home. The maid had left a cold chicken and some salad and fresh bread out on the table covered in some clean drying up towels. Alfredo took cold beers out of the fridge and poured a glass for them both.

'That looks delicious,' said Saul. 'I could eat a horse.'

'Half a chicken will have to do instead.'

'Let's start with that, then. Sorry for sleeping on the way home. You must be bursting to discuss old mother Hermann and her scary helper.'

'That's okay. Travelling always makes me weary, too. It was rather a strange morning. I can't believe we got such great information from Mrs Hermann. That Kleber person's someone to stay well clear of. He's a psychopath, setting the dogs on us for no reason. I'm convinced he's the man we saw running away from here yesterday.'

'What do you want to do next?'

'We should travel to San Blas del Lago to find Dr

Becker. The Schmidt brothers may be there too if they haven't left the country. Have you got walking shoes and some wet weather gear with you?'

'Yes, I came prepared for a hike or two.'

'Excellent. I've got to go out for an hour. Can you get ready meanwhile?'

***

Alfredo went straight to Gloria's apartment building and rang her bell. The maid answered.

'Good morning. Who's there?'

'Hello, it's Dr Vargas. Is Miss Gloria in?'

'Oh, I'm sorry Dr Vargas, she has gone shopping to the mall and I think she is having lunch with a friend. She didn't say what time she would be back.'

'Oh, well, please can you tell her I'm going on a trip to the mountains with my colleague from America and that we should be back in a few days?'

'Yes, Dr Vargas. I'll tell her. Do you want to leave her a note?'

'No need, I shouldn't be gone long. Thank you.'

Alfredo stood outside for a while wondering if he should tell her where they were going but he left without writing a note. The mission was becoming more dangerous than he had expected and he didn't want her getting hurt. He would never get back in her father's good books if he put Gloria in danger. He forced himself to go home and pack.

CHAPTER XI

Sam and Gloria, September 1988

The Klein sisters, Heidi and Liesel, lived in the family home with their mother, a woman bedridden with multiple sclerosis. Built in the style of a German country house, it was set back from the road down a mud driveway lined with eucalyptus trees. The outskirts of Calderon would swallow it up in its dingy concrete and zinc petticoat but meanwhile it still had a rural charm and a chocolate box prettiness alien to the Andean landscape. Sam held on to the handle over the door to prevent herself being thrown around in the front seat as Gloria tried to negate the huge dusty potholes by driving over them at high speed. The car stopped in a cloud of powder which settled on the bonnet. Sam almost fell out of the car with relief.

Gloria shook herself clean and raised the eagle's head door knocker on the front door, letting it fall twice. Sam's stomach flipped over. She was not a good actress and a worse liar. *Gloria should do most of the talking.* The door opened with a loud theatrical creak and a young woman with bright blonde hair stood in the sunlight.

'Gloria, how nice of you to pay us a visit. And this must be your friend?'

'Yes, hello, I'm Sam, which one are you?' she blurted out.

'I'm Liesel, and my sister Heidi is inside. Won't you come in?'

Gloria already pushed past her into the hall and making her way to the sitting room in a way that suggested this was not her first visit to the house. Sam smiled and followed them into a cold room with wooden furniture which would have looked more at home in a monastery. They had sat down when Heidi came in with a tray of coffee and a mild chaos reigned as the women got up and sat down again several times to greet the other and to serve the coffee and add milk and sugar. At last, they settled down with their coffee served.

'It's been a long-time, Gloria,' said Heidi.

'Yes, it has. Where does the time go?'

'You look wonderful.'

'Thank you. I try. You girls are identical to when you were at school, down to your beautiful blonde hair.'

Sam detected a slight stiffening of the woman's back at this pointed compliment. An uncomfortable silence.

'Don't tease her, Gloria, you know about our hair already. It got to be such a habit. I can't imagine going back to being brunette again. Well, the truth is I started so young I don't remember ever having brown hair. It's our trademark,' said Liesel

Her sister nodded in assent, mollified.

'I remember now. Your father liked you to have blond hair. Where is he? I haven't seen him for years,' said Gloria.

The two sisters glanced at each other. Sam had the distinct impression they were deciding which story to tell. Heidi replied.

'He went to live in Argentina years ago. We don't know where he is now.'

'I didn't know he had left. I wanted to ask him if he could help me search for Sam's relatives.'

'Why come to us? Isn't Sam English?'

'Yes, but her great aunt was German.'

'What was her surname?'

'Becker,' said Sam. 'She left Germany after the war and there are rumours she travelled to Sierramar.'

'Becker?' asked Liesel.

'Yes, she may have travelled with her brother. I'm told he was a doctor. Do you know him?'

Liesel's cup slid off her lap and crashed to the floor. The thin rug cushioned the fall but coffee flooded across it. She bent down to the floor, bright red in the face trying to pick up the crockery and wipe at the coffee with a paper napkin at the same time. Her sister glared at her.

'Talking of fathers, how is yours, Gloria?' asked Heidi. 'I was sorry to hear your mother died. That must have been hard for him.'

Smooth. Heidi impressed Sam with the apparent sincerity of the statement even though it was intended to change the subject without appearing to, thus avoiding answering Sam's question. The conversation changed to that of old school friends trying to remember tyrannical teachers and the name of that dishy boy in upper sixth, but Sam's question remained unanswered. Liesel had turned a funny colour and despite going out to the kitchen for fresh coffee, still looked shaken. Dropping a cup couldn't have affected her that much.

Sam took a risk.

'Um, can I use your bathroom, please?'

'It's straight up the stairs in the corridor. First door on the left.'

Sam headed up the steps and tried a couple of doors. One opened into a bedroom with the smell of hospital. An old woman slept slumped in a wheelchair by the window. Sam glanced around the room. Spotting some photographs on a chest of drawers, she crept over to examine them. One was of a slim older man who resembled Liesel dressed in tweed. In another he stood with several other Germanic looking men outside a pub or hotel called Lago Verde. They were doing a Nazi salute. She felt her blood run cold. The old woman sighed. Sam jumped, and she backed out of the room bumping into Heidi coming in.

'What are you doing in here?'

'Oh, I'm sorry. I heard moaning, and I wanted to help.'

'There is nothing you can do here. Please leave.'

'I should mind my own business. Sorry.'

She slid along the passage to the bathroom where she threw water on her face. That was close! Had Heidi seen her looking at the photograph? She composed herself and came back down the stairs finding the three women in the hall.

'Are you ready? We're going now,' said Gloria.

'Yes, I'm ready. Thank you for the coffee, ladies.'

'Liesel will help you out. Goodbye.'

Before they got into the car, Gloria pulled Liesel aside.

'I can tell that you are hiding something,' Gloria hissed. 'My fiancé, Alfredo, is missing and it may involve your father. I'm worried about him. If you think of anything that might help, can you please call us?'

Before Liesel could answer, a shout came from the house.

'Hurry, Liesel, our mother needs her lunch.'Heidi's voice had a nasty edge. Liesel ran back to the house without answering.

'Let's go, for God's sake,' Sam muttered as she got into the car.

'I hear you. Put some nice music on. I need some rock-and-roll to drive to after that little meeting. Aren't they sinister?'

'I felt as if I were talking to Barbie and Cindy. They didn't tell us the whole truth about their father though.'

'Definitely not. What did you do upstairs?'

'I found a shocking photo of their father in his wife's room. He was doing a Nazi salute with his friends.'

'Jesus, Sam, you could've got caught.'

'I sort of was. Heidi came in as I left the room. I made up some excuse about hearing a moan.'

'That was risky. Did she believe you?'

'I don't know, but I want to help Alfredo and I'm confident they hold the key.'

'Well, it's too late now, anyway. Was it an old photograph?'

'No. They had grey hair. I'd say they were in their late sixties.'

'Recent? Huh. But where did they take the photograph?'

'Outside a hotel called Lago Verde with mountains in the background.'

'I've been to Lago Verde. There's a German tourist village up there, San Blas, where they make cheese and beer. They must have been on a day trip. I can't imagine they are plotting a coup with Hansel and Gretel. I'm not sure how much this helps us.'

'Let's go home.'

***

'What are we going to do? How did Gloria know about our father? He left so long ago, I thought people had forgotten about him,' said Liesel.

'He's safe where he is. No one has any idea that he's still in the county. It's a coincidence,' said Heidi.

'What if they find him?'

'There are people protecting him. Don't worry. Tell the maid to make some lunch.'

'I wish he and his friends would forget about Hitler and the wonderful Third Reich.'

'Don't you dare say that! Don't you ever say that again. You don't understand what you're talking about.'

'You're the one who's delusional. I want to live in 1990 not 1940. The war is over. I don't want to live like Nazis anymore.'

'It's hard for you, but you will be glad we did when the next Reich comes. Run along now. I've got a call to make.'

Liesel stomped off to the kitchen, slamming the door behind her, but she stayed there with her ear against it.

Heidi picked up the receiver in the hallway and dialled a number in Calderon. Someone answered the phone on the first ring.

'Hello, Holger Ponce here.'

'Minister, it's me, Heidi Klein.'

'Well, hello there, Heidi. How's the prettiest woman in Calderon?'

'Well, thank you. And you?'

'Oh, can't grumble. What can I do for you?'

'We have a problem. Hernan Sanchez' daughter Gloria has been here today asking questions about our father. It turns out that she has been dating Dr Vargas and has noticed his disappearance. Her friend was nosing around upstairs and she may have seen a photograph Papa took with his friends in Lago Verde.'

'Oh, that's unfortunate. I'd hate for something to happen to Miss Sanchez. Hernan would not be happy.'

'Will you speak to him? Someone must dissuade her from looking for Dr Vargas at all cost.'

'Yes, I'll speak to him. Don't worry. He's old school. It's not in his interest to lose good contacts over a slight inconvenience.'

'Okay, I'll leave it with you. It's vital that Gloria gives up the search for Dr Vargas. The timing is critical. We are so close.'

'I fear that we must do something about him, and our Jewish friend, too. I hoped we could release them later but they are a liability.'

'Make it appear like an accident.'

'I'll inform you when it's done.'

'Thank you, Minister. I'll leave it in your hands.'

She replaced the receiver and opened the door into the kitchen. Liesel was standing on the other side looking in a cupboard.

'You shouldn't listen to other people's conversations,' she said and stalked past her sister into the kitchen.

***

Sam and Gloria were eating a supper of leftovers in the kitchen when the phone rang. Gloria picked it up chewing hard so she could swallow her mouthful of cold chicken.

'Can we meet?' said a voice.

Gloria stopped chewing.

'Yes, where and when?'

'I'll be at the German market in the valley tomorrow with my sister. Can you be at the Austrian Café at midday?'

'What about your sister?'

'Oh, she's meeting a boyfriend. I've an hour or so free before she comes to find me.'

'Okay, we'll be there.'

The phone went dead.

'Wrong number?' asked Sam when Gloria reappeared.

'I wouldn't say that,' said Gloria, 'It was Liesel Klein.'

'What did she say?'

'She wants to meet us tomorrow.'

'Tomorrow? What about her sister?'

'She will be alone at midday. We are meeting her at the German market.'

'Isn't that risky?'

'We won't stay long. It can't be safe for her either.'

***

The next morning, they drove down the winding roads to the same valley that Ramon had lived in.

'Remind me to pass by the local police station on our way back. I want to ask Inspector Torres about the fire at Ramon's house. As far as I'm aware, they still haven't identified the bodies and the cause of the fire.'

'Will do,' said Sam.

The fair heaved with the foreign population of Calderon who liked to shop for European style cold cuts and cheeses made by the immigrants. The Austrian coffee shop was one of the most popular

places there. It sold huge slices of Black Forest Gateau topped with fresh whipped cream. There was no stopping Sam once she had seen it in the window. She had to have some. It reminded her of the time she went to Munich with Simon and they had some in their hotel room. The whipped cream did not stay on the cake long.   She   sighed.
They settled into a window seat and watched the world go by as they waited for their order. Gloria sipped her double espresso. The waitress, dressed like a French maid in a porn movie, plonked the tray down on their table splashing some of Sam's tea into her saucer. Gloria glared at her with an intensity that almost melted her frilly top.

'Sorry, madam,' she said.

'I should think so, too,' muttered Gloria.

Sam was about to dig into her enormous piece of cake when she spotted Liesel Klein coming into the café. She readied herself to greet her when she realised that she was being shadowed by her sister Heidi. The two women swept up to the counter and ordered coffees. Sam kicked Gloria's leg under the table and pursed her lips in their direction.

'Why are you kicking me?'

'Heidi Klein at twelve o'clock.'

'Don't be silly. It's Liesel who is coming.'

'No, Heidi, behind you. At the counter.'

Sam tried to hide behind her cake as the Klein sisters turned around to find a table. A furious expression flashed across Heidi's face immediately replaced by a big public smile of recognition. They had been spotted.

'Gloria! Sam! What are you doing here?'

'Oh, Sam wanted to try the Black Forest Gateau. She loves cherries.'

'Can we join you? I am meeting someone in about fifteen minutes.'

'That'd be lovely.'

There followed the usual pantomime of moving seats from other tables over the heads of other patrons of the café and much shuffling of chairs. Heidi seemed convinced by Sam's noisy enjoyment of the gateau which was real. She refused to taste it on the grounds that she might have to have a slice if she did. Liesel sat on the edge of her seat looking out through the window to prevent her having to speak. Gloria took it in her stride, smoking with an intensity that suggested it was her first of the day but Sam could testify that it was not. After what seemed an age, Heidi rose to her feet and set off to meet her friend with Liesel in tow.

'Bye, see you soon.'

'Bye,' Sam said, waving. 'God, I thought they had rumbled us there.'

'Just a coincidence. Calm down.'

'What about Liesel? Will she come back?'

'I don't know. We should wait about half an hour but after that it looks suspicious.'

They stayed twenty minutes blocking the table when other clients were waiting for it. Finally, the waitress asked them to leave. They came outside into the bleaching sun and squinted into the crowd. Liesel Klein appeared, pink faced, running towards them. She shoved a piece of paper into Sam's hand and turned to run back the way she had come.

'What does it say?' asked Gloria.

'San Blas del Lago Verde.'

***

'Maybe she felt guilty.'

'At least it confirms what you saw in the

photograph. San Blas is a hotbed of intrigue.'

'What should we do next?'

'The police station. We need to find out about the fire.'

'Well done, at least one of us has a few memory cells working. Let's go.'

They drove up to the station when it opened for the afternoon shift. Gloria parked in a random officer's parking space and strode into the office in her cowboy boots.

'Hello. My name is Gloria Sanchez. I've come for information about the fire last week.'

Gloria was formidable in full flow and the policeman behind the desk was not in the mood, after his large lunch, to get into a fight that might spoil his siesta.

'Yes, madam, please follow me.'

He directed them into the shabby den of the station chief, Inspector Torres, who jumped to his feet as they entered.

'Inspector Torres, what a pleasure to meet you again.'

'And you, Miss Sanchez. How can I help you?'

'I wondered if you had any further information about the fire and who started it?'

'It was definitely arson but we don't have a motive and there were no leads that we could follow. Mr Vega did not appear to have any obvious enemies and although we are investigating a possible lead, we are not at liberty to give you any information right now.'

'I understand. Can you confirm that the body was Ramon Vega?'

Here, the policeman shifted in his seat and looked uncomfortable.

'I'm afraid we can't. There has been a complication.

It's delicate.'

Gloria understood. He must have found clues which led him to someone important. Cases like these almost always got covered up or the policemen investigating could disappear, too. She didn't push it. Sam squirmed but Gloria shook her head and mouthed 'No'.

'I understand, Inspector.'

The man relaxed. Sam bristled with fury but Gloria didn't explain.

'Well, you've my number. Please ring me if you've any further information about this case.'

'Thank you, madam. I am at your service.'

'Okay, let's go. Now.'

She had to get Sam out of there before she stuck her large gringa feet into the problem.

Once outside, Sam spat out a question.

'What the hell was that about? He had more information about the case that he didn't tell us.'

'Yes, and if you had a government minister threatening you with violence or worse, you'd probably lie, too.'

'Oh. I understand. Sorry.'

'Don't worry. You don't get how we do things around here. Trust me. If he can, he will tell me.'

'Okay, so where's San Blas del Lago?'

'It's a couple of day's drive from Calderon, up in the mountains. We need a map.'

'A map might help but there is something even better. Do they sell aerial photographs here? If the Nazis are hiding up there, they must have a concealed compound or something similar. We may spot it on an aerial photograph.'

'Aerial photographs? Mike Morton bought some when we searched for good alluvial deposits from the air, but there was a lot of red tape and we don't have time. I suggest a visit to our friend the Colonel in the Geographical Institute. We need short skirts and lots of sauce.'

'Sauce?'

'Honestly, Sam, anyone would think you hadn't hit puberty yet. S.A.U.C.E. Hot sauce.'

'Oh, that kind of sauce.'

'Come on, we need to buy you a tight dress.'

CHAPTER XII

Alfredo and Saul August 1988

By the time Alfredo got back to his house, Saul had packed his bag and was raring to go. Alfredo threw some things in a rucksack including his trusty explorer's hat and ancient walking boots. He searched for his SLR camera until he removed his coat from the stand in the hall and found it hanging underneath tangled up with a pair of battered binoculars which he also put in his bag. Several unused films hid in the fridge keeping fresh behind the jar of ancient olives. He put one of them straight into the back of the camera and stuffed the others in the front pocket of the rucksack. Just before they left, he dashed into the toilet and removed a new packet of toilet paper from the cupboard.

'Don't they have toilet paper in San Blas?' said Saul.

'I take no chances when it comes to my ablutions,' said Alfredo.

They locked the house and drove to the gas station where they filled the car with fuel and bought supplies of clean water and snack food. They also bought a bottle of whisky to keep Alfredo's blood alcohol up at normal levels.

'Have we got a map of the area?' asked Saul.

'The roads up to San Blas are not on any map yet as they were built twenty years ago and they completed the survey of Sierramar in the 1940s.'

'So how are we going to find it?'

'By asking the locals and aiming the car at the volcano behind the Lago Verde.'

'That sounds scientific.'

'Yes, it is haphazard, but that's how we do things around here. We'll get there. You'll see.'

They set off on the southern road out of town through the tumbledown, colonial cottages on the outskirts and into the countryside, along roads lined with dry eucalyptus trees and sisal plants, some of which had been stripped of their leaves. Their fibres hung out to dry on the wire fencing waiting to be turned into sacks.

'This is so exciting,' said Saul, 'I haven't ever been involved in the chase before. I do the research and other people get to hunt the Nazis.'

'I've no idea if we will find anything to chase or not,' said Alfredo, 'but it is thrilling.'

'It may also be risky. I'm not paying you enough to risk getting hurt or even killed on this trip. I never asked you why you're doing this.'

'I want to avenge my friend Ramon. We fought a few years ago because I was drunk and insulted him in front of our friends. It was my fault. I made peace with him before he died. He deserved better. And what are you doing here Saul? You told me you are *not a practicing Jew*. I find it odd that you'd risk your life to hunt some random Germans in Sierramar. Is there anything you haven't told me?'

Saul avoided Alfredo's glance and stared out of the window. His jaw muscles tightened.

'Can we talk about that tonight? I need some Dutch courage.'

'I understand more than you can imagine.'

The rest of the day passed almost without incident. A puncture held them up for about half an hour but a mechanic from a small shed on the side of the road repaired it for a couple of dollars. He impressed Saul who gave them a big tip.

'Hey, that's kind of cheap and they are so fast. I don't think we have anything like this in the States.'

'You probably have better roads where punctures are a lot rarer.'

'Well, that's true I s'pose.'

After driving for most of the day the two men got addled by the bumping and shaking and they stopped for the night in an inn off the main road chosen by Alfredo for its good home cooking and flea-free beds. They ate a substantial supper of goat stew and rice and then they sat beside a fire in the bar digesting their meal with a glass of whisky. Alfredo turned to Saul who fiddled with his glass. 'It's time for you to reveal your motives for coming on this trip. I want to understand what we're getting into.'

'Fair enough. I wouldn't blame you if you change your mind after what I'm about to tell you.'

'Okay, so why don't you start at the very beginning?'

Both men chorused 'it's a very good place to start' and then smiled. The ironic reference to the *Sound of Music* was not out of place.

'So, as you've noticed, I'm a Jew, born in Brussels and lived there as a boy with my parents and my sister.

My family had money, and we lived a comfortable life. We had lots of Jewish friends in our district. The war seemed far away from us when it started in Poland. Belgium had declared neutrality in the conflict but this didn't stop the Germans from invading. In 1940, they crossed our borders and eighteen days later the fight was over.'

'How awful.'

'When the Germans invaded Belgium, we became trapped. From then on, a German military government ran Belgium and levied the costs of the military occupation on the Belgians through taxes, nearly two-thirds of its national income. For a while, life went on almost as normal but they enacted anti-Jewish legislation in October 1940, and several pogroms took place. Many people collaborated with the Germans and helped them round up the Jews.

People avoided us and whispered behind our backs. Some other Jewish families had left for America and Britain but my father wouldn't go because the whole family fortune was tied up in Brussels. Then it got worse. The Germans seized economic assets belonging to Jews and threw us out of our home. They ordered us to report to the Mechelen transit camp. My father persuaded our neighbours to live in our house and hide me and my sister in the attic. He and my mother hid somewhere else and used to visit us when they could. One day they disappeared and we never saw them again'

'That must have been terrible.'

'Not so much. I was young and for me the whole thing seemed like an adventure. I didn't understand what was going on until the day when both my parents vanished. The Gestapo must have been picked them up. The people who lived in our house risked their lives to save us. Also, the rationing had got worse, and we were eating from their share, starving by degrees. Then one day soldiers tore down the wall concealing us and they dragged us out onto the street over the bodies of the people who had hidden us. It was April 1943. People hissed and spat at us as the Germans took us through the streets to the railway station.'

'How old were you?'

'Nine years old, and my sister was fifteen.'

'Christ wept. You must've been terrified.'

'Yes, I think it was then that it became real. People disappeared all the time, but we did not know where, only that we never saw again them. The same as my parents.'

Saul drained his glass and asked for a refill. He seemed to gather himself.

'Anyway, they put us all into a freight car with about fifty or sixty other people and one bucket in the middle of the floor. It was frightening, but we got to the corner where it was safer and received some air from the crack in the door. The freight car contained some desperate people who whispered about a place called Auschwitz. A man told us that this was the twentieth convoy of Jews to be taken to the camp. The train moved off after standing for a couple of hours in the station heading for Poland. It crawled along the track. They didn't give us any food or water and almost no air entered the carriage. People fainted from hunger and fear.

During the night, three members of the Belgian Resistance stopped the train using a red light made from a lantern covered in tissue paper. It caused the train driver to brake. This was the only time during the war that any Nazi transport carrying Jewish people got intercepted.

While his friends created a diversion by shooting at the train drivers, one of the resistance fighters opened the door of our freight car by cutting the wire binding it shut with pliers. He slid it open right opposite to me and my sister. He shouted at people to jump. They hesitated but my sister pushed me through the crowd and I jumped down into his arms. She came to the door, but she wouldn't, couldn't, jump. I begged her to leap, but she got pulled backwards as other people leapt to freedom.

The train began moving again. I screamed and screamed, but she had disappeared into the wagon and I never saw her again. The men took me back to town with them and put me in a safe house where I stayed until the end of the war. The Red Cross sent me to New York by ship in 1945 because I had an aunt who lived there. I have since found out that my parents and sister died at Auschwitz within a couple of days of their arrival.'

'I don't know what to say. It's too awful to contemplate. What a harrowing experience for a child. I'm so sorry.'

'I don't think I've ever got over it. I still prefer to sit with my back to the wall if I can.'

'I'm surprised you've managed at all. What a terrible tragedy.'

'I'm not finished yet. A Gestapo officer took charge of the searches in Brussels. A real sadistic monster. He was a medical doctor who ended up going to look after Hitler in his last days in the bunker. When the Russians took Berlin, he fled to South America and came to Sierramar.'

'What was his name?'

'His name was Doctor Kurt Becker.'

'Becker? Isn't that the name of the man we are

searching for?'

'The same. So now you know. You're not the only person who's looking for revenge.'

'Hence the gun? Jesus! I forgot the gun. You have it with you, don't you?'

CHAPTER XIII

Sam and Gloria, September 1988

She needed to alert Simon to their predicament. It was still possible Sam wasn't pregnant. She didn't have any symptoms. But she didn't want to leave it too long and reduce her options for action. She couldn't guess his reaction although she had fantasised about telling him many times and it always thrilled him in her daydreams. They had been through a lot together and come through as a pair. He was the one who had asked her to try again, so she assumed that he was now serious about them. Serious enough to have a baby? She sighed.

'Speak to him,' said Gloria.

'Okay, wish me luck.'

Sam went out into the hall and took a few deep breaths. The enormity of the situation had hit her now that she had to share their dilemma with Simon. Perhaps this wasn't the best time? But in her heart, she knew that she had to tell him sooner or later. It would be his baby, too. She rang the operator and asked for a call to England. Five minutes later the phone rang.

'Hello, I have connected you to England.'

'Thank you, operator. Hello?'

'Hello? Sam, is that you?'

'Yes, hi darling, how are you?'

'Oh, I'm fine. Missing you.'

'I've just got here. You must be braver than that.'

'It's not my fault I miss you. You're the one who left. How's Gloria? Still bonkers?'

'Yes, she hasn't changed. Still driving as fast as Santa Claus on Christmas eve.'

'And Alfredo? Any sign of him?'

'No, he's vanished without a trace. It's odd.'

'You don't think he's gone on a bender? It's common for alcoholics.'

'His disappearance may be more sinister than that. His friend Ramon died in a fire the day after Alfredo went to get some information from him about some fugitive Nazis.'

'Wow, that's a nasty coincidence. Did you say Nazis? The line's bad.'

'Alfredo didn't disappear alone. He went with an investigative journalist from New York to search for a village in the mountains and they haven't come back.'

'That sounds as if it should be a job for the police.'

'Well, that's the problem. The police are not a lot of use in Sierramar.'

'Sam, this doesn't sound safe. Are you sure you should get involved?'

'Don't worry about me. Gloria has a lot of powerful contacts. We'll be safe enough. I promise not to be reckless.'

'Well, you'd better not because I decided we should move in together when you get back. Maybe, share a flat.'

'Wow! You have been missing me. Are you

convinced that's what you want? It's a big step.'

'I want us to make more permanent arrangements.'

It's now or never. Spit it out, woman. Sam took a deep breath.

'I'm glad you feel that way, because the thing is, I think I might be pregnant.'

Simon went quiet. Sam could hear him breathing. Was he shocked or thrilled? His reaction froze her blood.

'Is it mine?'

It was Sam's turn to be silent. Stunned, no retort came to mind. What was wrong with him? How could anyone be so callous at such a moment? Was anyone on earth as self-centred as Simon?

'I'm not as free with my favours as you, Simon,' she said in a whisper, 'You are the father.'

She put the receiver back on the telephone and slid down to the floor, trying not to cry.

After about five minutes of silence, Gloria came to find her. Sam still sat on the floor hugging her knees, her eyes red with fury and pain. Gloria joined her, putting an arm around her shoulders in solidarity.

'I hate him,' said Sam.

'What did he say?'

'He asked me if the baby was his.'

Gloria's mouth fell open and she choked. 'What? The bastard. Oh my God, I'm so sorry. How would he even ask that? He's the one with the wandering dick.'

Sam smiled despite her distress.

'He is a complete bastard. But he always has been. I don't understand why I keep going back for more. Am I some sort of masochist?'

'That's love, I'm afraid.'

'It's not love, it's something far more addictive.

Drugs would be a relief compared to this. And what am I going to do about this baby?'

'We can share it.'

'What?'

'We can share him or her. I can babysit while you work and you can look after the baby when you are not working. It's the perfect solution.'

Rendered speechless with astonishment, Sam checked to see if it was a joke, but Gloria was serious. Her forehead furrowed in concentration as she imagined the mechanics of her plan. 'I need a cigarette,' she said.

***

Sam's news horrified Simon. The fact that she had only suggested she might be pregnant had gone right over his head. He was going to be a father. A horrible chill crept up his back as the news sunk in. Of all the scenarios he had imagined, being a parent hadn't been one of them. He was not ready. Panic grabbed him and the walls seemed to move in. He blamed Sam. She was the one taking the pill. The silly fool must have forgotten to take one. *She should get rid of the child.* She was pragmatic about most things but if he told her what to do, she would react badly. How could he influence her decision with her so far away? He didn't know anyone to whom he could turn for advice. Did he?

The door opened on her sulky face. His presence registered, but she didn't seem pleased to see him. He didn't let that put him off.

'Hi, here I am again.'

'Simon, you are becoming like a bad penny.'

'Please Hannah, I need to speak to you about Sam. You may be the only person on the planet who can help me right now.'

She looked at him with doubt in her eyes.

'It's obvious that you don't understand who you're dealing with. You can come in, but only for a short while. Do you want a glass of wine?'

Simon couldn't tell whether she was referring to her sister or herself. Disoriented by the strong feelings of lust she engendered in him, he followed her shapely figure into the cosy sitting room. She had decorated her flat in conventional beige and pink colours with tasteful cushions and fresh flowers on the table. A framed poster of Moulin Rouge hung on the wall. She indicated he should sit on the sofa and she passed him a glass of red wine before sitting cross-legged on a floral armchair.

'Cheers,' she said raising the glass to her lips and spilling some down her t-shirt. She didn't wipe it off. He realised that she was drunk.

'Cheers.'

'So, Mr Lonely Hearts. What can I do for you?'

CHAPTER XIV

The gates to the Geographical Institute were closed and the security guards refused to let them drive up the hill and park outside. They even turned down Gloria's offer of a cigarette. Gloria parked the car as near as she could to the entrance and they started up the hill on foot. Sam was wearing a pair of heels that felt as if they had been designed by the Marquis de Sade. Blisters were erupting over her feet as she tottered into the entrance.

'How can you bear to wear these bloody things? I'm crippled already.'

'Stop fussing. Compared to childbirth it's nothing.'

'A comparison I may soon make,' snapped Sam, who regretted it.

Gloria was already storming up the staircase towards the Colonel's office and didn't appear to hear her. As usual, the Colonel's assistant made them wait in the anteroom where Gloria gave Sam some fresh lipstick and enhanced her own cleavage by shifting her bosoms forward in her bra.

'This is important, Sam. Don't forget the sauce.'

'I won't. I'm perfectly capable of flirting when I need to.'

Gloria sniffed and rolled her eyes to heaven in a manner that conveyed her scepticism. This annoyed Sam who was convinced that she could flirt with the best of them.

After a twenty-minute wait, the secretary came out and beckoned them in. Sam's shoes almost made her cry, but she thrust her chest out and sashayed into the Colonel's office behind Gloria. The Colonel was signing some documents and took a minute to look up. When he did, he stood up and gestured towards the chairs in front of his desk.

'Please ladies, sit down. I am so sorry to keep you waiting.'

'Oh, that's no problem sir, we know how busy you are.'

'Miss Sanchez, we meet again.' He came around the desk and kissed her on both cheeks. 'And the gringa, Sam, isn't it? Welcome back to Sierramar.' He kissed her, too, gazing down her cleavage with undisguised lust. She forced her breasts a little higher with a deep intake of breath.

'Yes sir, that's right.'

'I can hear that your Spanish is much improved. Have you married a man from Calderon yet?'

'No, not yet.' Batting her eyelashes, she asked; 'Are you single, Colonel?'

Gloria squeaked in delight. The Colonel blushed to the roots of his hair and returned to his chair. Sam was stranded by her courage, having no follow up line with which to strike. The Colonel recovered first.

'So, what can I do for you today, ladies?'

'We have a problem that only a man in your position can solve,' said Gloria, swinging into heavy flattery mode. 'We need some aerial photographs of Lago Verde as soon as possible.'

'Is this an emergency?'

'It's not clear yet. A friend of ours is missing and we want to narrow down the places we have to search. That is why we need the photographs now, to check for farm houses and outbuildings in the area. We need your help to speed up the process.'

'This is irregular but then nothing with you ladies is straightforward. At least it's not a restricted area. If it were, I wouldn't be able to help you. As it is, I don't think there is any harm in skipping a couple of steps in the protocol. You mustn't tell anyone though, and you must promise to ask the police for help if you need it.'

'We can have them?' said Sam.

'Don't sound so surprised. Every man has his price and I prefer tight dresses.' He winked. Bureaucracy was a random system, thought Sam. You never knew when it would block you but sometimes it worked in your favour.

The Colonel picked up his phone and dialled a number.

'Mr Chiriboga, I am sending two ladies to see you. Can you please make up an order for the aerial photographs of the Lago Verde region? What scale have you got? Okay, that's fine. They are on their way.'

'Thank you, Colonel,' said Gloria, 'we are so grateful.'

'It will take a couple of days to print if they are not in stock. I will sign the order straight away if you send it up to me when you have paid for it. Now get out of here. Your outfits are distracting me, which I'm confident was your plan. Next time, just ask.'

The photographs were not in stock but Mr

Chiriboga promised to have them ready in forty-eight hours. They paid the cashier and left the order form with the Colonel's secretary. Then they walked down the hill with the receipt tucked into Gloria's ample bosom for safety. Sam could not bear her shoes any longer and risked the walk in her bare feet, swinging her heels by the straps.

'Amazing what a tight dress or two will do.'

'It made our Colonel jump to attention.'

'You're so rude.'

'Yes, so you noticed, too, huh?'

Gloria laughed. 'Yes, he had to hide it under the desk.'

***

Holger Ponce arrived at Hernan Sanchez' condominium in a ministerial car, ensuring that he got a parking space and obsequious attention from the security guard at the entrance.

'Minister, what an honour. Who are you visiting today?'

'Senor Sanchez and be quick about it. I don't have all day.'

'Of course, Minister. Is he expecting you?'

'No, he is not.'

'One moment please and I will check that he is in. Hello? Can you please tell Senor Sanchez that the Minister of Foreign Affairs is here to see him? Thank you.'

Holger Ponce lit a cigarette and puffed on it but he could not rush the guard. The Minister was important but Senor Sanchez was a lot more intimidating. The buzzer sounded.

'Rosita? Okay, I'll send him up. Thank you. Minister, please go up to the fifth floor. Mr Sanchez is waiting for you there.'

He opened the door of the lift and pressed the button with as much ceremony as he could muster. Holger Ponce stalked into the elevator, dropping his cigarette on the floor of the lobby. He was not expecting a difficult chat. Hernan Sanchez always had the best scotch in town, with which he was always generous.

'Minister, you are welcome. Come on through to the sitting room. Senor Sanchez is waiting.'

'Thank you.'

Hernan Sanchez was waiting beside the drinks cabinet in anticipation. A big welcoming smile creased his features but was not reflected in his eyes. He was not used to unannounced visits by government ministers.

'Thank you, Rosa. I'll do the drinks. Good afternoon, Minister Ponce.'

'Holger, for heaven's sake, Hernan. Do we need to be so formal?'

Holger crossed the room in a couple of long strides and extended his bony fingers which he withdrew almost as soon as Sanchez tried to grasp them. Sanchez hated wimpy handshakes. Being robbed of the big shake and the mutual grasping of elbows favoured by the menfolk in Calderon made him more uneasy.

'Do you want a whisky, Holger? It's a nice triple malt.'

'Yes please. Two fingers with a little ice.'

To avoid a long meeting, Hernan directed Holger to the hard-backed sofa instead of the armchairs. They sat down and swung around to face each other.

'To whom or what do I owe the honour of your visit?' asked Hernan.

'It's about your daughter.'

'My daughter? What on earth has she been up to this

time?' He found it hard to believe that Gloria had attracted the cabinet's attention. She had been on her best behaviour since Sam had arrived.

'Well, not so much your daughter as the company she has been keeping.'

'I don't follow you.'

'Dr Alfredo Vargas, to be precise.'

'Alfredo? But she is not going out with him anymore. They broke up.'

'Not according to my sources.' He rubbed his nose and chin, playing for time. 'The thing is, Hernan, that Dr Vargas has been associating with a man named Ramon Vega, who is investigating the collaboration of our government with certain fugitive German officers after the second world war. Many of the people involved are still connected to the government and, as you can imagine, it is a sensitive subject.'

'What's that got to do with Gloria?'

'This Dr Vargas is missing and your daughter is upsetting people by asking intrusive questions concerning his whereabouts.'

'How does that concern me?'

'I should've thought it was obvious. Your ability to get government contracts relies on a bit of give and take. It would be a pity if your standing took a knock, and it was no longer possible for us to look with favour on your bids for work.'

'I get her to back off or my contracts disappear?'

'In a nutshell. I hope you understand. These matters can be vexing. We want to shut this down before a can of worms gets opened.'

'Naturally.' Hernan Sanchez took a couple of deep breaths. He stood up and gestured towards the door. 'Well, it was good of you to visit. I'm afraid I wasn't expecting you and I have a previous appointment. My apologies.'

Taken aback, Holger hid his emotions, and his disappointment at having to abandon his whisky. He considered gulping it down but there was no polite way of doing so.

'Of course, my friend. I'm assured we understand each other. There is no need for this to interfere with our relationship.'

Hernan rang a silver bell on the mantelpiece and Rosa appeared.

'Yes, sir?'

'The Minister is leaving. Can you show him out, please?'

The maid looked surprised. Most visits from the Minister lasted for hours and he almost had to be carried out of them.

'Yes, sir. Minister?'

Holger travelled down in the lift feeling as if he had accomplished his mission. He was also smug at taking Hernan Sanchez down a peg or two. Insufferable jumped-up street urchin! He'd put him back in his box and no mistake. His driver was lounging on a bench across the street chatting up a maid from the other building. He ran across the road.

'Everything okay, Minister?'

'Perfect, thank you. Take me home, please.'

***

Hernan Sanchez was shaking with anger after Holger Ponce left. The bare faced cheek of that man threatening him in his own house had left him quite discombobulated. He poured himself another whisky and sat in one of his more comfortable chairs trying to slow down his heart rate. One of these days he would have a serious heart attack if he didn't lose weight and stop smoking but these were not the ideal circumstances.

He marvelled at Gloria's ability to get herself in trouble. It annoyed him that she had disobeyed his request and gone back to Alfredo but he understood affairs of the heart were not that simple. Her loyalty to Alfredo was quite touching, and he felt pleased that she had found someone about whom she cared enough to defy him. What on earth was Vargas researching that had made the government so paranoid? He had to find out.

And then he remembered. Standing up, he made his way to the chest on his wife's side of the bed. He opened the drawers with reverence and he ferreted around until he found the sheath of paper hidden amongst the clothes. The faintest waft of his wife's perfume from the untouched legacy of her presence crept into his nostrils and made him sigh. The document was heavy, and he dropped it as he removed it from the drawer, scattering pages over the bedroom.

It took him quite an effort to retrieve them again, especially those that had floated under the bed. Puffing with exertion, he laid them out on the bed and reordered them, holding them together with the bulldog clip he found in his dresser drawer. Then he took the report back into the sitting room, poured himself yet another whisky and made himself comfortable.

CHAPTER XV

Alfredo and Saul September 1988

The next morning Alfredo made Saul remove his gun from his rucksack and put it behind the side panel at the back of the jeep, along with the jack and other tools for changing the tyre. There was always the chance that they would encounter a random police checkpoint on the roads leading south, manned by individuals who wanted to augment their paltry salaries. The police would invent some infraction and the victim would pay an instant fine, almost like a toll. However, if they found a weapon, things could get nasty, especially if it was in the hands of a foreigner. This gave the police licence to extort much greater sums of money and to employ violence if they didn't get what they wanted.

Alfredo and Saul didn't need any extra trouble on this trip which was dangerous enough already. Alfredo had assessed the risks without taking into account the fact that one half of his team had been hiding his light under a bushel, posing as a mild-mannered investigative journalist while he was a vengeful Jew with a gun. The stakes were much higher than he had anticipated. They would need more whisky.

Some of his worry soon dissipated. Saul was full of the joys of Spring, humming as they drove along. He had never been to South America before and was in a constant state of amazement. They made unplanned stops for perusing vistas and a sampling of local delicacies. Alfredo was happy to let him relax and forget about his mission of revenge for as long as possible. He was not confident he could control Saul if they ever found Kurt Becker but he would not get between them if things went wrong. That gun needed to stay hidden.

They had lunch at an ancient food stand in a village along the main road after Saul spotted that it had a primitive barbecue with a rotating spit from the car. As they pulled in to the side of the road, Alfredo realised what was cooking and waiting for the inevitable reaction as Saul took in the skinned guinea pigs with accusing faces, bucked toothed grimaces and begging paws turning on their skewers.

'What are those animals? Are they rabbits?'

'No, they are guinea pigs. The local people farm them for food.'

'Oh my! Are you serious?'

'They are tasty.'

'Well, what are we waiting for?'

To Alfredo's surprise, Saul ate two of them, sucking the bones with gusto, as if he were a local. The owner of the stand, a toothless old crone who smelt like a corpse, encouraged him and brought him extra rice and corn to mop up the juices. A loud burp from Saul broke the silence of a good lunch and brought it to an end. Alfredo paid for their meal and they got back into the car.

'You are the first gringo I ever saw who ate guinea

pig with such gusto,' said Alfredo.

'Oh, we ate rat often when we were children. I used to think it was normal. And now I can see that it is. Life is super weird, huh?'

This comment rendered Alfredo speechless. The phrase 'the condemned man enjoyed a last meal' ran through his brain like the electric advertisements in Times Square. Maybe they wouldn't find anything, and they would remember it as a nice trip to the mountains. Maybe.

They drove south for a couple of hours between the two rows of volcanoes that form the peaks of the Andes. Then they turned east into the plains and valleys of the upper reaches. The road became narrow, and the tarmac patchy, as they drove towards the lakes. The roads, which were empty, got steeper and narrower with precipitous drops into green patchwork alleys. They passed some over-loaded open wooden buses which bumped along at bicycle speed and could only get overtaken with great caution on wider stretches of the roads. There were few of these, so progress was glacial.

To make matters worse, as the evening drew in, sheep and cattle making for home blocked their route and kept them waiting in fading light. Finally, they entered an area where the road flattened out again. A village loomed out of the darkness, the whitewashed walls of the thatched houses bright in the gloom. There was an old inn on the main square named Lago Verde.

'We'll stay here tonight,' said Alfredo.

'Looks good to me,' said Saul, 'can we order some whisky?'

There was no whisky but their host produced a bottle of cheap local rum which they drank with the local version of Coca Cola and some dubious looking ice. They ate a piece of well stewed beef with some fried yucca and rice before bedding down for the night. The bathroom was a little primitive but, as Alfredo observed, at least it had a flushing toilet and their precious supply of toilet paper would come in handy.

The next morning, they arose early and ate some eggs scrambled with onion and bell peppers before setting out for San Blas. Alfredo stopped the car three times to ask different people for directions before taking the way indicated by them. Saul got a little irritated.

'Why did we need to get instructions from three people? Didn't they give you the same answer?'

'Yes, they did. However, it's local custom to send people on a wild goose chase so I had to check.'

The road got even narrower and it sank into the peat until they travelling along a sunken ditch with the sods of turf piled up into walls on either side.

'I hope there's not much traffic,' said Saul.

'It's unlikely. We must reverse into a gateway if we meet another vehicle.'

'This place is hidden from view. It's a wonder you know where it is. How ever did you hear about it?'

'I had a girlfriend whose father was German and she told me about it years ago, I guess it stuck in my mind. I'd forgotten about it until this came up.'

'They may not be here anymore.'

'Some of them will have died by now, too, but there may be some who have stayed put. We will soon find out.'

There was one road to follow, so it was hard to get lost. It wound on through the boggy terrain skirting the snow-topped peaks. Suddenly, like a cork out of a champagne bottle, the jeep popped out into a street of neat houses with carved window sills and wooden tiled roofs. It was like a Swiss alpine town.

'Jesus!' said Alfredo, 'all we need now is Heidi and a flock of goats.'

'Man, it's creepy as hell.'

'This must be the place.'

'Yes, sir.'

They drove down what looked like the main street of San Blas and came out into a neat square with precision cut box hedges and a carousel in the centre. There was a hotel on one side of the square which was so picturesque that it looked as if it belonged on the lid of a box of chocolates. It had window frames with carved hearts and birds in relief and wooden balconies with baskets of geraniums still dripping from a recent watering. Alfredo drove through a side entrance into a car park at the back of the hotel. They sat there for a while with their thoughts. A large cat emerged from some bushes and jumped up on the bonnet where it curled up and went to sleep.

'What do we do now?' said Alfredo. 'We haven't thought this through.'

'I imagine they'll come to us rather than the other way around.'

'You could be right. We'd better see if we can book a room then.'

'Lead on, Dr Vargas.'

They stepped into the foyer which was also ornate and decorated like a Swiss chalet. There was no one at the reception. A cuckoo clock chimed making them both jump. They watched mesmerised as a couple of dolls emerged from the doors of the clock and spun around in a circle before going back inside. One of them appeared to be wearing a uniform of some sort.

'Nice, isn't it?' said a voice behind them. 'My name is Franz Schmidt; I am the hotel manager. How can I help you?'

They both spun around in an uncanny imitation of the figures in the cuckoo clock. There was a large blonde man in lederhosen behind the reception desk. All he needs is a Tyrolean hat to complete the hallucination.

'Good afternoon, Mr Schmidt. Myself and my companion here would like a room each for tonight please and possibly tomorrow night as well.'

'Certainly, sir. We have en-suite rooms if you are interested?'

'Yes, please, that would be wonderful.'

'Are you here for the cheese making or the Germanic culture?'

'Oh, We'll do both.'

'Excellent. Can I have your passports, please? I need to get your details for the tourist log.'

'My passport is in my suitcase,' said Saul. 'Can I bring it down later, please?'

'Of course, sir, as long as I have the details of this other gentleman here, that will be fine.'

Thank goodness Saul had been so quick thinking. If the hotel manager had realised that a New York Jew was staying at the hotel, the news of their presence would have travelled fast. This might not be a bad move. Perhaps it would speed things up. He wasn't clear how they should proceed if they met a Nazi. That eventuality was still fuzzy in his mind. What they needed was a nice shower and a big supper with ample liquid fortification to give them some breathing time.

'Let me show you to your rooms,' said Schmidt.

***

Saul knocked on Alfredo's door.

'Hello, can I come in?'

'What's up?'

'We should give the manager my passport. He said his name was Franz Schmidt. Isn't that one of the Schmidt brothers that you used to play football with?'

'Wow, I was so freaked out by the hotel décor that I didn't recognise him. Mind you, I don't think he recognised me either. We're definitely in the right place. Are you confident about this? These people may be dangerous. We don't know what they are capable of.'

'I do. I saw first hand, but it's worth the risk. Think of us as bait.'

'Okay but be careful.'

Saul descended the stairs to the reception. Franz Schmidt was bent over the ledger and jumped when Saul put his passport on the desk.

'Here is my ID,' he said.

'Thank you. If you wait a moment, I will take down your details and give it back to you.'

Schmidt opened the passport and turned to the page with Saul's data on it. A slight widening of the eyes was the only visible reaction. He copied the information into the ledger without looking up. The pencil bit into the page and left a furrow due to the exaggerated pressure placed on it. The lead snapped and he took a deep breath.

'Is there anything else I can do for you, gentlemen?' he said, emphasising every syllable of the last word.

'Yes, we'd like to have dinner. What do you recommend?' said Saul, ignoring the ferocious re-sharpening of the pencil.

'We've a nice restaurant here in the hotel,' said Schmidt through gritted teeth. 'To tell you the truth, our restaurant is the only place in the village that opens at night. The village is built for day trippers and we don't get many people staying overnight.'

'Sounds good to me,' Saul said.

***

The two men came down for dinner at eight o'clock. They followed Schmidt into a quaint dining room with chequered red and white table cloths and carved wooden chairs with cut outs of deer on the seat-backs. There was a log fire burning in the grate. The mantelpiece had a set of elaborate candle holders on either side, framing a shadow on the wall where an image had been removed. It looked like a shrine. Schmidt caught Saul looking at the square of fresh paint revealed by the image's absence.

'Some tourist got drunk and damaged the painting we had there. It's in for repairs.'

'What was the painting of?'

'Oh, a local dignitary. No harm done.' His tone of voice suggested otherwise but Alfredo shook his head at Saul, who looked like he was about to interject. The manager must have removed the painting when they arrived at the hotel to prevent them seeing it. But why?

'Drunks, eh?' said Alfredo.

'Quite. And on that note, what can I get you to drink, gentlemen?'

They laughed. It is not religion but humour that is the opiate of the masses.

'I'll have a beer,' he said.

'Me, too,' said Saul.

'Is there a menu?'

'Not as such. We have typical German dishes here like Wiener Schnitzel with potato salad, wurst with red cabbage and sauerbraten with dumplings or any combination of these. We also have potato pancakes, potato dumplings and potatoes fried with bacon and onion but I don't expect you'll want that,' and here he looked at Saul.

'Two Wiener Schnitzels with sauerkraut and potato dumplings please. Is it veal or chicken?'

'It's veal.'

'Excellent, thank you.'

Saul had changed colour and was clutching the armrests of his chair.

'Hang in there,' said Alfredo, 'remember what you came for.'

The beer was cold. Saul drank his in long swallows and Alfredo asked for two more. By the time the new drinks arrived, both men had controlled their emotions. The food followed not long after and the plates groaned with huge portions of soothing calories which had the desired effect. Their progress had slowed to a crawl and they were playing with the remnants of their meals, when two men walked into the restaurant and sat down at the opposite end of the room. Both me had grey-hair and a military bearing and they had dressed in tweed suits with cravats at their necks.

'It seems that the neck tie is de rigueur in San Blas,' murmured Alfredo.

Saul had stiffened like a cornered dog. He was staring at one of the two men.

'Easy there, old chap,' said Alfredo, 'don't want to set the cat among the pigeons yet, do we?'

'It's him. Kurt Becker, the scourge of Brussels.'

'Are you positive? It's been forty years since you last saw him.'

'How can you ask me that? He took my family from me and sent them to Auschwitz. Do you imagine I could forget something like that? And that other man, I recognise him from the photos. That's Boris Klein. I'm convinced of it'

'Okay. Calm down. We need to find out where they live and how many others there are in San Blas. If there are more, we will need help to catch them. Don't let him see your reaction.'

'Reaction? He's a fucking mass murderer.'

'Yes, and we will get him for it. But not this minute. Trust me. We need to leave now. Stand up, there's a good chap.'

Saul stood up and Alfredo grabbed his arm and frogmarched him out of the restaurant as if forcing a drunk friend to go to bed. He smiled at the two men and raised his eyebrows in mock distress. There was no reaction.

They started up the stairs, Saul tripping in his reluctance to abandon the scene. Alfredo kept a firm grip on him and pushed him onwards. 'Goodnight,' he said to Schmidt. 'Can you put the meal on our bill, please?'

***

'I knew that bastard Ramon Vega was trouble,' said Kurt Becker when Alfredo and Saul had left the restaurant and gone to their rooms.

'They told me that we'd snuffed him out. Didn't Ponce say that Vega was working on his own? You should never trust a politician,' said Boris Klein.

'I'm confident Vega didn't collaborate with anyone on his report. He was working on his own for months. Kleber Perez saw this Dr Vargas fellow poking around in the archives asking for information about German settlers and became suspicious.'

'Kleber who?'

'Perez. The lad who works for us at the archives. He comes from Rolf Hermann's farm.'

'Oh yes, that boy. Is he the one who told us a Jew

had visited Mrs Hermann with Dr Vargas?'

'The same. He claims that he followed Dr Vargas to Ramon Vega's house after Dr Vargas found the address in the archives. Kleber told us that he suspects that Vargas was given the final report by Ramon Vega before the house burned down. He even tried to search for it in Dr Vargas' house but he was thwarted when Vargas returned from the airport with the Jew sooner than expected.'

'How come we didn't know about these jokers? The Jew and Dr Vargas. Where did they spring from and who the fuck are they, anyway?'

'The Jew is a journalist from New York. My sources tell me that he is a survivor from the pogrom in Brussels. He's a minor celebrity. He was on that transport that got held up by the resistance.'

'The one that got away. He may be dangerous. Revenge is a powerful motive. I wonder if he had family on that train. How about the doctor?'

'Dr Alfredo Vargas is an expert on the Inca and Valdivia cultures. He is rumoured to be a lush. Ponce tells me that Vargas has lost the respect of his colleagues because of his drunken escapades. We don't understand what his connection with Vega is. They may have studied together or been childhood friends.'

'A Jew and a drunk? Well, we may be old but we can deal with this little inconvenience without too much trouble.'

'That's what I said. Anyway, the Jew is about the same age as the Führer when he died so that may prove ideal for our purposes.'

'Huh, I never thought of that. You may be right. Well, I must get on if we are to deal with this tomorrow. Do you want a lift home?'

***

The next morning, Alfredo and Saul breakfasted on eggs and black bread before setting out to tour the sites. There was not much point pretending to be tourists anymore, but they carried on with the charade. As Alfredo pointed out, it was too much of a coincidence that Becker and Klein had turned up to eat the same evening they did. He was positive that Schmidt had alerted them after he had seen Saul's passport. Jewish journalists were not a dime a dozen in German theme villages, especially a village hidden in the mountains of Sierramar. If there was a conspiracy, Franz Schmidt had to be part of it.

Alfredo went up to his room and tried to ring Gloria. He dialled several times but there was no connection. He went back downstairs.

'Mr Schmidt, I need to speak to someone but I cannot get through to Calderon. Can you help me?

'Oh, I'm sorry, Dr Vargas. The telephones are not working. The line may be down. It's windy in the valley.'

Alfredo had seen Schmidt on the telephone when they came out of the dining room after breakfast but it was more evidence that something untoward was going on. He would contact her from Lago Verde when they got there. They told Scmidt that they would be back for dinner and would check out the next morning. Then they left on foot and worked their way through the town, criss-crossing the main street as they looked for evidence of the hidden community.

It was difficult to look for something that was already on display. They did not see any evidence of swastikas, heel clicking or pencil moustaches but the whole village reeked of German culture and history and they did not find a single native local working or living in the village. While they ate lunch in a local bar, barmaids dressed in white blouses surrounded them singing songs about beer and flirting.

'It's like Disneyland on drugs,' said Alfredo in wonder.

'More like Springtime for Hitler,' said Saul, shaken by the overload of Germanic bonhomie. 'I'm not sure what I expected to find, but this isn't it. What we do next?'

'Search me, I'm Germanated right now. However, cheese making and bad singing are not illegal in Sierramar as far as I am aware so we can't take matters into our own hands yet. Things may get nasty around here so we'd better make ourselves scarce. Let's go back to the hotel.'

'It's not like we haven't spotted any Nazis. They almost had dinner with us last night but how can we confirm their identities? We can't go up to them and ask them who they are.'

'That's not a bad idea.'

'What? Asking them to incriminate themselves? I don't think that's likely.'

'No, but Schmidt knows who they are. Why don't we ask him?'

CHAPTER XVI

Sam and Gloria, September 1988

Gloria fielded a phone call from Mr Chiriboga at the Geographical Institute who informed her that the aerial photographs were ready for collection.

'Sam, hurry up, we've got to pick up the photos of San Blas.'

'Okay, just putting my shoes on. How are we going to search for clues using the photographs? We need a special viewer to see them in three dimensions.'

'I've already thought of that. I've a friend who works in the seismic monitoring centre. They've every kind of equipment and he has a crush on me so the combination is promising.'

It did not surprise Sam to learn that Gloria had another admirer. She was the sort of woman that men lost their heads over, being as beautiful as Venus, as rich as Croesus and ultra-high maintenance.

'Sounds perfect. I'm ready. Let's go, then.'

They drove to the Geographical Mapping institute and parked outside, walking up the hill to the atrium, and through to the aerial photograph department. Mr

Chiriboga had already put the photographs in a big brown envelope for them.

'Has the Seismic Monitoring Centre got the correct viewers for seeing these in three dimensions?'

'Yes, they do. There will be someone up there who can help you. Good luck, ladies.'

The Centre lay on the flank of the large volcano that towered over Calderon and threatened to engulf the population of one million inhabitants with its next eruption. It was five hundred metres higher than the city and Sam's heart and lungs worked overtime trying to combat the lack of oxygen in the thin air. Gloria, unconcerned, lit a cigarette and surveyed the view from the car park.

'Amazing, huh? Calderon gets bigger and bigger.'

'Fantastic,' panted Sam.

When Gloria had finished her cigarette, they entered the nondescript concrete building and found themselves in a plain orange room with a scruffy reception desk. A bored looking woman was plaiting her hair behind it.

'Good morning. What can I do for you?'

'I'd want to see Guillermo Palacios, please.'

'Go into the room on the right and keep walking. His desk is the last one on the left at the end of the office.'

No security, no I.D. checks? It was almost disappointing. They walked through the long office through parallel lines of cubicles, each with an earnest looking occupant scrutinising their screen and taking notes. They stopped at the last cubicle and looked in. A man wearing thick glasses and a big moustache that resembled a fat caterpillar balancing on his lip, was peering at a print-out on his desk. He was worrying the cuticle on the side of one finger, which looked inflamed already. Gloria coughed.

'Ahem. Guillermo? It's me, Gloria.'

He spun around to face them, his face going deep red in pleasure and embarrassment.

'Gloria? Oh goodness. It's been far too long. You're still as beautiful as a flower. The roses must be jealous when you walk by.'

'Thank you. I should come here more often if I want to receive compliments.'

'But what're you doing here? And who's your friend?'

'This is Sam. We need your help. If you've time?'

'Hello, Sam. Nice to meet you. I've all the time in the world when it comes to you, Gloria. How can I help?'

'We need to examine some aerial photographs in three dimensions and to blow them up to a bigger size if possible. Is that something you can do?'

'Oh yes, I can do that. Have you got them here?'

Gloria handed over the envelope.

'What're you looking for?'

'It sounds strange but we're looking for concealed buildings outside the village of San Blas de Lago Verde.'

'Isn't that the village where they make the cheese? I'm guessing you're not looking for secret cheese makers?'

'Not exactly. It's more like a game of hide and seek. We're looking for some people who don't want to be found.'

'Sounds mysterious. Okay, let's see what we can do.'

He crossed over to the opposite cubicle where there was a flat table and a pair of thick lenses suspended above the table on tripods. Selecting two of the photographs, he placed them under the lenses and moved them around muttering. At last, what he saw satisfied him.

'There you go. Nice clear images, I'd say.'

Sam leaned over the table and looked through the lenses at the photographs which merged and came towards her in relief. She made out individual trees and people.

'That's fantastic.'

'Good, I'm glad that's what you needed. Now in return I want a favour, too.'

'Name your price.'

'If you'd like to stay here and search through the photographs, I want to take Gloria for a coffee.'

Sam looked at Gloria for confirmation. She nodded.

'That'll be perfect.'

Gloria stuck her arm through Guillermo's preventing him from floating off in a cloud of happiness and left to have coffee with him in a nearby café. Sam stayed behind examining the photographs for any clues to the secret hide-out of the Nazi officers. It was painstaking work but she could be meticulous and she had refined observational skills, part and parcel of being a geologist. She had reviewed four of the pairs of photographs spotting nothing of note when something caught her eye.

The image taken of the eastern part of the village had some raised bumps that didn't appear natural due to some straight lines in their formation. They had a covering of grass but they had dark depressions which could have been entrances in their sides.

Even more interesting were the human figures in the photograph. It might have been a trick of the light but they appeared to be wearing white coats. They might have been dairy workers, but they weren't wearing rubber boots. Then she realised what she was looking at. Laboratory coats. They were so out of place that she didn't believe her eyes even when she magnified the figures by lowering the lenses. What the hell was going on? Why would someone be wearing a lab coat in the outskirts of a village miles away from anywhere? It made little sense.

By the time that Gloria and Guillermo came back, Sam was almost hysterical with pent up excitement. Guillermo looked as if he had been smoking a psychotropic substance, and Gloria had the smug look of an opera singer that has just got a standing ovation.

'Did you find what you were looking for?' asked Guillermo.

'I think so,' said Sam. 'Can you tell me what you see?'

He leaned into the glasses and moved the photographs into focus. He grunted in surprise and moved the lenses around again.

'They look like doctors. Is there a clinic in the village?'

'Yes,' said Gloria, 'I believe there is, paid for by the dairy.'

She looked through the lenses and turned to face Sam, raising her eyebrow.

'We need to go now, Guillermo,' she said. 'I've got to pick up something at the chemist before it closes.'

'Please don't leave such a large gap between visits next time flower. I'll miss you.'

'Off course I won't, poppet. Thank you for your help.'

'Yes, thank you. It's been so useful,' said Sam.

They made their way to the car where Gloria lit another cigarette. She sucked in a deep breath and blew it out. The day had become overcast and dark clouds smothered the top of the volcano which brooded over them. Sam shivered and Gloria offered her a drag of her cigarette which she didn't refuse.

'What the hell is going on?' she asked Sam.

'Something weird. I've no idea. Don't panic, I'm convinced we're on the right track now.'

'We must go there straight away. I've a horrible feeling about this.'

'We should leave tomorrow at dawn. You ought to tell your father that we're going. Just in case.'

'My father? Are you mad? He'll be furious.'

'Yes, he will be, but not for long. We need to take someone trustworthy with us. Someone who can protect us should the worst happen.'

'You mean Segundo?'

'Yes, I do. If Alfredo and Saul are in trouble, we'll need help to rescue them.'

'Okay, I hate to admit it but you're right. However, we will stop at the chemist's first.'

'What for?'

'We're going to buy a pregnancy test.'

***

Hernan Sanchez' face lit up with pleasure when the two women arrived at his apartment. He had been in a quandary ever since he had read the report written by Ramon Vega. Whether he liked it or not, it implicated him in some shadier goings on of that era. He was ashamed that he had profited from the expulsion of the Jews from Calderon, having never imagined that similar policies would lead to the death camps in Germany and Poland. He had been young and influenced by the macho vibe of the fascist slogans and uniforms and talk of world domination. This fascination had disappeared when he learned about the final solution but not before he had earned some money building roads and houses for the new arrivals. He had not told Gloria about any of this and he wanted it to stay that way. Ramon's report would stay secret.

Despite his misgivings on the subject he had decided not to warn Gloria off the search for Alfredo. He did not appreciate being told what to do and Holger Ponce had crossed a line with his rude intervention. But he had a condition.

'Papi, how are you?' said Gloria.

'Mr Sanchez, it's so nice to see you again,' said Sam

'I'm well, thank you. How nice to see you both. I was bored by myself.'

'Our visit will vex you but I need your help, Papi.'

'Does it have anything to do with that rogue, Alfredo Vargas?' said Hernan, wrinkling his brow in a mock serious manner that even Sam found amusing.

'How did you know?'

'Honestly, darling, you don't imagine that you can keep secrets from me?'

'I should have realised that it was unlikely. I'm so sorry that I've been lying to you about him. I meant to tell you. It's difficult to be apart from someone you love.'

'I'm not pleased, but I love you and I understand how it is.'

'Papi, Alfredo is missing. I'm so worried about him. He travelled to the mountains with an American journalist and they've not come back. They may be injured or stranded somewhere.'

'And what're they doing up there, may I ask?'

'They were looking for a fugitive German officer from the second world war,' said Sam. 'It's likely to be a rumour, but there might be some truth to the matter, and we're worried that they have got themselves in trouble.'

'So, you two fine young women are going to rescue the men from peril? There's something wrong with this story.'

'That's why we're here. You don't imagine we would try to do this without your help, do you?'

'I can guess what help you want, or should I say whose? That's my condition for allowing you to go on this mad adventure so we're in agreement. I'll ring Segundo tonight and have him meet you at your apartment tomorrow at dawn.'

'Thank you, Mr Sanchez. We'll be a lot safer if Segundo is with us. He's quite a formidable person.'

'Ha! That's one way of putting it, Sam. Now what can I offer you to drink?'

After the women had left, Hernan rang his enforcer, Segundo Duarte.

'Good evening. Who is it?'

'Segundo, good evening. How are you?'

'Don Sanchez, what an honour. I'm well, thank you, sir. And you?'

'Not bad, old friend. I have a job for you.'

'What can I do for you?

'I want you to babysit my daughter and her friend, Sam. They're going to search for Alfredo, Gloria's boyfriend, who is missing in the mountains. I understand you learned about Alfredo and Sam on your trip to Riccuarte. I want you to make certain that they get home safe.'

'Okay, boss. I'll do that. And don't worry about a thing. I'll guard your daughter with my life. When do you need me?'

'Can you be here tomorrow morning?'

'Tomorrow is impossible I'm afraid. I've got an

appointment to renew my identity card. I can't travel without it, or the police might pick me up.'

'What about the day after?'

'Yes, that will be fine. Where shall I meet them?'

'Can you wait at the crossroads at San Francisco after lunch? That way you won't have to come in to town and then go back out again.'

'I'll be there.'

'Thank you. I will reward your loyal service well.'

'I can never repay you the debt I owe, Don Sanchez.'

'Be careful. We don't know what has happened to them. They were looking for fugitives from Nazi Germany.'

'I'll take my gun.'

***

Gloria wanted to send Sam into the toilet with the pregnancy testing kit as soon as they got home.

'But I don't need to do a pee.'

'You haven't done one all day. So, unless you're a camel, you're a poor liar. Pee on the stick and let's get this over with.'

'But what if it's positive? I don't want to find out before we leave, in case it makes me afraid.'

'Afraid of what?'

'Afraid of losing the baby. Afraid of being a mother. Afraid in general.'

'So, you've decided that you want it?'

'Yes, no, I don't know. But I don't want to find out yet. Let's do the test when we get back? Please?'

'Hmm, I'm uncertain if that's a good idea. Wouldn't you rather be put out of your misery? We should bring it with us and decide on the trip.'

'Being sure I'm pregnant will not make me less

miserable than I am already. I'll put the kit in my rucksack, I promise. I might change my mind on the road.'

'I don't understand how putting off the result will help you decide, but if you can't face doing it now I guess we can wait for a while.'

'Thanks, I don't want to do this right now. It's the rest of my life in the balance.'

'Go to the toilet anyway and I'll make some tea to refill your bladder.'

Gloria went to the kitchen and set the table with cups and saucers and put a kettle on to boil. Sam's arguments against doing the test did not convinced her but she could understand the reluctance. She lit a cigarette and leaned against the counter and waited for the kettle to whistle. The phone rang and she carried an ashtray out to the hall in case it was going to be a long one.

'Hello. Who's speaking, please?'

No one spoke. The sound of coins being dropped into a payphone vibrated in her ear. She waited.

'Hello? Is that Gloria Sanchez?'

'Yes, it is. Please speak up, I can't hear you well.'

'It's Ramon.'

'Ramon? Ramon who?'

'Ramon Vega, Alfredo's friend.'

Now it was Gloria's turn to be silent.

'Hello? Are you still there, Gloria?'

'You're alive? But they told us you'd died in the fire. How did you get my number?'

'Alfredo's maid gave it to me. I wanted people to think that I'd died in the fire so they would leave me alone, but I'm alive.'

'Whose were the bodies that the police found in the house? They found one in the maid's room and the other in your room. I presume the maid was in her bed, but who was in yours?

'I was having an affair with someone who came over to see me that night. We were in bed together and then she sent me to the off-licence to buy some wine. When I got back, the house was a furnace. There was nothing I could do.'

'Have you told the police?'

'They are aware of it but they are keeping it quiet because the husband doesn't want anyone to know how she died. He wants to pretend she died in a car crash.'

'Alfredo's devastated. He thinks you're dead.'

'Where is he? I gave him an important document that I need to get back. He's not answering his phone.'

'Alfredo's missing. He went into the mountains with an American journalist looking for the Nazis and they've disappeared.'

'That's awful news and it will get worse. We need to publish the document as soon as possible to expose those people before they escape. Do you have any idea where it is?'

'Yes, I hid it in my father's house but I didn't tell him. It's safe. Where are you?'

'I'm in Miami. I flew out after the fire as I was afraid they would hunt me down if they realised that I was still alive.'

'My father can send you the document by courier if you let him have the address. You need to ring him but wait until tomorrow. I'll ring him myself today and tell him to give it to you.'

'Okay, what's his number?'

Gloria dictated the number and then the beeps went. Ramon swore as he tried to force more coins into the slot to no avail. The phone cut off.

She stood in the hall composing herself for a minute

and then rang her father.

'Papi, it's me.'

'Hello, darling. I was about to ring you. I've news about Segundo.'

'I have news, too. Who should go first?'

'Tell me.'

'Ramon Vega, Alfredo's friend, contacted me. He's in Miami.'

'Ramon? Didn't he die in a fire?'

'It's a long story. I'll tell you another time.'

'Okay, so what did this fellow want?'

'He asked me about a report he had written. He gave it to Alfredo and he was trying to track it down.'

'What's this report about then?'

'It's an exposé of the collaboration between Germany and Sierramar during and after the war.'

'Would this be the document that is hidden in a drawer of your mother's chest in my bedroom?'

'I should've known you'd find it. It contains incriminating research. There are people who don't want it published and are prepared to do anything to stop it. Ramon's house burnt down last week and he left the country because he was worried about his safety.'

'So why do you have it?'

'Alfredo gave to me after someone tried to burgle his house to steal it. I didn't imagine anyone would dare to search for it in your house. I'm sorry I didn't tell you.'

'This document's a dangerous piece of paper. Perhaps I should destroy it.'

'Don't do that, Papi. Ramon wants to publish it in Miami. He contacted me this evening and asked me if I would send it to him. I told him that you have it and he will ring you tomorrow.'

Hernan Sanchez was in a quandary. If they published the document, Holger Ponce and the rest of the collaborators might find out who kept it safe and that would be the end of his lucrative public contracts. On the other hand, the truth would not remain hidden much longer anyway, and the right thing to do was publish and be damned. He hedged his bets.

'Off course, darling. I'll talk to him and see what I can do.'

'It's vital, Papi. If we publish the truth, there is no reason for anyone to harm Alfredo and his friend for discovering the secret.'

'I understand. Now listen to me. Segundo cannot be here until tomorrow evening so I don't want you to set out until he arrives. Is that clear?'

'But…'

'No buts. That's an order.'

'Okay.'

'It's too dangerous to go without him. I'm serious about this.'

'Okay, Papi. I promise.'

'Bye, darling. Ring me before you set out.'

'I will. Bye.'

Gloria was not happy, but he was right. One day shouldn't make any difference but who knew what was going on? She returned to the kitchen where Sam cradled a cup of tea.

'So?' she asked, 'who was that?'

CHAPTER XVII

Simon was in a complete panic. Talk about bad timing. How had he been so stupid? He had dug himself a couple of holes in his life but this time he had tunnelled to the centre of the earth. And the worst thing was that he had done it because Hannah reminded him of Sam and he was feeling abandoned. He didn't even tell her about Sam and the possible pregnancy. He doubted that she even remembered what happened, she was so drunk. She was so similar to Sam, and so different, it was like being in a parallel universe until he woke up the next morning and realised what he had done.

He snuck out of Hannah's flat without waking her, and he hadn't been brave enough to contact her since. She was going to be shell-shocked, too. Why didn't Hannah know about Sam's pregnancy? He was so dumbstruck when Sam told him the news that he couldn't remember what he had said. It hadn't been good because she left him holding the phone with a dialling tone ringing in his ear. What a bloody mess.

He blamed Sam for going away and leaving him alone. She knew that he resisted everything except temptation. The worse thing was that having found himself in bed with Hannah only made him long for Sam. He wanted to live with her and keep her close to stop him from roaming. Now he had done something unforgivable.

He moaned and paced the room, gesticulating and talking to himself. *How would he convince Hannah not to tell? Surely, she would agree rather than hurt her sister?* She must be feeling worse than him. No matter how awkward, he would have to talk to Hannah and get her to agree to a vow of silence. Sam need never find out. He would deal with the baby thing if it became a reality. *Should they move in together and work from there?* He found his address book and looked up Hannah's number.

***

Simon was not the only one in a panic. Hannah woke up alone, tangled up in bed linen smelling of sex and wine. Her head was throbbing in a way that suggested it might explode. The nasty pain behind her eyes made her screw them up, stopping all but the tiniest glint of light from entering. This did not prevent her from noticing the stains on the bottom sheet that belonged to both types of liquid. It wasn't a dream? She shouldn't have slept with him, but the evidence spoke for itself.

No one must ever find out. She didn't want to imagine what her parents would think. And Sam? She blamed Sam for going away again. None of this would have happened if she had not gone prancing off to Sierramar leaving Simon home alone. She bundled the sheets up and stuffed them into the washing machine with her underwear and some random tea towels. Switching on the hottest wash, she went into the bathroom and immersed herself in the shower, trying to scrub herself free of fault with a loofah.

***

'I don't understand what the point of this is.'

Hannah stirred her coffee, avoiding Simon's pleading look and staring past him out of the window at the plastic bags being blown around the bus stop.

'We need to talk. You know we do.'

'And what can you say, Simon? You took advantage of me when I was drunk and now you want me to forget it ever happened. Or did I get that wrong?'

Simon spluttered. 'How can you say that? You took advantage of me and not the other way around. I showed my vulnerable side and you went for the jugular. You're no angel, either.'

He put his head in his hands and ran his fingers through the tufts of hair above his ears. His shoulders slumped.

'Okay, don't panic, we're both guilty. I needed attention after my breakup and Indiana Jane had deserted you. It was only sex.'

'Just sex, huh? How come I can't get you out of my head?'

'Perhaps you enjoyed it?' Hannah looked him straight in the face. 'Or you like me? Has that ever occurred to you? This wouldn't be the first time a man fancied more than one member of a family.'

'I like you. You're funny and beautiful, but I love your sister.'

'You can't love her after sleeping with me and shouting with passion.'

This was true. But he was thinking about Sam at the time and the two bodies mingled in his mind and drove him crazy with desire. The drink and the passion had befuddled his mind to the extent that he wasn't clear who he was with, but he wouldn't admit that. He fancied Hannah and he was certain it was mutual which was why he avoided her in the past. Why had he gone to her house? That was the sixty-four-thousand-dollar question. This scenario was always a possibility, for him anyway. He had told himself that he only wanted to bask in her resemblance to Sam and flirt a bit. He hadn't banked on her being drunk and lonely and open to suggestion.

And she smelt great and he was dying to touch her again and make her moan. He leant forward and breathed in her scent as she bent to place her cup on the table. They stopped with their faces almost touching, hardly daring to breathe. She went pink with desire. He put his hand behind her head and pulled her in for a kiss.

***

The phone rang when Hernan Sanchez was walking by on his way to the bathroom. He tutted at the bad timing and picked the receiver up.

'Yes?'

'Good morning, Senor Sanchez.'

'Good morning. Who is this? I'm in a hurry.'

'Ramon Vega, sir. I told your daughter that I'd contact you today.'

'Oh, yes, how can I help you?'

'I understand you have my report in your possession. I'd be most obliged if you would send it to me.'

'Where are you? Why can't you come and collect it?'

'I am in Miami. I can't come to Sierramar right now.'

'The report is inflammatory. Sierramar's reputation

will be at stake if outsiders read the content.'

'You have read the document? Didn't Gloria hide it?'

'My daughter cannot hide anything from me. I have the right to read something that was hidden in my house.'

'Aren't you ashamed about the collaboration of our government? You are not blameless, either. This can not be kept secret forever. Sooner or later the truth will get out.'

'You've no right to judge me. I was a young hothead. We did things differently then.'

'I'm sorry. You're right. I can't judge the things that happened then, but I know how things are now, and Alfredo is in danger. We must publish.'

'I can't decide right now. Tell me where you are and I'll send the report to you if I decide that this is the right thing to do.'

'But this is not your decision. The document is mine. You must send it.'

'Possession is nine tenths of the law, young man. You don't get to tell me what to do.'

'I can't force you to send it. That's true. But I'm begging you. That report represents two year's work, my livelihood. If you destroy the contents, you're vandalising history.'

'Tough. I'll decide what to do without your help. Where are you?'

'I'm staying at the Hotel Franklin, on South Beach.'

'Okay, let me meditate on this.'

'Please send it soon. Time is of the essence. Alfredo may not survive if I do not publish as soon as possible.'

'Goodbye, Mr Vega.'

Hernan Sanchez replaced the telephone and continued on his way to the bathroom.

*** * * *

Gloria was not happy. She was determined to set out for San Blas to find Alfredo but now they had to wait for Segundo. They had only been delayed for a day but it seemed like a week to her. She stomped around the house trying to find things to do.

'This is the problem with having a maid,' she said to Sam, 'the ironing is done, the floors are shining, the beds are made. I've nothing to do.'

Sam, who considered having a maid to be a luxury, was happy doing nothing for a change. She was lying on her bed dreaming about Simon and the baby. The pregnancy test lay on the quilt beside her, still in its plastic container. There was no escape. She needed the result.

'I'm going to the corner shop to buy a newspaper and some cigarettes,' said Gloria, 'are you coming with me?'

'No, I'll stay here, thanks.'

'Okay, I'll be back in a minute.'

As soon as she heard the front door shut, Sam jumped off the bed and grabbed the pregnancy test. The world began to spin as her low blood pressure made her world black for an instant. She grasped the door handle and waited until the moment passed, then she went into the bathroom and locked the door. The plastic packaging was difficult to take off and Sam swore as the wand flew out of her hand, across the tiles and landed in a pool of liquid under the toilet bowl.

She reached under the bowl and picked the wand up. Would the chemicals still work? She imagined Gloria's fury at her incompetence. Did she drop it on purpose? It had seemed like an accident. She shook off the excess liquid and balanced the wand on the bath, removing her underwear and sitting down on the seat of the toilet. She held the wand between her legs and tried to pee.

Predictably, her desire to urinate had disappeared and no matter how she pushed, none would emerge. She reached over and open one tap on the bath. She tried to concentrate on water, cool streams and lazy rivers. Suddenly, like a cork firing out of a champagne bottle, a strong stream of urine shot out hitting her in the hand and knocking the wand onto the side of the bowl.

'Bloody hell,' she said, and reached down to grab the stick before it fell into the water. It soaked the whole thing with urine. She shook it dry and placed it beside the sink. There was no reason to think it wouldn't work. The whole point was to soak the stick in pee. She washed her hands and checked the packaging again. Three minutes for results. Even Sam could wait three minutes.

Three interminable minutes. Sam tried to distract herself by plucking her eyebrows but it didn't take long to realise that she was not brave enough. The hairdresser did this for her at such high speed that she didn't have time to complain. She examined her face in the mirror. Was this the face of a mother? She didn't look old enough to order a drink even though she was almost thirty. Her face was unlined and still had the dew of youth. Her worried green eyes stared back at her.

Time was up. She picked up the wand and examined the little box for a blue line that would signify a seismic shift in her existence. She squinted and the window came into focus. Oh, bugger! The line of doom. How could a line so faint be a harbinger of such a life-changing event? Bad luck seemed to follow her around. Why couldn't she win the lottery instead?

She let out the breath she had been holding and looked in the mirror again. What on earth was she going to do? The walls of the bathroom started closing in like a blue womb. She wanted to curl up in a foetal position. She was screwed. Where was Gloria? How long did she take to buy a lousy packet of cigarettes?

She sat on the edge of the bath with the stick in her hand willing the blue line to disappear. Telling Gloria seemed like a worse idea with every passing minute. Wasn't she suffering enough with the whole Alfredo drama without burdening her with the news of Sam's pregnancy? She had to tell someone or she might burst. With Simon eliminated as an option there was one person on the planet she wanted to tell. Gloria wouldn't mind if she used the phone.

***

'Hello?'

'Sam? Hi! How are you? How is Calderon?' asked her sister

'Great, thanks. Complicated, but you there's never a dull moment with Gloria around.'

'She definitely fits into the interesting category. What's up?'

'Nothing. Why should anything be up?'

'It's so obvious that something has happened. You never ring me from Calderon unless a drama has occurred. And your voice sounds funny.'

'Well, I wouldn't call it a drama, more of a tragedy.'

'Spit it out!'

'I'm pregnant, up the duff, I have a bun in the oven.'

'What? How? When? Who's the father?'

'Don't be ridiculous. Simon. How can you even ask?'

A long silence followed.

'Hannah? Are you still listening? I need you.'

'I'm here, sis. Shocked. I will be an aunty.'

'If that's shocking, imagine how I feel. Anyway, who said I will have the baby? Simon wasn't enthusiastic.'

'Simon? You've told him? When?'

'I spoke to him last week before I took the test to warn him.'

'What did he say?'

'He asked me if it was his. Bastard.'

'This is a nightmare.'

'Wow, you sound more worried than me. I have made no decisions yet. I rang for reassurance and I have to tell you, you're not doing a good job.'

'No, I'm sorry. It's a lot to take in. What are you going to do?'

'Nothing right now. The pregnancy is still at an early stage, only two months, so I have plenty of time to decide.'

'Have you told Gloria? What does she say?'

'I told you first, sis. You're my rock.'

'Gosh, thanks. Look, if you're okay, I need to make tea and digest this news. Will you ring me again when we've both had time to digest this?'

'That sounds good. Please Hannah, don't tell Mummy. I may not keep the baby and I would prefer she never finds out. You know how upset she would be.'

'I promise.'

'Okay, got to go now, these calls are expensive and this is Gloria's line.'

CHAPTER XVIII

Alfredo and Saul, August 1988

Franz Schmidt's eyes open wide and his mouth fell open before he recovered.

'The man with Dr Becker? Boris something, Klein I think. They come here often. I'm expecting them tomorrow.' He hesitated. 'Have you met Dr Becker?'

'I knew him a long time ago.' Saul's voice was tight.

'We're leaving in the morning so we won't get the chance to meet them this time. Perhaps on another occasion,' said Alfredo, moving away and pushing Saul up the stairs with him.

'Don't do anything foolish,' said Alfredo in Saul's ear, 'you've come this far. We should leave first thing in the morning.'

'Those bastards must pay. What if they try to get away?'

'I think it's us who need to get away now. Trust me.'

He led Saul to his room. Then he realised that he had left his wallet on the reception desk. 'Get packing.

I left something downstairs.'

He started down the stairs and a voice floated up towards him.

'Boris, we need to act now. These men are on to you.'

Alfredo stopped with his foot in mid-air, still hidden from the reception desk, but he could hear quite clearly what was said.

'Yes, they're leaving tomorrow. We have to stop them.' There was a pause.

'Okay, I'll do that. Leave it to me. Goodbye.'

Alfredo crept back up the stairs and then turned around and descended again making certain Schmidt could hear his footsteps. Schmidt looked up as he heard him coming.

'Yes? Ah, your wallet? I have it here.'

Alfredo took it and returned up the stairs where he knocked on the door of Saul's room.

'Saul? Let me in.'

'What's up?'

'We need to leave this evening. The hotel manager has told Boris Klein we know who he is.'

'Okay, what do you suggest?'

'We need to sneak down the fire escape into the car park and get out of here as soon as possible. It's better in the dark. How about ten o'clock?'

'Sounds good. See you then.'

Alfredo left Saul's room and went back to his own to pack. His heart was thumping. He felt like he was in a movie. And he still hadn't called Gloria. But now he knew that people might listen, he waited. He wanted to get out of San Blas before it was too late.

***

At ten o'clock, the two men made their way to the back

of the hotel. A door locked with a heavy padlock blocked the entrance to the fire escape. Someone had screwed the hasp onto a rotten piece of wood. Alfredo gave it a sharp tug and it came away with ease. The door swung open with a loud creak onto a clear and cold night. The almost full moon flooded the car park with light, their jeep caught in the spotlight of its ghostly shimmer.

'Not a great night for sneaking away,' said Alfredo. 'I could read a book in this light.'

'It's beautiful,' said Saul.

'Come on. Let's get out of here.'

They crept down the rusting stairs to the car park. Their car stood on its own in the middle. There was something strange about it. It was listing to one side. Alfredo ran towards it across the open space and he knew what was wrong.

'The tyres on the left side of the car,' he said, 'they're both flat. This can't be a coincidence. Someone has sabotaged it.'

'Shit. What'll we do now?'

'We can't stay here. Let's walk out. It's our only chance and the next village isn't that far away. We should get there in a few hours. The moonlight is perfect for a nice stroll.'

'Okay, I didn't like this hotel, anyway. Can you open the back for me?'

'Did you forget something?'

'Alfredo, you must be crazy if you think I will leave my gun behind.'

'The gun, I forgot. I think we should abandon most of our stuff and take the essentials.'

Saul threw his bag into the back of the car and opened the side panel to take out the gun.

'Well, I've got bullets, a gun, some cash and my

passport. How about you?'

'I'm going for my ID, cash and two bars of chocolate.'

'Okay then, let's make ourselves scarce.'

***

The moon also illuminated the road out of San Blas, making their shadows precede them and walking a little difficult, but they did not slow down. The village lights receded into the blackness and the two men began to breathe easier.

'I'll need double rate for field trips,' said Alfredo.

'If we get out of here, I'll pay you overtime as well.'

They kept up the pace for an hour and then sat down for a rest and some chocolate. The sound of an engine broke the silence.

'Did you hear that?'

'I did. It might be a bus.'

'I hope so because these peat banks are steep and I can't see an exit.'

They started to walk again, their breath visible in the cold night air. The engine grew louder. Headlights picked them out on the road. They flattened themselves against the banks as a car drove past and went around the corner.

'Phew, that was close,' said Alfredo.

But as they walked around the bend, they noticed the car had stopped and the doors were open. Two men stood waiting for them.

'Dr Vargas, isn't it rather late for a walk?' said a voice. Boris Klein stepped into the moonlight.

'Well, it was such a clear night.'

'How foolish of you to think that we would let you leave with your little Jewish friend after he recognised my colleague Dr Becker.'

'It was worth a try,' said Alfredo.

Boris Klein turned to his companion, a burly man with blonde hair.

'Have you got the rope?' he said.

Saul moved closer to Alfredo. 'Be ready to run,' he hissed.

'Don't be a fool. They're armed.'

'So are we. Have you forgotten? I have the Glock. They won't take me alive.'

'Use your head man, we don't need to die here. Get a grip.'

Boris and the young man approached them. Saul Rosen's cheekbones stuck out in the moonlight making him look like a corpse.

'Face the bank and put your hands behind your back.'

Alfredo did as he was asked but Saul stayed where he was.

'Oi, Jew, turn around or I will make you.'

'No.'

He took the Glock out of his waistband where he had concealed it under his shirt and pointed it at Boris Klein.

'Make me,' he said. 'Go on. I dare you.'

The young man with Klein hurled himself at Saul. The gun went off and Boris Klein grunted as the bullet hit him in the shoulder. Alfredo threw himself on the ground as Saul kept shooting at the prone body, his arms flailing as he wrestled with his attacker. They fell to the ground. There was another shot. Alfredo lay in the mud afraid to move. There was a groan. Boris Klein sat up cursing.

'What the fuck is going on? Where did he get that gun? Jesus, Hans, get up and stop messing about.'

'Sorry boss, I didn't see the gun until it was too late.

Are you wounded?'

'It's a scratch. Get up, Jew.'

'He's not going anywhere, boss.'

'Is he alive?' said Alfredo

'I think so. Get up,' said Klein

'I can't stand up. My legs won't work,' said Saul.

'You won't be needing them. Hans, get him into the car. We have to take him to the lab right now.'

Hans gave Alfredo a poke with his boot.

'Are you hurt?'

'No, I don't think so.'

'Okay, stand up and no funny stuff or you will end up like your friend.'

Alfredo stumbled to his feet. Hans gestured at Saul. 'Help me get him into the car.'

Saul lay in the mud with his face to the sky. He tried to speak but bright bubbles of blood came out of his mouth. They had shot him through the spine and when they tried to lift him, his legs flopped about like strands of spaghetti. The two men strained and struggled for ten minutes before they were successful. By the time they finished, they had covered Alfredo with Saul's blood which added to his distress. His hands tied, they manhandled him into the back seat of the jeep beside Saul, who was slumped but still breathing. He opened his eyes and muttered something that sounded like revenge, but it was hard to tell.

'Did you find the gun,' said Boris.

'No, it too dark. I think it sank into the mud somewhere,' said Hans.

Somehow, Hans turned the car around in the narrow, high-banked road by driving back and forward and twisting the wheel to its limit. Alfredo held onto Saul to stop him falling off the seat. The smell of blood was overpowering and his hands fell sticky. He drove them back through the village of San Blas and out of the other side along a crude gravel road with large potholes. They did not drive far and when they stopped on the edge of the forest, there were no buildings in the area. It struck Alfredo with the thought that they were being taken there to for burial. He hoped that it would be quick. Would Gloria ever find out what happened to him? He wished he had told her where they were going. Too late now.

'Quickly,' said Boris, 'don't let him die'.

Hans sounded the horn of the car and then he and Alfredo pulled Saul out of the seat and gave him an improvised chair lift towards a grassy mound in the clearing. To Alfredo's bewilderment, a door opened in the hillside and a man put his head outside.

'Get a stretcher. Now!' yelled Boris.

Less than a minute later, the man ran outside pushing a stretcher on wheels. They placed Saul onto it and disappeared into the door in the hill.

'I don't understand,' said Alfredo, 'why are you keeping him alive?'

'He won't be alive for long,' said Boris and laughed. 'Take Dr Vargas to the guest suite, Hans.'

***

They led Alfredo down a dark passageway with flickering fluorescent lighting. His ordeal had disorientated and shocked him, and stumbled several times on the smooth flooring. Hans pushed him into a pokey room with two single camp beds.

'There you are. Luxury. You can choose your bed.'
'I need to use the bathroom.'
'It's under one of the beds. Sleep tight, Dr Vargas.'
'What about Saul?'
'What about the nasty Jew? He's dead by now.'

'Dead? But he was still alive when we arrived.'

'You understand nothing, do you? We had to take his fingers before he died or they can't be used.'

'His fingers? Oh my God…'

It was too much for Alfredo, who fainted. Klein chuckled. 'And you are next, Dr Vargas,' he said and shut the door.

***

Saul Rosen struggled to stay conscious. Blood was choking him and he kept floating off the stretcher towards the lights in the ceiling. The Glock was still in his jacket pocket where he had managed to secret it whilst lying in the mud. The cold metal felt good in his hand. He could hear people talking.

'A fucking disaster. How were we to guess that he was armed?' said Hans

'Well, he's here now. I need to get on with it. Can you tell Boris to hold out longer? I'll take the bullet out of his shoulder as soon as I finish here.'

'Okay, doc. Jewish bastard!' Hans walked up to the stretcher and said it again, right into Saul's ear. 'Jewish bastard. You're going to die in the Führer's service.'

Saul smiled at him, coughing blood out of his throat so that he could speak.

'So are you,' he said.

There was a sharp retort and Hans fell to the floor, a large red stain spreading across his chest. His face had an expression of surprise frozen on it. Becker swore and ran to his side to feel his pulse, but it was too late.

'Hans? You bastard! He's dead.'

The gun fell to the floor making Becker jump, and Saul Rosen slipped out of consciousness for the last time. He was still smiling. Boris Klein came running into the laboratory.

'Jesus, what happened?'

'He kept the gun. Hans is dead. I have to get the fingers now or it will be too late.'

'How can I help?'

***

'What a fucking train wreck,' said Klein washing the blood off his hands.

'it will devastate his father,' said Kurt Becker

'The Schmidt brothers were always a little half-hearted about this project. Franz fancies the local women. He's never been Aryan enough.'

'Well, his nephew was Aryan enough to die for it.'

'That's true. I'll tell them tomorrow and alert them to the fact that we have to leave.'

'I need more time,' said Becker, sitting in the corner with his head lowered. 'People may come looking for Dr Vargas and the Jew. We have to put them off our trail.'

Klein rubbed his chin and examined his fingers.

'I've an idea but we will have to be careful that no one sees us.'

'Go on.'

'We need Vargas for a bit to talk to him about Vega's report and find out who knows what before we dispose of him. We may also want more fingers before we're ready for the final step.'

'That makes sense. So?'

'Their car is at the hotel. If we bring it here, we can fix the punctures and put the two bodies in it. If we set it on fire and push it down the cliffs outside Lago Verde, people will think that they had an accident on the way home. It will take them weeks to identify the bodies and realise that Dr Vargas is not one of them.

We'll be long gone by then.'

'Brilliant. I like it. Send one of the boys to change the tyres. Then drive the car here and we will load it up with the bodies and dump it tomorrow. There is no one on the roads at night here. It will be straightforward.'

'I'll get on with it.'

'We still need a human incubator.'

'Trust me.'

CHAPTER XIX

Sam and Gloria September 1988

After what seemed like an age, the front door opened. Sam flew out of the kitchen and down the corridor waving the pregnancy-test stick.

'I have news,' she said and stopped in mid-sentence. Gloria's face was white with shock. She was holding a newspaper which she thrust into Sam's hand.

'The car,' said Gloria, 'it's Alfredo's car.'

It took Sam a few seconds to realise what she should read, a report on the discovery of a crashed car near Lago Verde. 'Are you positive?'

'I remember the registration and you can see most of the number plate in the photograph. It can't be a coincidence.'

Sam looked at the photograph which showed a mobile crane on a narrow road pulling a car back up over the edge of a precipice. To her horror, the car appeared carbonised. No-one could have survived that.

'Did they find the driver? What about passengers?'

'The article doesn't say. What shall we do?'

'What about your friend Inspector Torres? Perhaps he can find out for us?'

'Yes, I'll ring him now. Oh God, what will I do if I lose Alfredo?'

'Don't panic. You need to stay calm and ring the Inspector. I'll make you a coffee.'

Gloria started rummaging in her bag for the Inspector's card. She found it and rushed out to dial the number of the police station in the valley.

'Hello, this is Gloria Sanchez, can I speak to Inspector Torres, please?'

Gloria balanced the receiver on her shoulder and lit a cigarette. She took a long pull and breathed out, draining her lungs. Then she fumbled with the receiver and put it back to her ear.

'Yes, Inspector, thank you, I understand you're busy but I need your help.'

She frowned.

'What? No, it's not about the fire. My friend Alfredo is missing, and they have found his car near Lago Verde. Can you tell me if the police found him and his friend too? Did they escape or are they injured and in hospital?'

Gloria nodded.

'Yes, I can. I'll be there after lunch. Thank you, Inspector.'

She hung up the phone and turned to Sam.

'He will ring the police station nearest to Lago Verde and get the details. He wants us to come and see him in the station this afternoon so he can give us the details in person.'

'Okay. I made the coffee. Let's have a cup with our lunch and we can head down to the station.'

'I can't eat. I'm so worried.'

'Come and sit down. You might manage

something.'

Sam had to shout at Gloria to slow down on the way to the police station. She was driving even faster than usual and Sam feared that they would also end up at the bottom of a precipice. They swept into the car park almost hitting a police car on its way out. Gloria jumped out of the car and made for the station entrance, Sam trailing in her wake. Then she stopped and stood there as if in a trance. Sam caught up with her.

'Gloria? Come on.'

'I'm afraid.'

'Me too.'

Sam slipped her arm through Gloria's and they walked into the station. The desk sergeant was expecting them and directed them straight into the office of Inspector Torres who was standing up facing the window with his back to them.

He didn't need to turn around.

***

Sam drove back to Calderon, heading straight for the apartment of Hernan Sanchez, reasoning that if she lost someone she loved, she would need her parents. Gloria sobbed all the way there. Her mascara had spread over her cheeks. She said nothing except for 'Alfredo' over and over, rocking in her seat like a lunatic. Sam got out first and asked the guard to inform Rosa, Hernan's maid that Alfredo Vargas was dead and Gloria needed her father.

They travelled up together in the lift with Gloria weeping into Sam's chest making a damp black patch on her shirt. The doors opened and Hernan Sanchez stood there with his arms open. Sam passed Gloria into his care without being able to comfort either of them.

'I'll come over tomorrow,' she said.

'Why don't you stay, too? There's plenty of room.'
'I can't. She needs you to herself. I'm sure I would.'
'Okay, but I'm here if you need anything.'
'Thank you.'

Sam pressed the button to descend, waving a sad goodbye. Enveloped in her father's arms, Gloria sobbed her heart out. Her friend's desolation was too much for Sam to bear. She drove back to Gloria's flat and parked the car in the garage. It was a cold evening turning her hands to ice. She sat on the sofa and looked out at the volcano, as lonely as the last person on earth.

She wrapped herself in a blanket and recalled the inspector's face as he explained that they had found two bodies in the car. They had been impossible to identify on site as it had burned them beyond recognition. There was one tall thin man who appeared to be missing his fingers, and one stocky man of about five feet nine who had been driving. The taller man had a tattoo from a concentration camp visible on an unburned part of his wrist, a sure sign that he was Saul Rosen. There was no certainty about the identity of the smaller man.

The inspector told them he would receive information about any identification for the smaller man in the next day or two. He reminded them of the unexpected body at Ramon Vega's house, trying to give them a little hope. He didn't sound as if he believed what he was saying. Gloria, who had cried even before she sat down, did not take in any of this. The inspector was used to being the bearer of awful news, but seemed quite overcome by Gloria's distress.

'I'm sorry,' he said to Sam. 'So sorry.'

***

The next couple of days were the saddest that Sam had

ever experienced. Gloria was inconsolable and Sam could not think of anything to say to make the hurt diminish. Hernan Sanchez had taken on the role of full-time care-giver. He did not need Sam who languished like an extra wheel, racked with guilt because she had not taken Alfredo's disappearance seriously, using it as an excuse to escape from her own life. And now he was dead.

It didn't seem real. How did he die like that? It didn't compute. Old people died. She didn't have any experience of death and it made her feel inadequate. What did you say to someone who was so sad they wanted to die, too? She tried walking around town to distract herself but her light hair and green eyes made her the target of would-be lotharios on most street corners. Their cat-calls and lewd suggestions intruded on her grief and confusion.

One morning when out early to avoid them, she noticed a slim young man who appeared to be following her up the hill to Gloria's building. She tried speeding up and slowing down to check if he did the same but when he overtook her; it seemed ridiculous. Why would he be following her?

When she got to the entrance, he was leaning against the wall outside, smoking a cigarette, leering at her. She pushed the door open at pace and pressed the button on the lift. The door opened, and she got into the lift waiting for the doors to shut. As they closed, the man jumped in and stood right next to her.

His hand brushed her breast as he leaned over and pressed the button for the floor above Sam's. He apologised, but Sam flinched and stood as far from him as was possible. She guessed he was visiting a friend and was chancing his arm with the gringa. He smelt of old sweat and garlic. He had combed his greasy hair into submission and stuck down with pomade. His smug presence so close to her repulsed her and it was with relief she got out at Gloria's flat. Something told her she might have seen him before, hanging around on the street but she couldn't be sure. Alfredo's death had taken away a lot of her certainties.

When she got inside, she had a lingering doubt about him. She pulled the net curtains open a crack and peered down at the street. There he was, leaving the building again. Perhaps his friend wasn't in. He looked up at the window. She snapped back the curtain. He must have seen the movement. *Was she being paranoid?* She didn't know any more.

***

Kleber saw the curtain flicker out of the corner of his eye. There was no way the gringa realised he was following her. He kept walking, taking his time to reach the Ministry, buying some banana chifles on the way. Holger Ponce was waiting for him, sitting in the back of his ministerial limousine.

'What kept you?' he snapped.

'Sorry Minister, surveillance doesn't always go to plan.'

'What have you found out?'

'Miss Sanchez is staying with her father. The gringa is still in her apartment. She goes walking by herself with a face like a wet Wednesday.'

'They've definitely seen the article?'

'I'd say so. I spotted the daughter in the lobby of Senor Sanchez' building and her face was puffy and swollen from crying.'

'Hah! Vargas is dead then. That will stop them interfering in our plans.'

'No one can stop the Reich, sir.'

'No, that's what I meant. You've done well. Monitor them just in case.'

'Yes, sir.'

***

Gloria came home on the fourth day, her face still swollen with weeping. It was strange to see her without make-up; her whole glamorous image having been washed away by the tears. She had shoved her hair into a chaotic bird's-nest bun which hung uncertainly to one side of her head. She was wearing some ancient tracksuit bottoms and an oversized t-shirt. She crawled into bed and hid under the duvets and seemed unable to put her sorrow into words.

Sam was ill equipped to deal with such a depth of mourning. She did not understand how to comfort her friend, so she went into kitchen mode. She made coffee, and tea, and bowls of soup that went uneaten. Washing up gave her something to do besides looking out at the grey skies. She emptied ashtrays and went to the local shop to buy more cigarettes and escape the claustrophobic atmosphere in the apartment.

She was also having to deal with the knowledge that she was carrying a child she didn't want. Alfredo's death had made it clear to her she was in a relationship with a man with whom she should not be having a baby. This was difficult to admit. She remembered how she had defended him when people who loved her tried to point out the inevitability of the failure of their relationship. She hated him for his duplicity and the misery he had caused her. There would be no future for them as a couple with a child. Why had she been so blind? And now she had a horrible choice to make with no support.

Gloria was not in a fit state to help her and needed

support herself. Hannah had seemed disinterested on the telephone. There was no point talking to Simon. Loneliness enveloped her like a cold sea. She needed to abort the foetus as soon as possible. Despite Gloria's offer of help, she didn't want a child under any circumstances. Her career was just beginning, and it would be difficult enough to get past the ring of prejudice that fenced her off from mining without adding a metre to the height of it. She was not ready and she couldn't face bringing up a child who looked like Simon, or worse, behaved like him.

***

Sam was sitting on the sofa trying to warm her hands on a hot cup of coffee when the telephone rang. Gloria had hidden under a pile of duvets in her bedroom and did not come out. Sam made her way to the telephone with trepidation. They had told no one about Alfredo yet, because the police had not made the information public, but the rumour about him being missing was spreading. She dreaded fielding the inquiries from their circle of friends.

'Hello?'

'Is that the gringa? I need to speak to Miss Sanchez.'

'Inspector Torres? I'm afraid that won't be possible. She's sleeping.'

'Wake her up. I must talk to her right now. I have to ask her a question.'

His voice contained a suppressed excitement that was contagious.

'Okay, give me a minute.'

Sam put down the receiver and went into Gloria's bedroom, switching on the light. The curtains hung shut and the duvets rose and fell almost imperceptibly.

A stick of incense had left its scent and a long trail of ash on the bedside table.

'Gloria, it's the inspector on the phone. He wants to talk to you. It's urgent.'

There was a snuffling noise and a nest of hair emerged from the covers.

'Urgent? I don't think I can bear to talk to him.'

'Come on, you can do it.'

Gloria got out of bed with a big sigh and walked to the phone dragging a duvet with her and leaving a trail of bedclothes in her wake. She picked up the phone and held it to her ear.

'Hello? Inspector? It's Gloria Sanchez, here.'

'Miss Sanchez, sorry to disturb you. I understand that you are going through hell but there's been a development.'

'A development? What do you mean?'

'We have some new information about the bodies in the car. It will distress you, but I need you to confirm something for me.'

'Okay, go ahead.' Her voice trembled. Sam grabbed her free hand and squeezed it.

'Did Dr Vargas ever have a serious break in his leg?'

'A broken leg? No, I don't think so. We compared our scars and broken bones once for fun. I've broken everything you can break, but he claimed that he'd never had so much as a fracture.'

There was the sound of air escaping from the Inspector's lungs, a big relieved sigh which even Sam could hear. His voice rose with excitement.

'The body that we are trying to identify has metal plates screwed into his right shin. We are tracing the serial number now but I think I can tell you...'

Gloria started to sob again, collapsing in a heap on

the floor.

'What?' said Sam. 'What is it? Tell me for God's sake.'

Gloria gulped. She turned to face Sam, her eyes shining like beacons in her face.

'It's not him. It's not Alfredo.' She lifted the receiver which she had left hanging in the air.

'Inspector?'

'Yes, well as you have guessed, we can confirm that the body is not that of Dr Vargas.'

'Thank you. Thank you so much.'

'My pleasure, Miss Sanchez. Please don't tell anyone. It won't be made official for weeks until we discover who he is.'

Gloria put the receiver back on the telephone and the two women hugged in excitement. 'I'll speak to my father' said Gloria. 'We need to leave today. Segundo should be available now.'

'Okay, I'll get packed.'

'I hope we can get there in time. If the Nazi's didn't kill him, that means they are keeping him alive. At least we have a location for the search now. Fingers crossed.'

A shiver ran up Sam's spine as she remembered Saul Rosen's missing fingers. They might have reprieved Alfredo for some sinister purpose that hadn't yet become clear, and a foreboding swamped any passing euphoria at the news of his survival. *To travel hopefully might be better than to arrive.*

CHAPTER XX

Guilt overwhelmed Hannah. She was used to getting her own way. Being the older and more beautiful sister, she got a lot of positive attention as a child, making her feel invincible. Sam had not represented competition in the beginning. Hannah was the centre of attention and Sam trailed in her wake.

That lasted until the trip to Sierramar, and the Indiana Jones-like adventure she had. After that, Hannah had lost her advantage, as her mundane job and the string of pointless boyfriends paled beside Sam's career. She had become short-tempered and resorted to sabotage to get the better of her sister as the spotlight shifted away. Sam, who didn't possess a jealous bone in her body, was unaware of this shift, which would have made her uncomfortable.

For Hannah, Simon was the last straw. What on earth did he see in Sam that Hannah didn't have more of, and better quality? She was mystified and envious. When Simon had come to her house, she grabbed the opportunity to prove her superiority. She didn't like him that much, although he had an animal magnetism that made her feel sick, she had intended to seduce him and then blackmail him into leaving Sam for good. She had been drunk at the time and had not examined the ramifications of her plan before they consummated it. She hadn't expected to like him. Or for him to like her.

When Sam had dropped her bombshell about the pregnancy, it horrified Hannah. Somehow, she got to the end of the conversation without blurting out the truth. The awful reality of what she had done to her only sister, who had never done her any harm and had always supported her, sunk in. She realised what a vile coward Simon was. He had come to her house to tell her about the pregnancy but been side-tracked by the possibility of a quick shag. Now, his own libido had screwed him. How were they going to talk their way out of this one? What if Sam wanted to keep the baby? Worse still would she ever talk to Hannah again if she found out?

There was only one thing to do. Nothing. She would wait and see who cracked first. Either Sam would decide not to have the baby or Simon would have to tell Hannah the truth about Sam's pregnancy. Either way, if she did nothing, there were no consequences for her. She could support Sam through the abortion if she had one, or blame Simon for seducing her when he knew Sam might be pregnant. She was in a win-win situation if she sat on her hands.

Simon turned out to be the weakest link and came to her house a couple of days later. She heard his timid knock on the door as she was folding her laundry in the kitchen. Opening the front door, it surprised her to find him standing there with a large bunch of flowers. It made her even more irritated.

'Why are you here?'

Simon's face fell.

'Wow. That's not the welcome I was expecting.'

'I suppose you imagined I'd fall down in the hall with my legs open if you brought me some flowers?'

'Please. Don't say things like that. It's unfair.'

'So, I'm being unfair? That's interesting coming from a man who forgot to tell me that his girlfriend, my sister, is pregnant with his baby.'

'She told you? Oh, Christ. Let me in. I need to explain.'

'Yes, you do, because I'm confused right now.' She headed for the kitchen, Simon following her with his redundant gift. She nodded her head towards a kitchen stool and went back to folding her laundry.

'Okay, I'm listening.'

Simon looked trapped. He kneaded his hands together as if trying to extract the blame from them. 'It's not that easy to explain. I've always fancied you and when you came on so strong, I thought it would be the only chance I'd ever have to be with you. It was selfish and stupid.'

'You've got that right.'

'But I haven't. Because now that I've been with you, and I understand you better. I don't want it to be the last time.'

'But Sam is pregnant. You can't walk away from her.'

'Sam hasn't confirmed that she is pregnant. She only said that she might be. I'm hoping she isn't, and anyway, there's no chance she'll keep it. Sam is not maternal, and that was part of the attraction. For a man like me, a woman who doesn't want to get married and have children straight away is a big bonus. But the bits of Sam that I like, you have them, too. And more.'

'So, what are you saying, Simon?'

'I chose the wrong sister.'

***

Sam's mother, Matilda Harris, was fretting. She had a terrible secret. There was no way she could keep quiet without tearing herself in half. Try as she might, she couldn't forget what she had seen. She had dropped some of Hannah's belongings back to her at her flat one morning on her way into town. It was early, but her daughter would be at home on a Saturday so she didn't bother letting her know that she was coming.

She pulled in to the pavement near the house where Hannah lived and noticed the front door opening. She was about to wave when Simon came out. This was odd but not as awful as what happened next. Hannah followed him out in her pyjamas. He turned around, took her in his arms and kissed her passionately before leaving. Waving back at Hannah, he did not see Matilda Harris in the car parked beside the pavement as he walked past whistling.

'I couldn't believe my eyes,' she told her husband. 'I was so shocked, I slid down in my seat so he didn't spot me.'

'What did Hannah say about it?'

'I didn't confront her. I just drove off.'

'Did she see you?'

'I don't think so.'

'Christ. What a mess. What on earth is going on? Does Sam know?'

'Simon won't have told her while she was in Sierramar. She'll be looking forward to seeing him after being away.'

'Poor old Sam. She has no luck. What are you going to do?'

'Do?' She sighed and pushed back her hair. 'What can I do? Hannah is so selfish. She always gets her own way, but I never thought it would come to this. I

187

suppose I'd better talk to her. It will not be pretty.'

'Rather you than me. I would offer to talk to Simon, but my opinion of him has just got a lot worse. I might do something stupid.'

'I feel like slapping her. She's gone too far this time. I can't understand where we went wrong. They are so different; I sometimes wonder if one of them got swapped in the hospital.'

'Except that they look like twins.'

'Well, Hannah definitely qualifies as the evil twin right now. I will give her a good talking to.'

'And Sam?'

CHAPTER XXI

Alfredo, August 1988

Alfredo came to on the floor, shivering from a combination of shock and cold in his tiny prison, his body stiff and sore. From where he lay, he spotted a chamber pot under one of the camp beds, surrounded by the corpses of beetles and millipedes. He reached underneath and pulled it out. Levering himself up on the bed frame, he relieved himself into the pot and pushed it back under the bed. It got stuck on something protruding from the concrete, and urine splashed over the side and floated some insects off the dusty floor. He snorted in disgust.

He sat on the opposite bed and reviewed the contents of the room in the strong moonlight that entered from a skylight set in a mirrored funnel. There were two beds, with thin blankets, and a table, beneath which there was a rickety-looking wooden chair. The walls were whitewashed and flaking onto the floor which was painted red and had an odd sheen. A single bulb hung from the ceiling. He pushed his shoes off, dropping them between the beds, but kept the rest of his clothes on.

He crawled into bed, wondering if this was a dream. It seemed real, but he struggled to focus on his surroundings which made him doubt its existence. His teeth chattered. He sat up again and reached across to take the second blanket from the other bed pulling it over himself. There was no pillow, so he rolled up his waxed jacket with the cotton lining on the outside. Lying in the moonlight, he forced himself to shut his eyes and slow his breathing and he was soon asleep.

The next morning, he awoke exhausted and disorientated, traumatised by the events of the night before. Where was Saul? There was something wrong, but he did not remember what it was or why he was sleeping in this tiny room. He caught sight of his shirt cuff, covered in dried blood. Lots of it. Was he injured? There was no pain. He waited for something to happen.

When someone knocked on the door of his room, fear gripped him and did not answer. His heart was hammering out of control even though he was lying in bed. He pulled the blankets right up to his nose exposing his feet. The door swung open, and a man stood looking at him. Alfredo stared back. He thought he knew this man, but it confused him. He tried to stand; the room spun, and he sank to the bed again.

'Are you unwell, Dr Vargas?' A voice floated across the room. Alfredo smiled as it landed on his bed and purred in his ear. Then he fainted again.

***

The first days of his captivity went by in a blur. It became clear to his captors he was suffering from shock. Dr Becker made him stay in bed under some old covers. They gave him soup and hot sweet drinks laced with sleeping pills. When he surfaced, he was clammy and filthy, still wearing the same bloodstained clothes as on the night they captured him. He surveyed the room as if he had never seen it before and was surprised to see Kurt Becker standing in the doorway.

'Dr Vargas, welcome back. How are you today?'

'A troll has taken up residence in my mouth but apart from that, not too bad.'

'I regret to inform you that your colleague is dead and you will soon join him. However, I don't see why your last days should be miserable. You do not deserve your fate, you were a pawn in Mr Rosen's game.'

Alfredo digested this information. He felt at a disadvantage lying in his bed and he attempted to pull off the covers and swing his feet down to the floor.

'I'm a dead man walking? So why did you keep me alive?'

'I may need you.'

'It's nice to feel needed,' said Alfredo, with patent insincerity that went right over the top of Becker's head.

'Well, I am alone here, except for the guards. If you promise not to escape, I will allow you to come and go in the laboratory at your leisure. Since there is no chance of you ever telling anyone what we are doing here, I will share our story with you. As a historian, you are in a privileged position to be at the birth of the future and get an understanding the past.'

'Until you kill me.'

'Yes, there is that disadvantage but I can make it painless.'

'Do I have a choice?'

'No. I mean, you can stay in this room until you die if you prefer, but that's the alternative.

The idea that Kurt Becker might be bored and not following orders struck Alfredo. If he could convince

Becker of the futility of murdering him, he might stand a chance and he was always being told how witty and charming he was. This was the acid test of his character. It was like an exam where you either passed or failed, except that it was life or death. Alfredo chose life.

'I'd love some breakfast,' he said.

'Will you eat eggs?' said Becker as if he were hosting a weekend in the country.

Breakfast was delicious. Alfredo found his enjoyment of the food embarrassing. And the condemned man devoured a last meal. Dr Becker looked at him as if to say something but stopped.

'What?' said Alfredo, 'what did you want to ask me?'

'I was wondering what our friend Mr Rosen told you about me.'

'He said that you sent his family to Auschwitz, and that he had escaped from the transport but that his sister and parents had died in the concentration camp. Is it true?'

'Yes. I was acting under orders.'

'Ah, that old chestnut. I hope you will be frank with me or I would rather die now,' he drawled.

Dr Becker looked startled, and unable to find a suitable retort, he roared with laughter. Alfredo was a little disconcerted. He realised that the man was like a cat toying with his prey, thrilled to see it running away far enough to slam a paw on its tail to make it more exciting. Resistance is futile, schweinhund.

Dr Becker stood up.

'Come on, bring your coffee with you and I'll tell you a story.'

They walked into the laboratory and Dr Becker gestured at an old armchair.

'Sit there. Oh, there are some clean clothes on your bed and the toilet is down the hall to the right. It has a handheld shower with hot water in one corner. It's primitive, but it works. Use it when you like. Please do nothing foolish or you will force me to shoot you.'

Alfredo sat down, changed his mind and stood up again.

'I'll go now if it's okay with you,' he said.

When Alfredo came back from his shower, Dr Becker had put on his lab coat and a pair of surgical gloves and he was absorbed in his work. It horrified Alfredo to see that he was removing the flesh from what looked like a finger. The finger was long and thin and fresh. Nauseated, he shut his eyes and tried to pretend that he hadn't seen it. Inside he knew. It's meat now. Saul is gone. When he opened his eyes, he saw that Dr Becker was still working on his gory task.

'Why did you come here?' asked Dr Becker. 'What did you hope to gain?'

'We were investigating a report that a group of high ranking Nazi officers, who are wanted by the War Crimes Commission, had escaped to Sierramar at the end of the war. Saul had heard that you were one of them and he enlisted me to help him find you. My friend Ramon Vega gave me a copy of his research, which backed up the story about the fugitives arriving here, and then he was murdered in a fire. I don't suppose you have anything to do with that?'

Dr Becker did not answer.

'Saul was trying to find you so he could get his revenge for his family. He didn't tell me that was his plan,' said Alfredo, 'I thought we were trying to track down the whole group.'

'He almost succeeded.'

'What happened last night?'

'It was last week. You have been asleep for days. He shot Hans from the operating table and killed him I'm afraid.'

'You weren't able to save him?'

'Hans? No.'

'I meant Saul.'

'We didn't try.'

'What's so secret that he had to die? The war has been over for decades. Why didn't you save him? He was harmless.'

'I can see that you do not understand what we are trying to achieve here. You pair of idiots almost ruined our plans.'

'Achieve? I thought you were in hiding from the authorities.'

And what would they achieve in a cheese-making, lederhosen-wearing village in the Andes?

'That's unfortunate. We are so close, and we were almost foiled by a pair of ignorant, glory hunters.'

'I resent being called ignorant, although I can see your point. I've no clue what you're doing in this laboratory. We didn't expect to stumble across an amateur science project run by a bunch of Nazis.'

Dr Becker was not amused and drew himself to his full height.

'Be careful, Dr Vargas. If you cross the line, you cannot come back.'

'I apologise. I get sarcastic when I'm nervous, and you have me at a disadvantage.'

'I understand. Did you go to school in England? You have an English sense of humour.'

'So I'm told. It's a bit of a blur because of the amount of drink I consumed being proportional to the number of memory cells that I have obliterated.'

'Well, you won't need to remember any of this. I'll

start at the beginning, shall I?'

The parallels of his conversation with Saul struck Alfredo hard, and he almost cried. He took a deep breath.

'I'm listening.'

***

As he lay on his bed that night Alfredo wondered if Gloria had realised that he should have been back by then. His regret at not leaving her a detailed note of their itinerary, and how long they would be away, increased as he reviewed the missed opportunities to speak to her and tell her where he was. He knew how resourceful she was but she was not psychic. Her absence felt like someone had removed one of his body parts.

The knowledge of his forthcoming execution had not reduced the ache in his heart. He still hoped that he might somehow prevent it but with what he knew now, he had to be realistic. Dr Becker would have to kill him, and Boris Klein would carry out the execution without a qualm. It was a pity that they were wasting their talents in a laboratory stuck in a hillside in the middle of nowhere but the central idea was the product of insane minds stuck in the past.

'We'll start with the basic science behind our project. Have you ever heard of cloning?' asked Dr Becker.

'No, not really. Perhaps you would elaborate?

'We remove The DNA contents of an animal cell and inject them into an unfertilized egg cell of the same species which had already been emptied of its DNA content. Then we fuse the genetic material and the egg cell together using electric pulses. We implant this cell into a womb and grow it as normal. This is the technique that we are using here.'

'I recall hearing about it before. Weren't they experimenting on sheep? But I understood that there were hundreds of failures. As far as I'm aware, they haven't produced a healthy adult sheep. Is this technology reliable?'

'Ah, Dr Vargas, you're an innocent abroad. I was doing experiments on human cells in Auschwitz before you were a twinkle in your father's eye. We have fifty years of research on our side. Our first lamb was born years and years ago.'

'But why do this research in secret? What's the point? Are you creating a flock of killer sheep or something? A new secret weapon?'

'You need to learn some respect, Dr Vargas. They told me you're a drunk. It has made you reckless.'

'If you will murder me anyway, I'd prefer to go out fighting. So why are you doing this?'

'I have a sacred duty to perform and I need to be one hundred percent certain that I can carry it out. I have practiced for years and we are on the brink of success.'

'What are you trying to clone?'

'Before I tell you that, I must give you the background to this project so you understand our motives.'

'I'm listening.'

'When the Second World War was coming to a close, we members of the Third Reich realised that we had to accept defeat or become extinct as a culture. I was one of a group of loyal Nazis who swore to make it their mission to establish a Fourth Reich in the fullness of time.'

'A Fourth Reich?'

'Yes, A pan-Aryan world empire encompassing the

land populated by European-descended peoples. We escaped from Germany to various countries in South America to wait for the moment to try again. That time is approaching with the dominant role of Germany in Europe. In thirty years' time, we will once again rule the continent.'

'Who will lead this Fourth Reich?' asked Alfredo, who was afraid that he might be hallucinating.

'Adolf Hitler.'

This convinced Alfredo that he had entered a parallel universe. *Perhaps they had drugged his coffee? Was he having an epic dream?*

'The Adolf Hitler? Or a descendant?'

'There is only one Adolf Hitler.'

'Look, I hate to be rude but isn't he dead?'

'The Führer will never die.'

'I understand that his ideas might live forever, but it will be hard for a ghost to run an empire.'

Dr Becker smiled. It was a smile so evil that Alfredo thought his organs had melted.

'If we carry out the final part of my research within the next couple of weeks, as planned, he will be thirty years old.'

The penny dropped.

'Oh my God, you plan to create a clone? How?'

***

Alfredo found it hard to accept what he had heard. *Was it caused by the delirium tremens?* He hadn't had a drink for days. Perhaps he imagined this whole episode? Had they been in a car crash? Perhaps he was in a coma and dreaming. But it was so real. Even the cockroaches were convincing. It was hard to imagine that grown men believed that they should reincarnate a human being because they had his finger, which they had kept frozen for fifty years. His maid wouldn't keep any meat in the freezer over three months. And worse, Kurt Becker, an educated man, a scientist, had experimented on his prisoners in the concentration camps, and was now planning to impregnate some unsuspecting female with a cloned cell from Hitler. It was harder to accept that such an urbane man could be so evil, whereas with Boris Klein, it was too easy.

'I have repeated the steps to the cloning thousands of times. We have had success creating human embryos but so far, we have not implanted them in a human womb. It shouldn't be any different to a sheep's womb. Same principle applies.'

'So that's why you needed the fingers?'

'Yes, your friend did not need them anymore. Besides, he was about the same age as the Führer so it was good to practice on genetic material of that age. I am sorry you found that distressing.'

'And who will carry this baby for you?'

'It's time for lunch Dr Vargas.'

CHAPTER XXII

Sam and Gloria September 1988

Hernan Sanchez shouted at his daughter. He pleaded with her. He begged her. But Gloria would not change her mind.

'Papi, I have to go. When my mother was in trouble, did you not move heaven and earth to save her? Alfredo's the love of my life. I've a second chance because he survived. I must go.'

'But what if something happens to you?'

'What if there's an eruption while I'm away? Life's full of risk in Sierramar. It's not full of love and that's more important to me.'

'You're so stubborn. You won't change your mind?'

'I'm going, and so is Sam.'

'You'll take Segundo?'

'Will you call him now?'

'I will. Promise me to listen to what he says and not put yourself in any danger.'

'I promise.'

'Please be careful. And let me know you are safe.'

'Papi, I'm uncertain if there will be a telephone in any of the villages, but I'll call you as often as I can.'

***

'Segundo? The trip is on again. I need you to wait for the car at the crossroads in San Francisco,' said Hernan Sanchez

'Okay boss, I'll be there,' said Segundo Duarte.

'My daughter will travel with Sam Harris. Do you remember her?'

'I didn't meet her, boss. I took Wilson Ortega to El Loco's house before she came out of the jungle with Alfredo last year.' He paused. Hernan waited. 'Sorry to ask this, but do we need her as well? Another woman on the trip will only add to the difficulties.'

'Honestly Segundo, sometimes I don't understand where you get your caveman ideas. Both my daughter and the gringa are resourceful and intelligent. They're the only reason that we found out where Alfredo's being held. Please don't doubt me. Gloria's always safer with Sam around.'

'Yes, boss, I'm sorry. The twentieth century left me behind I guess.'

But he wasn't sorry. Segundo thought women were trouble and only slowed men down. They were always crossing themselves when they met him, making him feel like a monster, because of his crooked mouth. He didn't need the help of a gringa who probably didn't even speak Spanish.

***

In London, Hannah opened the door to find her mother standing on the doorstep.

'Hi, Mummy, was I expecting you? My memory is terrible.'

Her mother pushed past her and walked straight into the kitchen where she filled the kettle.

'Mummy? Is something wrong?'

Her mother turned around grasping the counter behind her for support and looked her in the eye.

'How can you ask me that? You're the one who should realise what's wrong.'

A feeling of panic overcame Hannah. Oh God, she knew. But how? She couldn't find any suitable words.

'What do you mean?'

'You don't fool me with that act missy, you know exactly what I mean. You and Mr Slimy. I saw you.'

'So, we had coffee together. What's the big deal? Can't I have a coffee with Simon if I want? You should have come in and joined us.'

'Joined you? Are you mad? It was a lot more than coffee I saw him sharing with you last week. Snogging in the street like teenagers. How could you? What about your sister?'

Hannah sank down onto a chair. Things were much worse than she suspected. There was no easy way out of this conversation.

'You saw us kissing? When was that?'

'Who cares what day it was? You were kissing your sister's boyfriend at nine in the morning. He came out of your house. It's bloody obvious he stayed the night with you. You were still in your dressing gown. Don't lie to me.'

Hannah sighed. Even an inveterate liar like her, couldn't think of a reasonable explanation for that.

'Mum, I'm sorry, it happened. Simon's hard to resist and I was drunk when he turned up. What else can I say?'

'You're a wicked girl trying to use alcohol as an excuse. What about your sister? Didn't it occur to you how much this will hurt her?'

'It has, and I was determined that it would never happen again, but Simon and I like each other a lot. We're better suited than they are. It's not the first time in history a man has seduced more than one sister in a family.'

'How can you say that? How can you trample over Sam's heart without a care in the world? I don't understand. What are you going to say when she comes home?'

'Look, Mum, I don't know if this will last that long but we had to try because there was that atmosphere between us every time we met. Our feelings needed to be explored, to see if they were real.'

'What about Sam's feelings? Haven't you hurt her enough?'

'That's the thing, Mummy. She should find someone else who won't hurt her instead of hanging on like grim death to someone who always will. And don't lie to me, either. You don't think he's good enough for Sam. You'd be relieved if she broke up with him for good.'

Matilda Harris sighed. Hannah had hit the nail on the head.

'Yes, that much is true. But why did it have to be you? That's a double betrayal for Sam. She won't understand. And don't fool yourself, you'll be crying on my shoulder in several months' time when he gets bored and finds someone else. How much sympathy do you imagine you'll get from us?'

'I'm a big girl, and much better at this than Sam. Simon can't fool me.'

Matilda shook her head. Her face was a collage of different expressions fighting for supremacy. Finally, she shrugged.

'On your head, be it.'

***

Sam packed her rucksack with essentials: penknife, chocolate, camera, tea bags, floppy hat, passport, collapsible water bottle. At the last minute she put in the snake bite zapper, just in case. She could see her father nodding in approval. Bags packed, she lounged on the sofa staring at the volcano in its white cloak of snow. While Sam waited, Gloria floated around the house chain smoking and singing out of tune and throwing random things into her bag. Suddenly she went quiet and dived into the bathroom. Sam could hear her retching.

'Gloria, are you okay?'

'Yes, I think so, I felt nauseous suddenly. I guess it's the shock of learning that Alfredo is still alive. It's quite a lot to take in.'

'You poor thing. I can't believe you have to go through this.'

'It was a lot worse when I thought he was dead.'

'Hilarious.'

'Are you ready?'

'Yes.'

'Okay then, let's load the car. Segundo should be waiting at a crossroads outside of Calderon. We must try to find him before dark.'

They drove out of the underground garage in time to miss the evening traffic. Gloria pulled into the pavement and went to talk to the building's security guard.

'Washington, I will be away for a few days. Please don't let anyone go up to the apartment until I come home.'

He noted it into his book while she stood there with

her hands on her hips.

'Can I ask where you are going Miss Sanchez, in case anyone asks?'

'I'm going to pick up Dr Vargas,' she said. Then she remembered what Inspector Torres had told them and didn't elaborate. She didn't see Kleber Perez, who was hidden behind a van, copying the number plate of the car onto a piece of paper. Jumping into the car again, she turned to Sam. 'Right, let's go then.'

As they drove off, Kleber approached the guard.

'Good afternoon,' he said, 'I see that Miss Sanchez has left. I was hoping to talk to her about Alfredo Vargas.'

'Oh, well, she's going to collect him, I believe,' said the guard.

'Where?'

'I'm sorry, I don't know. Who are you?'

'Kleber Perez. I work for the Ministry of Public Works. We need Dr Vargas' advice on a project we are undertaking.'

Washington, who was not an educated man, was no fool. He knew it was unlikely that the Ministry of Public Works would consult anyone about anything. They did whatever they wanted. He was extra-protective of the glamorous Miss Sanchez and fancied himself as her bodyguard.

'I am not at liberty to tell you,' he said.

***

It annoyed Perez that he couldn't get any gossip from the guard but he saw the stubborn look on the man's face and he knew it was hopeless. They had to stop the women before they stumbled across the truth. He went straight to the nearest phone booth and rang Holger Ponce.

'Minister, I'm sorry to disturb you, but the Sanchez woman and her gringa friend have left Calderon in a car loaded up with supplies. It looks like they are going to San Blas.'

'Why are they going? Don't they read the newspapers? I had that article put on the front pages. I can't believe they are so stubborn. They will ruin everything.'

Kleber waited while the Minister ranted on.

'I am sorry Minister, they believe Alfredo Vargas is alive.'

'Who told you that?'

'I heard Miss Sanchez tell the guard in her building. Would you like the registration number of the car?'

'What? Oh, yes. Tell me.'

'PG2 36S'

'Thank you Kleber. That will be all. I'll contact you if I need you.'

***

Holger Ponce rummaged through a drawer in his desk and pulled out an address book. He leafed through the pages, panting with agitation. Having found the number, he was looking for; he pulled the telephone towards him and dialled. Despite the care with which he entered the numbers, the call took several tries to go through. The high-pitched tone which indicated congestion on the lines seemed to go straight through his head. He could feel his heart tightening in his chest with panic. The phone rang for almost a minute before Boris Klein answered it, panting as if he had been running.

'Hello, Klein here.'

'Boris? It's Holger Ponce. I need to talk to you. I received some important information from Kleber

Perez.'

'Who?'

'Kleber, the boy who works with me in the Ministry.'

'Oh yes, that boy. What did he have to say for himself?'

'He has been watching the block of flats where Hernan Sanchez' daughter lives and he saw her leave with the English woman. They were travelling in a car full of supplies. He thinks they are heading for San Blas to look for Dr Vargas.'

'For fuck's sake! Didn't you plant the article like I told you?'

Yes, it was on the front page of the newspapers. Miss Sanchez ignored it. It's not my fault.'

'No, I'm sorry, but it's still a disaster as far as our timing is concerned. We are so close now.'

'I thought I ought to give you fair warning. I expect it will take them a couple of days to get there.'

'At least. Thank you, Holger. You can fool some people some of the time but not Miss Sanchez. She must have received some information that made her think Dr Vargas was not dead.'

'What do you want me to do?'

'I need you to put some pressure on Hernan Sanchez. She's certain to ring her father from the road. Warn him of the consequences if she sticks her neck out too far.'

'I'll ring him now.'

'Oh, and Holger, how old is the gringa?'

'Hang on, I have a copy of her passport here somewhere.'

He opened the drawer again and pulled out a piece of paper.

'According to her passport, she's about thirty.'

'Is she white?'

'Yes, and it says here that she has brown hair and green eyes. What are you getting at?'

'Nothing to concern you. Contact Hernan Sanchez and do everything you can to force him to stop her interfering.'

'I will.'

Holger Ponce hung up the telephone and lit a cigarette. He took several long drags, holding the smoke in his lungs until he felt his pulse slow and his panic diminish. Stubbing out the cigarette, he reopened his address book and looked up Hernan Sanchez's number. He dialled it with care, listening to the clicks as each number registered.

'Hello?'

'Hernan? It's Holger Ponce.'

A grumpy voice asked, 'What do you want now?'

'Your daughter has set off for San Blas. No good can come of this. I want you to tell her to return.'

'How do you find out? Are you having her watched?'

'It's none of your business. I can't answer for her safety if she doesn't stop now.'

'What on earth is going on down there, Holger? This is getting out of hand. Can't you do something?'

'They are working on a top-secret project and have been for forty years. These people are fanatics and I can't stop them. You must tell your daughter to come home before it's too late.'

'And who says that she will call me?'

'She'll check in with you. Let's hope for her sake that she does. Those roads are dangerous. Look what happened to Dr Vargas.'

'You bastard, how dare you threaten me? If anything happens to her, I shall cut off your dick and shove it down your throat.'

'It's not in my hands now. I suggest you follow instructions or I won't be responsible for what happens.'

He hung up before Hernan Sanchez could come up with a retort.

***

Sanchez swore and threw the receiver back into its cradle. This was getting out of hand. As much as he trusted Segundo Duarte to keep the women safe, he couldn't risk anything happening to them. When he had built the road to San Blas, there had been no sign of anything strange going on. The speed with which the Germans were building the village had impressed him but they wouldn't let him bid for any of the contracts there. He couldn't imagine what was going on that was so secret and so deadly to anyone who found out. There had to be something he could do to even the playing field. If only there was some way of exposing them. And then he remembered Ramon Vega's report. What better way of opening the whole can of worms than to reveal the real identities of these people? It would force them to abandon the project and flee the country.

He went to his wife's dresser and removed the report again. Finding DHL's number in the phone book, he contacted them and asked them to come and collect a document for immediate transport to Miami. Then he put the report in an envelope and sealed it with tape. He went into the kitchen and put it on the table.

'Rosa? The man from DHL will be here in an hour or so. Can you please give him this envelope?'

'Of course, sir.'

He still felt a little emotional and panicky. He was

exposing himself to the criticism that would result from publishing such inflammatory information. It was tempting to change his mind but his daughter was his life. To the surprise of Rosa and the building security guard, he took a walk to calm his nerves. It had been years since he had walked anywhere and he felt self-conscious. It took him a while to get into the rhythm but soon he had gathered speed. He walked around the block, stopping to eat an ice cream in the pizza place, and by the time he got home again, he was calm but his blood was still boiling. He'd had about enough of Holger Ponce. That bastard was going down this time, but not until the girls were safe.

***

Night fell in San Blas where Dr Becker and Boris Klein were eating at the hotel. Klein wolfed down his dinner, disgusting Kurt Becker who was a stickler for good manners. He spoke before swallowing, giving Becker an unwanted view of his last mouthful.

'The Sanchez bitch is on her way with the Englishwoman. They think they can rescue Dr Vargas. This is a complete farce.'

'It's becoming like a soap opera.'

'However, I venture to suggest that it presents us with an opportunity.'

'How so?'

'The Englishwoman is the perfect incubator. She's Anglo-Saxon, in her thirties. I didn't want you to use a non-Aryan. The blood of the Führer must not be contaminated.'

'But we can't keep her here, they will find her.'

'I have been thinking we should contact Argentina. It's about time we moved down there. Sierramar is no longer safe. How close are you?'

'In theory, I am ready. We may only get one chance at this rate.'

'I can't believe it. After all these years of work, a Jew, a drunk and an Indian may thwart us at the last hurdle.'

'Sounds like a joke.'

'There's nothing funny about it. Get ready for the implantation. We can't permit anything to go wrong.'

CHAPTER XXIII

There's a package for you, Mr Vega,' said the receptionist, flicking her hair back and giving him a laser-beam smile.

Ramon Vega, who had been crossing the lobby of the Miami hotel at speed in order to avoid her, turned reluctantly back to the desk.

'A package? Excellent.'

She handed it to him without letting go and stared at him. There was an awkward silence.

'Thank you, Silvia,' he said, tugging it out of her grasp, 'much appreciated.'

'Have a nice day,' she replied, with an insincerity that made him feel even more guilty.

Was it his fault that American women loved Latino men? She had practically begged for it and now he had to put up with her resentful stares. He had been going to change hotels, but the thought that Hernan Sanchez might repent and send his research report to him had kept him there. His luck had changed. He recognised the weight and thickness of his report in the courier's envelope. Gloria must have convinced her father to

211

send it. Now it was up to him to get it published and he knew the place. Without opening it, he spun around and walked back through the revolving door into the pouring rain.

The hotel concierge got him a cab and he jumped in, tipping the man a couple of dollars.

'Take me to the offices of the *Miami Herald* please.'

'The one in Biscayne Bay?'

'Yes, that's the one.'

During the ride to the offices, Ramon took his report out of the package and read some of it again. He had no doubt that it was explosive stuff and that his life would never be the same after he handed it over. Would he even be able to go home again? Could he claim refugee status in Miami? Mostly, he wondered why Hernan Sanchez had changed his mind.

'Here we are, sir,'

'Thanks. Keep the change.'

Ramon walked to the main doors and went in unchallenged. He breezed up to the reception wearing his best smile and looking into the woman's eyes from under his dark, floppy fringe.

'Good afternoon. I need to see Guido Luna, please.'

'I'm afraid that Mr Luna is in a meeting. Do you have an appointment?'

It was not often that his full-on charm had no effect. He decided to change tack.

'No. I don't. But this is a matter of life and death.'

'Life and death? That sounds serious.' She smiled at him.

'It is,' he said, making his best sad puppy dog face, the one that always worked on other people's wives.

'Hmm, let me see what I can do.'

'Hello, Nadia? Yes, I have a man here who says he has to talk to Guido Luna.' She put her hand over the receiver. 'What did you say your name was?'

'Ramon Vega.'

'He says his name is Ramon Vega. No, he doesn't. Okay.'

She put down the phone.

'Guido can't see you today. He is busy. Can you come back tomorrow? I could try and get you a meeting.'

'No, it's urgent. I need to see him today.'

'I'm sorry sir. It can't be done.' Seeing the real devastation on Ramon's face, she added, 'he does like to have a cigar outside in the afternoon, though. No guarantees.'

***

The meeting went on longer than an hour but Ramon was so absorbed in reading his report that he didn't notice time passing. He was sitting outside the newspaper building on a bench in the sun and sweat soaked his shirt and ran into his trousers. Finally, a short man with a bushy moustache and a big mop of grey hair stepped through the revolving door and lit up a cigar. He smoked it in short puffs as if impatient to finish. The pungent smell wafted over to the bench making him wrinkle up his nose and look for the source of the odour. That must be Guido Luna. It was now or never. Ramon stood up and approached him with his hand held out.

'Mr Luna?'

His hand was ignored and the piercing grey eyes gave him a once over that seared his flesh.

'Yes. And you are?'

'Ramon. Ramon Vega, at your service, sir.'

'So, what do you want Mr Vega? I'm a busy man.'

He didn't look that busy but Ramon wasn't stupid

enough to comment.

'I have a scoop for you.'

'A scoop, eh? We'll soon see about that. You have thirty seconds.'

'I have proof that there is a group of fugitive Nazis hiding in the mountains in Sierramar.'

'Seriously?'

'Cross my heart and hope to die.'

'That's an irresistible bait for a journalist. Perhaps you knew that already?'

His piercing blue eyes examined Ramon's face for signs of trickery but he found none. He took a deep drag on his cigar and then threw it into the bin with a look of sorrow.

'You'd better not be leading me on. That was Cuban.'

'No sir, I'm serious. It's a matter of life and death.'

'Come on, we'll talk in my office.'

***

When Ramon finished talking, Guido ran his fingers through his mop of grey hair a couple of times. He lit a cigarette and leaned back in his chair.

'Good God man! This is dynamite. Why have we never heard about this before? Where's this proof you were talking about?'

Ramon handed him the report. 'I have only one original,' he said. 'I'd appreciate it if you could make a photocopy and give it back to me.'

'Nadia!' Guido shouted, and she appeared in an instant. Ramon wondered if she had been eavesdropping. 'Go get a copy of this for me right now. Do you want a coffee, Ramon?'

He didn't. 'Yes, please,' he said.

They sipped their coffees while Nadia copied the

document, lost in their own thoughts.

'If I publish an article on these revelations, I imagine that things at home might become a bit difficult for you.'

'Once the horse has left, it's a bit late to shut the barn door. I'm more inclined to think that they might improve.'

Guido nodded. Nadia handed the original to Ramon and Guido put the copy on his desk. He bent over the document and leafed through it, stopping to gaze at the photographs and other facsimiles. A couple of times, he whistled and shook his head. At last, he glanced up, his eyes sparkling. He looked ten years younger.

'A scoop! It's been years since I had a proper scoop.' He dashed out of the room, leaving a startled Ramon behind. 'He'll be back,' said Nadia, 'he'll be trying to get it in tomorrow's edition.'

'Stop the presses,' said Guido, who had returned at the same speed as he had left. 'Well, it's too late for tomorrow's edition but we will mock up the front page and a double page spread for the following day. How does that sound?'

'That's excellent. Thank you.'

'I'll pay you for an exclusive. We will do an interview with you as a follow up.' He rubbed his hands together in glee. 'That'll teach them to label me as washed up,' he said to no-one in particular. Nadia beamed.

'Show Ramon out. We'll see you here tomorrow morning at ten for a photograph and an interview. I'll be here tonight if you need anything.'

'Thank you.'

'The pleasure's all mine.'

***

Back at the hotel, Ramon phoned Hernan Sanchez.

'Mr Sanchez, it's Ramon speaking. I received the document.'

'Ramon, that's great. I'm so sorry I didn't send it straight away. It took a tragedy to make me see sense.'

'A tragedy. What happened?'

'There was a car crash near Lago Verde and they found two burnt bodies. The police told us that one of them was Alfredo. We mourned him for three days.'

'Alfredo? Oh my God.'

'Don't panic, the autopsy proved that it couldn't be him. But there is no doubt that we were meant to think that it was. My daughter and her friend have set out to find him.'

'Is that a good idea? They may also be in danger. I never dreamt that my research would lead to this.'

'I sent my fixer with them so they should be safe, but I want insurance. I decided that if we published the report, the Nazis wouldn't have any reason to try and keep their presence a secret. It's up to you now. How soon can we have it on the front pages?'

'I managed to get into the *Miami Herald* today and talk to one of their longest standing journalists. He has agreed to do a write up on my report. The day after tomorrow, the revelation that some Nazis are hiding in Sierramar, and that the government has been complicit in hiding them, will be front page news.'

'I hope that will not be too late. I tried to stop the girls from going to find Alfredo but my daughter is so stubborn.'

'As soon as I have a copy of the article, I will fax it to every newspaper in Calderon. Can you please help me?'

'Anything.'

'I will need the fax numbers.'

CHAPTER XXIV

Sam and Gloria September 1988

It was almost dusk when Sam and Gloria got to the crossroads where Segundo Duarte was waiting. Hernan Sanchez's fixer was standing by himself outside a local shop festooned with baskets of fruit and footballs hanging in net bags. A woman crossed herself as she passed him on her way into the shop, his scarred face causing her superstitious soul to revolt. He didn't give her a second glance and came over to the car, a rucksack slung over his shoulder and a cigarette in his mouth.

'Good evening,' he said, lowering his head, and then, 'how are you, Miss Sanchez? I am at your service as always.'

'Segundo, how good to see you. Get in.'

Ignoring Sam, he climbed into the back seat of the four-wheel drive, flicking his cigarette into the gutter as he shut the door.

'Senor Duarte, buenas noches,' said Sam, determined not to be left out. 'Me llamo Sam.'

'Ya se, lo mismo a usted.' (I know, the same to

you).

He didn't look her in the eye or notice that she was looking at him with frank interest and had not crossed herself or shown any interest in his scar.

'Let's go. We should get to the hostel by midnight,' said Gloria, who hadn't noticed the chill in the air.

She released the brake, and they were off into the gloom. She put the music on full volume, making it impossible to chat. Sam wondered what Segundo made of Fleetwood Mac. They were singing 'you make loving fun' and Sam thought about Simon and the baby, and whether Alfredo would live to see it. She had not yet confessed the result of the pregnancy test to Gloria and as time went past, it seemed less easy to do. It was so ironic that she should get pregnant at the drop of a hat, while poor Gloria, who still hoped for children, would never do so. She wanted to talk about her fluctuating feelings about it and about Simon but Gloria's recent trauma had made this seem trivial in comparison so she kept a lid on it.

As usual, the passage of time was making her reconsider her decision to leave Simon, mostly because she didn't see anyone else doing better in the boyfriend stakes. There was always something wrong. Was it better to stay with the devil she knew or discover some other man's weakness? Should she prefer Simon, who couldn't say no to a seductive body, to a man like Alfredo who couldn't say no to a seductive bottle?

Compromise was difficult for Sam. Being inflexible when it came to her expectation of others, she thought if she resisted temptation; it was only logical that her other half should, too. Being iron willed led to success against the odds but it often caused her unhappiness as it was hard for her to accept that mere mortals were a lot more likely to succumb to the easy choices.

***

After driving for a good six hours, they stopped at the same hostel where Saul and Alfredo had stayed. They were weary and hungry when they arrived. It was close to midnight, but they persuaded the owner who was still drinking in his own bar with two friends, to rustle up some bowls of soup left over from the evening meal. Gloria questioned the owner about Saul and Alfredo.

'Yes, I remember those gentlemen,' he said, 'they stayed up late talking and drinking.'

'When was that?' said Gloria.

'Oh, I can't remember, perhaps two weeks ago.'

'Where were they headed?'

'They were off to San Blas but they were planning to stay in Lago Verde on their way there. They told me they'd need a room on their way back but they never turned up. I guess they went somewhere else. That American was interested in the local culture. Perhaps they went to the Indian Market at San Marco?'

Sam got Segundo alone. She didn't understand why they had started off on the wrong foot but she was determined to improve their communication. There was no way of estimating how much they might need each other on the trip.

'I'm glad you are with us. Senor Sanchez trusts you. Have you known him a long time?'

'Long enough.'

'Did you meet him in Calderon?'

'Why are you asking me questions about it? It's none of your business.'

Gloria, who joined them, interjected.

'Don't be rude to Sam. She's only being nice. Segundo met my father when he saved him and his family from the clutches of a loan shark who was holding his son for ransom. Segundo was looking for work and my father hired him to make a road or something.'

'It was the road to San Blas.'

'San Blas? But that's where we're going. What a coincidence,' said Sam.

'That's all it is,' said Segundo. 'Gloria's father found out that someone was threatening my family, and he sorted it out. I've been working with him ever since.'

'Senor Sanchez is a legend,' said Sam.

'He's a special man,' said Gloria.

'Amen,' said Segundo.

Sam didn't feel as if she had made any progress but at least now she understood the fanatical loyalty.

She shared a room with Gloria. They lay side by side in their single beds, wide awake despite the hour. The glow of Gloria's cigarette deepened in the darkness as her friend inhaled. Usually she would have complained about smoking in the bedroom but she hadn't the heart.

'Do you think he's still alive?' asked Gloria

'Yes. They would've put him in the car with Saul if he was dead. It seems like they were trying to put us off the trail.'

'What d'you mean?'

'Why push Saul off a cliff with a random body in the car? They could have pushed him off by himself. Also, why set fire to the car? I think they burned the bodies to slow down identification. They were hoping that the police would assume the body was Alfredo's and put it in the newspapers. It was a message.'

'A message? To whom?'

'To us. They must be aware we are on to them. I don't know how, but they must. That's the only explanation. They are trying to stop us going to San

Blas to look for Alfredo, by pretending he is already dead.'

'So, they were buying themselves time? But what for?'

'It's a mystery. I've no idea why they don't run away to Argentina if they realise we have discovered them. There must be a reason that they are staying in San Blas, when they should be leaving. I can't imagine what it is though.'

'It must be important.'

'Important enough to kill for. It must be related to those weird underground buildings we noticed on the aerial photographs.'

'I hope we're not too late.'

'We're on the right track.'

'I don't believe in God, but I'm doing a lot of praying.

'I hear you.'

***

The next morning, they ate breakfast at dawn. Despite the hour, Gloria was in a sunny mood for once. It didn't do her much good as she retched when the scrambled eggs arrived and stumbled outside. Segundo grunted and reached over for her plate.

'Waste not, want not,' he said.

Sam found Gloria smoking a cigarette outside.

'Are you okay?' said Sam

'I'm fine. I've picked up a stomach bug. Don't worry about me.'

'I'll finish my breakfast before Segundo does. We should go as soon as we are ready.'

'I'll be right there.'

Sam return inside and sat opposite Segundo who was finishing Gloria's breakfast.

'What are we looking for when we get there?' he asked.

Sam reached into her rucksack and pulled out the aerial photograph of the hidden laboratory. She handed it to Segundo who glanced at it and threw it back.

'It's a hill,' he said, 'why's a hill important?'

'You see those figures?' she said, pointing at the photograph. 'They are wearing lab coats. That hill is on the far side of San Blas at the end of the road to the forest.'

'I've been there before. I didn't see any buildings then.'

'We think it contains an underground laboratory. Why else is this truck parked here? Do you see that shadow? That might be a door.'

Segundo grunted. It wasn't clear whether in assent or disdain.

'Alfredo may have stumbled across a drug laboratory, or something like that, and is being held captive inside the hill.'

'Why would they keep him?'

'We don't understand.'

'You don't know much, do you?'

'There's no need to be rude. I'm doing my best.'

'I can't imagine why they got a girl to do a man's job.'

To her surprise, Sam realised that he was jealous of her for doing his job, protecting the Sanchez family. She didn't have time to argue.

'I'm a woman not a girl, and without me, you wouldn't have found anything. I don't care if you like me or not, but we need to work together on this before it's too late.'

'Against my better judgment.'

Sam let him have the last word and went to pay for

the hostel. Gloria was revving the engine by the time she came out with her bag. There didn't seem to be any ill effects from Gloria's dodgy tummy. Segundo was sitting in the back, his hat over his face, catching a nap. Sam got into the car and shoved a random cassette into the player.

'Let's go, then. It should take us about five hours to get to the spot where the car crashed,' said Gloria.

'Is that at ludicrous, or ridiculous, speed?'

'Shut up, gringa.'

***

Even with Gloria at the wheel, the journey took hours. The rainy weather had made the roads worse and their contents disguised the potholes, making them perilous at any speed. They passed through a village where the local people were following a statue of the Virgin Mary around the streets which delayed them an hour.

It was hard to get annoyed. Tiny people, slightly bigger than dwarfs, marched behind the Virgin, dressed in elaborate costumes. The women wore heavy felt skirts with multiple layered petticoats topped with white lace blouses. On their feet, they had espadrilles which did not seem to offer any protection against the weather. Most of the men wore trousers that looked like plus fours in shape, with multi-coloured waistcoats and baggy shirts. The adults were sporting bowler or trilby hats made of felt. They chanted as they marched, in odd, high nasal voices.

Behind them, a brass band with ancient battered instruments blasted out national favourites, sustained by a bottle of rum that was doing the rounds out of sight of the priest. Sam took surreptitious photographs out of the window, being careful that no one noticed her. She knew from experience that mountain people in Sierramar didn't like their photograph being taken.

As they crawled out of town, a woman approached the car and asked for money. Gloria handed over some coins from the cup holder in the divider between the seats. The woman tried to grab her hand. She was insistent.

'What does she want?' asked Sam.

'To tell my fortune.'

'It can't do any harm. Let her do it. At least it will feel less like begging if you have paid for a service.'

'Honestly Sam, sometimes I think you're related to Mother Teresa,' said Gloria, but she stuck her hand out of the window. The old woman gazed at it, tracing the lines with her forefinger and muttering invocations of some sort. She started talking, but not in Spanish.

'Segundo? Do you understand what she is saying?'

'She's speaking Quechua. She says that you will have a long life with children.'

Gloria snatched her hand back, furious and upset, but the woman did not stop talking.

'She is telling you to be careful. Great danger awaits in the mountains. You should turn back.'

Sam felt a chill down her spine which spread to her arms. The hairs stood on end. If she had been superstitious, she would have taken the hint.

'Silly old woman. Let's go,' said Gloria revving the engine. It cut out.

'The spirits are trying to tell us something,' said Sam, only half in jest.

Gloria turned the key and restarted the engine. She sped out of town without a word. Sam felt terrible. It was so predictable and yet she fell right into the trap. She should have known that all fortune tellers predict happy marriages and children for women. Give the customer what they want. Damn! Gloria smoked three cigarettes in a row, lighting the next one from the embers of the last. She drove with grim determination alone with her thoughts, worry etched on her face. Alfredo must still be alive, he had to be. A double death would be too much for her to bear. Sam resisted the temptation to put her hand on Gloria's shoulder and give it a squeeze.

Finally, they reached the crash site outside Lago Verde. The police tape which wafted in the breeze still identified it, tangled in the grasses on the roadside. There was a bulldozer working above the road. It appeared to be opening an entrance to a hacienda further up the hill. They got out of the car and approached the cliff edge.

The police had found the burnt-out wreck of Alfredo's car on a rock shelf, supported by some bushes about fifty metres down. They had reported that someone had probably pushed the car over the edge as there were no skid marks on the road to indicate an accident. The flames from the fire still blackened the cliffs. The bushes had prevented the vehicle from plunging to the bottom of the cliff and remaining unreachable for good.

'This doesn't tell us much,' said Sam.

'Now there's a surprise,' said Segundo, turning away.

Sam was composing a reply when there was a roaring noise from above. They turned towards the sound. A landslide thundered down the slope towards them. Sam threw herself to one side and Segundo and Gloria to the other. Gloria screamed as a rock hit her and she fell to the ground. Segundo rushed to help her move away. Material kept falling onto the road, separating them from Sam who had been trapped on the far side.

'Are you okay, Sam?' said Segundo, peering through the dust and dirt.

'Yes, I'm not injured.'

Suddenly, they heard a car sliding to a halt along the gravel on Sam's side of the landslide and doors being opened. Sam started shouting. 'Hey! Let me go. Help! Segundo, I am being kidnapped. It's them. Do something.'

But Segundo was more concerned about the possibility of Gloria being crushed by a rockfall. His first duty was to Hernan Sanchez, and he had to get Gloria to a hospital.

'I'll be back, Sam. Be strong.'

'No, don't leave me here.'

But it was too late. A rough hand pushed a rag over her face and she went limp. Someone her bundled into a car and drove away. Gloria heard the engine and tried to stand up.

'What's wrong? Where's Sam?'

'Don't you worry about her. I'll be back to rescue both Sam and Alfredo.'

'But Segundo, we can't leave them here.'

'You need to go to hospital. You have a broken arm. I must tell your father.'

'What happened to Sam?'

'Someone took her away. The landslide wasn't an accident.'

'They might have killed us. I don't want to leave Sam with those people.'

'We've got to get you to hospital. Trust me, Miss Sanchez. Everything will be fine.'

***

Segundo strapped Gloria up with a towel and helped her into the front seat of the car. Once he made her comfortable, he got in and drove to the main road. Every bump on the road made her grunt in pain but she did not complain.

'Are you okay, Miss Sanchez?' said Segundo.

'Drive faster. You must go back for Sam.'

'I can't drive fast. Your arm...'

'Forget my arm. I'm ordering you to speed up.'

Gloria was sick again on the way to the hospital but Segundo did not stop. He handed her a box of tissues without comment. Finally, they arrived at the nearest large town. It was on the main Andes corridor further south of Calderon. It had the advantage of having a local airport and a hospital so Hernan Sanchez could fly there without the discomfort of a long drive. Segundo drove up to the hospital and ran inside to get help. Dirt from the landslide covered his clothes and he had trouble convincing the paramedics to come outside. When they found Gloria, she had managed to slide out of the car seat and was smoking a cigarette with her good arm. Her bad arm hung by her side at a funny angle.

'Stop fussing, Segundo,' she said. 'I'm fine.'

'You need to put out that cigarette if you're coming in,' said the paramedic.

'Have you got a private room?'

'Yes, madam. Have you got a credit card?'

'My father is Hernan Sanchez.'

'We still need your card.'

After they took Gloria into accident and emergency for treatment on her arm, Segundo rang Hernan Sanchez.

'Hello Don Sanchez, it's me, Segundo.'

'Segundo, I wasn't expecting to hear from you so soon. Is there a problem?'

'Not exactly, sir. There was a landslide in the road

and a rock hit Gloria. She's hurt.'

'Hurt? How bad is it?'

'Sir, she's okay. It's only a fracture in her left arm.'

'Oh God, I knew it was too dangerous. I should never have let her go.'

'Did you have any choice, sir?'

Hernan laughed. 'No, I guess I didn't. She's as stubborn as me. What about Sam?

'I'm afraid they caused the landslide on purpose. Someone separated her from us and took her away in a car.'

'Was it them?'

'I don't know, sir, but it can't have been a coincidence.'

'This is terrible. Where are you? Is there an airport nearby?'

'We're in Llanos. The medics told me that there is a daily flight from Calderon at about midday. You should come tomorrow and visit Gloria, but I must go back today and look for Sam and Alfredo. I remember the lie of the land from when you and me built that road.'

'That was a long time ago. I hope you can get there in time.'

'If it's okay with you, I will set out now for Lago Verde. I need to do surveillance on the laboratory in San Blas, so I can find out how many men are there and work out a plan. Don't worry about me. Thirty men wouldn't stop me from rescuing Miss Sam and Mr Alfredo.'

'Be careful, Segundo. You're family to me. I'll get the first flight out there tomorrow morning. Gloria will be fine until then, please go back and rescue the others.'

'Thank you, Don Sanchez. I'm proud to work for

you. I will not disappoint you.'

Segundo hung up the phone and found Gloria who was sitting up in bed with her arm in plaster. She had a purple bruise on her cheekbone.

'Miss Sanchez, I've to go now. I won't come back unless I have Dr Alfredo and Miss Sam with me. Your father will take the next flight. He should be here tomorrow morning.'

'Segundo, don't worry about me. Time is of the essence. Good luck.'

CHAPTER XXV

Sam woke up in the back of the car as they were driving through San Blas. Her head was spinning, and she almost vomited. When she forced open her eyes, she thought she was hallucinating. She saw what looked like dolls' houses through the windows of the car. She tried to sit up, attracting the attention of Boris Klein who shoved her down so she was prone on the back seat. Her arm felt sore, as if they had vaccinated her. *Had a rock from the landslide hit her? The landslide! Where was Gloria and why was she in a car with people she had never seen before? What the hell was going on?*

'Where am I? Who are you?'

'Shut up! Stay quiet and we won't hurt you,' said Franz Schmidt.

'What happened?'

'The earth moved,' said Boris Klein and laughed, an evil choking sound.

She lay without moving, trying to check her limbs for damage. She reviewed her surroundings, searching for a weapon or some form of escape. To her horror, there appeared to be blood in the stitching channel on the seat near her face.

'Whose blood is this?'

'It will be yours if you don't keep quiet.'

The men sniggered at Klein's joke. Sam spotted her rucksack on the floor under the front passenger seat. She pulled it towards her by inches and edged the zip open with her finger dulling the sound. She slipped her hand into the main pocket and searched for her penknife. At the bottom of the bag she felt a box. What on earth was that? And then she remembered. She took it out of the rucksack and removed the snakebite zapper, which she shoved down her sock. She put her hand back into the rucksack where she found the penknife which she put in the side pocket of her khaki trousers. Some chocolate lurked in one of the pockets, but she knew they would smell it if she unwrapped it by mistake so she left it in the bag.

They drove out of town and stopped on the edge of a forest. Sam saw the trees and decided to make a run for it. She pulled hard on the door handle as they slowed down but the child locks were on. It didn't stay shut for long. Boris Klein opened it and pulled her along the seat by her t-shirt which pulled up over her breasts exposing them to his lustful stare. She grabbed it and pulled it down again, her fury making her strong.

'I wouldn't bother,' he said, 'I can have you any time I want.'

He put his hands under her arms and pulled her out onto the ground. The impact dispelled any illusions she had of escape.

'Stand up,' he said, 'and go into that doorway.'

'What doorway?'

But now she could see a dark crack opening in the hill and fluorescent lighting in a passageway that led into it.

'Can I bring my rucksack?'

'Do   you   think   I'm   stupid?'
He grabbed it and shook out the contents, removing the
camera and her passport and leaving her with the
chocolate and tea bags and some clean underwear.

'Take it!' He shoved her hard, and she stumbled
towards the door. The fact she had been right about the
secret building was no comfort as they entered and the
door closed behind them.

***

Segundo drove back to the place in the road the
landslide had blocked. His concern for Gloria, and his
preoccupation with the fate of Sam and Alfredo was
such that he drove straight past it without registering
as someone had cleared the blockage and pushed it off
the road and down the same cliff as Alfredo's car. It
wasn't until several kilometres down the road that he
realised what had happened. This was Segundo's first
experience with German efficiency.

But why had they cleared the road when the
landslide was doing a great job of preventing people
from going to San Blas? They must be planning to
make a getaway soon or they would have left the
blockage where it was. There was no other way in or
out of the area. The Nazis must be aware the people
looking for them now realised where they were. It
could not be long before they made a break for it. He
had to move fast.

The lights of Lago Verde welcomed him back after
two long days and he needed something to eat and go
straight to bed. He headed for the inn where he had
stayed years before and was relieved to find that it was
still in business. He wasn't certain when he would

sleep again and he wanted to rest before the final struggle. The owner took in his exhausted state and diagnosed extreme hunger. He served him a huge dinner with mountains of rice and chicken followed by big slices of banana bread and coffee.

After he had eaten the food on the table, he went up to his room and shut the door. He lay in bed rubbing his distended belly and groaning with pleasure. Feelings of guilt assailed him regarding his treatment of Sam. He had been rude to her because he felt usurped, not even acknowledging her efforts to include him in the mission. He resolved to be less hard on her when he rescued her. Don Sanchez was right, he was a caveman.

***

Alfredo couldn't believe his ears. He rushed over to the door of his room and put his ear against the metal.

'Let me go, you arsehole. Where is Alfredo? What have you done with him?'

'Sam?' he said, and then louder. 'Sam, is that you?'

'Alfredo? Let go of me you bastard!'

'Boris, let the woman see her friend. It may calm her down a bit.' Dr Becker's velvet tones seemed to have the required effect. Sam stopped shouting. There was the noise of a key in the lock of his door. Alfredo jumped backwards. The door swung open. Sam stood there, dishevelled and furious, with her eyes blazing. She shook herself free of Boris Klein's grip.

'Alfredo! I thought you were dead. We did. I mean...' Despite herself she burst into tears and stood sobbing in the passageway, arms hanging by her sides. Alfredo stepped out of his room and put his arms around her. Hot tears transferred to his cheeks.

'What are you doing in Sierramar?' he asked.

'Searching for you,' she snivelled.

'But how did you find me?' he said, astonished. 'I can't believe it.'

'It's a long story,' she said.

'Not one that will have a happy ending,' said Klein.

'How crass you are, Boris. Let them have their moment. There aren't many left for Dr Vargas.' Becker turned to go back to the laboratory. 'And get them some food,' he said.

Klein shoved them into Alfredo's room and slammed the door. They could hear him muttering as he walked away.

Sam pulled away from Alfredo and inspected him.

'You look like shit,' she said.

'Thanks. You don't look so hot yourself. How did you get here? Where is Gloria? Is she with you?'

'She's with Segundo. We were on our way to rescue you when we got separated by a landslide engineered by the Nazis. I think she got hurt but not badly.'

'Poor Gloria. She's such a heroine, no wonder I love her. So where are they now?'

'Segundo took her to hospital. He will get her to safety before he comes for us. What on earth is going on here? It's like a bad horror movie.'

'You've almost hit the nail on the head there. Let's eat first. I think you'll need your strength for what I'm about to tell you.'

***

Sam almost threw up her food when Alfredo told her about Saul's demise.

'But why did they kill him?'

'They didn't need him anymore. He was fatally injured when we tried to escape and they didn't try to save him. Besides, he was a Jew, worthless in their new

234

world. They would never have wasted time saving him.'

'They are using his fingers to practise making Hitler?'

'Yes, that about sums it up. They cut Hitler's finger off when he committed suicide and they had preserved it since then while they perfect their cloning techniques. Dr Becker has been most forthcoming about the plans, since he is planning to kill me too. We've freaked them out by finding their hideout. They're making plans to leave.'

'To leave? When?'

'Who knows? They can't go before they complete their mission.'

'But how will they do that? They don't have the time to bring anyone here so they can use her womb. Where will they...' Sam stopped talking. It had become crystal clear to her why they had kidnapped her.

'Oh my God, Alfredo, they intend to use me as Hitler's mother.'

'Don't be absurd. You aren't German. Why would they use you?'

'I'm Aryan stock, according to them. They don't have any choice.'

'How do we stop them?'

'I think I may be carrying the solution, but I don't think it will save us.'

'What do you mean?'

'I'm pregnant. They can't inseminate me if I'm already carrying a baby.'

'Jesus, Sam, when did this happen? Are you positive? You don't appear pregnant. In fact, you're skinny.'

Sam didn't want to tell him about the sad days when

they imagined him to be dead, and food tasted like cardboard, and their appetites died too. Normally, she would have been glad to lose weight. Simon was always grumbling about her eating habits. He liked her to be slim.

'Is that awful Simon the father?'

'I'm afraid so. Never mind him. What are we going to do? Segundo will be back in a couple of days. We must try to stay alive until then.'

'And your baby?'

'Let's not mention it again in case they hear us.'

'But…'

'No buts.' She made a zipping motion with her fingers across her mouth.

***

Kurt Becker sat alone in his laboratory looking at the frosted canister in front of him dripping onto the countertop. It had come down to this. Over forty years of secrecy and planning would now culminate in a rushed trial that was almost certain to fail. He had procrastinated for years because the possibility of failure terrified him. What if he destroyed the finger with no result?

Now there was no alternative. They couldn't guarantee they could get the canister out of the country without it defrosting. There were too many risks now that people were searching for them. Sierramar had been wonderful for many reasons but when it came down to it, it was too primitive. The electricity supply was unreliable, the water got cut off, landslides often blocked the roads. They could no longer rely on the village of San Blas as their cover. It was ironic that the Jew and his friend Dr Vargas did not understand what they were walking into and had destroyed their project by coincidence after they had been operating in plain sight for so many years.

He put on some gloves and wiped the frost off the catch, fiddling with it without attempting to dislodge it. Boris Klein appeared and watched him fumble.

'Are you ready, Kurt?'

'Ready? How can anyone be ready for this?'

'Come on, old friend. You can do it. You've done these hundreds of times.'

'Yes, I have. Thank you. I need to do this alone. You might break my concentration.'

'I understand. I will not disturb you. Let me know if you need help.'

Kurt Becker nodded. He heard the door close behind him. The canister was heavy, and he struggled to get a good grip on the catch. It opened with a pop as the air equalised and a short metal tube slid out onto the table. It looked intact and undamaged by forty years in various freezers, but there was only one way to find out.

With great care, Becker unscrewed the top and shook the contents out into a large petri dish. A grey slime ran out of the tube followed by what looked like a shrivelled piece of rubber which fell into the centre of the dish. The finger was grey, and the nail was hanging off. It looked like it had been mummified. He poked it with his scalpel, dread invading his being.

He reached over to the bench and picked up a bottle of sterilised saline, which had the same salt content as blood, and squirted it onto the finger. Then he cleaned off the slime by moving the digit around in the liquid and then transferred it into another petri dish. This he filled with more saline. The finger refused to assume a healthier colour and looked like a twig on a stream bed. He put the lid on the dish and put the finger in the fridge.

Half an hour later the finger had rehydrated and looked a little better. Becker cut a minute piece off the end and macerated it in saline. He dropped the resulting liquid onto a slide and put a glass cover on it. Then he put it under the powerful microscope. Bending over the lens, he searched the liquid for whole cells. He could only see a grey soup with broken bits of cell content and structure. This abortive trial run did not concern him as he had cut a piece from the extreme end of the finger. The extremity of the digit was bound to be rotten to some extent. He went back to the table and dissected the finger with precision cuts to reach the inner flesh.

The fresher material was not in great shape either but he could see some whole cells in the liquid, which he transferred to some clean saline. He put this liquid under the microscope in a petri dish and used a micropipette to breach the walls of one cell. With great care, he used the rubber bulb on the same pipette to suck up the contents of the cell. He then squeezed the bulb again and pushed the contents out into the saline and peered at them. They were whole, but they were a nasty grey colour. Perhaps they needed more hydration. Were they viable? There was no way of telling. He didn't have time to check.

He took another petri dish out of the fridge. This contained the empty egg cells harvested from German women undergoing fertility treatment in Calderon. A colleague had collected them over several months and kept them frozen for shipment to San Blas. When Kurt Becker questioned the ethics of using the eggs without permission, Klein dismissed his objections.

'Who will miss a couple of eggs?'

He used a clean micropipette to remove one of the

empty eggs and placed it in another petri dish beside the finger cells. Then he sucked the contents out of another finger cell and injected it with great care into the egg cell. With extreme caution, he removed this and placed it in a new petri dish half full of saline. He repeated this procedure, making twenty egg cells with new contents. Sweat dripped off his brow as he put a lid on the petri dish. He put the finger and the other cells in petri dishes into the fridge. Then he tipped the newly filled eggs into a warm dish with a weak electric current running through it.

He sat down exhausted by his effort. His watch said that it was nearly midnight. He felt like Dr Frankenstein. Was he creating a monster? He had never thought about it. All those years, missing his family and working for the good of the Reich, it had never occurred to him to ask himself if this was a good idea. The Führer was a great leader but there was little doubt that he was insane. What if that madness was genetic? He rubbed his eyes. This was not the time to develop cold feet. There was nothing more to do this evening. He cleaned the laboratory and the surfaces with meticulous care. As he left the laboratory, he bumped into Boris Klein who was waiting outside on a chair.

'Is it done?' he asked.

'Yes, the process of fusion is underway. Did you inject the woman with hormones?'

'Yes, while she was asleep in the car.'

'It should only take a day or two to make her ovulate and for her womb to accept the eggs.'

'She's a fine-looking young woman. I'd like to shut myself in a room with her for an hour or two.'

'Are you crazy? Don't you dare touch her. What if you impregnated her? She's our only chance, and it's a long shot.'

'Fingers crossed then. What are our chances of success?'

'I can't say. It's in the lap of the gods now.'

CHAPTER XXVI

Ramon Vega blinked in the bright lights. Beads of sweat clung to the makeup on his face, tempting him to rub it off.

'Stay still Mr Vega, we need to take readings from your skin tone.'

'Can you please hurry this up? I need to get out of here.'

'Will do. Darling, can you put the corduroy jacket on Mr Vega? There, that one looks more learned.'

'It's a pity you don't wear glasses Mr Vega, to add gravitas,' said his assistant, a short girl with blonde hair who leaned in close to his face, so close he could smell her breath mints.

'I can't help it if I'm handsome,' said Ramon, winking at her. 'And it's Dr Vega not Mr.'

'Apologies. Just another few minutes.'

With the photographer satisfied, Ramon returned upstairs to Guido Luna's office. He had to wait for him, because they were reviewing the final proofs of the article in another building. While he waited, Vega became uncomfortable with the close quarter flirting of

Nadia, so he felt relieved when he heard the elevator pinging and Guido Luna appeared clutching the proofs.

'Good morning, Ramon. I trust you slept well.'

'As well as expected. I should have stayed here with you.'

'Would you like to check the proofs?'

'Yes, please.'

Guido laid them out on the table. There was a big headline on the front page – Secret Nazi Enclave in Sierramar. The two-page spread had various images from the report reproduced with in-depth analysis of Ramon's report. The effect was stunning. Ramon imagined the reaction that it would provoke in Calderon. There was still a blank space for an interview and the photograph they had taken of him.

'Okay, so let's get that interview started,' said Guido.

'May I ask you something?'

'Is there anything wrong with the special? We can still edit it if you notice we are missing something or have got something wrong.'

'No, nothing like that. I have some friends who are in danger because of this Nazi cult. Can you help me get the article sent to the press in Sierramar?'

'Listen, there is no way we would let other newspapers steal this scoop in tomorrow's editions but I can give the story to the Reuters agency to distribute first thing tomorrow morning.'

'Reuters?'

'Yes, they will spread it around the globe and the newspapers in Sierramar will have the story by the afternoon. Does that help?'

***

After finishing his interview and making it clear to the

photographer he didn't care which picture of him would appear in the article, Ramon asked Guido if he could use a telephone to contact Sierramar. They directed him to the office of a journalist who was out doing some research into a story. He settled into the office chair and pulled out his notebook and looked for the number of Gloria's father. He tried ringing the operator but then remembered that he could ring straight through from Miami.

'Don Sanchez?'

'Yes. Is that Ramon? How are you, my boy? Any luck?'

'Great news, sir. They are publishing an exclusive article tomorrow and will pass it on to Reuters to send worldwide.'

'That's fantastic news. I'll go down to their offices in Calderon first thing in the morning and get the print-outs.'

'What will you do with them?'

'I'll take them to Holger Ponce. He's the source of most of the communications coming out of Calderon. He must be in touch with the group in San Blas. It may be our only hope of stalling them.'

'Good luck, sir.'

'Thank you, Ramon. It will be my pleasure. I hope we're not too late. My unwillingness to accept my past almost killed my daughter and has put Alfredo and Sam in terrible peril.'

'How could you realise that these people were still so fanatical? I can't believe it myself.'

'It's incredible. By the way, I'm going to the south tomorrow as my daughter is in hospital with a broken arm.'

'Oh no, how did that happen? I hope it wasn't related to my report. It has caused enough mayhem.'

'Don't worry. It's not serious. Another casualty of this saga.'

'Let's hope she's the last. Give her my best wishes and let me know if you get any updates on Alfredo and Sam.'

'I promise that I'll ring your hotel, if I get any news.'

'I'll be waiting for the chance to come home to Sierramar. I hope it will be soon.'

'If you're short of money, I can send you some. That's something I can do for you.'

'Thank you, but the Miami Herald are being most generous in their payment for the scoop and it's likely they'll ask me to appear on the news and talk shows in the USA so money won't be a problem from now on.'

'Okay, I'll keep you posted.'

***

Hernan Sanchez got up early the next morning and had a quick coffee before asking his driver to get the car out. They drove through the streets ahead of the rush hour and parked outside the Reuters offices. Hernan read the paper without interest, trying to will time forward. When they opened the office to the public, he climbed out of the car and was first through the door. Wheezing with the effort, he rushed straight to the reception desk where the receptionist was swallowing a couple of aspirin and looked as if she might faint.

'Can I meet the bureau chief right away, please?'

'I'm afraid he's not in until later.'

'This is urgent. Is there anyone else?'

'Yes, Javier Sanchez is in. How about him?'

'He'll do. Tell him Hernan Sanchez is here.'

'Is he a relative?'

'Yes.'

Her handover had taken the fight out of her and she waved him through. He entered Javier Sanchez's office and introduced himself. Javier Sanchez looked a little intimidated to have Hernan Sanchez in his office. An experience journalist, he was well aware of the reputation of the man standing in front of him.

'It is an honour to welcome you here, Don Sanchez. To what do I owe this pleasure?'

'I believe that you have received a report from Reuters in Miami about a breaking story in Sierramar. I'd like a copy.'

'We rarely give out that information.'

'I rarely ask for it.'

Twenty minutes later, Hernan Sanchez was on his way to Holger Ponce's house in the suburbs with several copies of a facsimile in a white envelope.

***

Hernan Sanchez waited in the sitting room until a bleary-eyed Holger Ponce staggered in, still wearing his silk dressing gown. His large gut poked out between the folds and he dragged them together with a grumpy gesture that suggested a fit of pique.

'This had better be important,' he said, falling back into a chair.

'Oh, you'll find that it's worth getting up for,' said Sanchez, who had not sat down. He threw the printout onto Holger's stomach and turned around to look out the window through a gap in the curtains. The early morning sun was pushing its way through the clouds like a boxer heading to the ring. The volcano looked at once magnificent and terrifying in its potential to take out the city of Calderon in one tantrum.

It was not long before he heard a gasp followed by something more like a gurgle. He was about to say something sarcastic when Holger clutched his left arm and mouthed something that would not come out. Holger sank into a chair fighting for breath. A smug smile crept across Hernan's features. Serves the bastard right. He bent over and whispered in his ear. 'That's what you get for threatening my daughter, you scum.' Then he called out to the maid.

'Senorita! You need to alert the hospital and get them to send an ambulance. The Minister's had a turn and I fear that it's life-threatening if he doesn't get attention soon.'

He picked up the print-out and was going to take it with him but changed his mind. He replaced it in the envelope and handed it to the maid who was trying to dial the hospital and looked like she might also succumb to a heart attack with fright.

'Senorita, I'm sorry to leave you in this situation but I must go to an important meeting. Can you give these papers to the Minister's aide? He'll deliver them.'

She nodded, struck dumb by shock.

'Good day.'

Sanchez could not stop smiling on the short journey to the airport. The treatment he had received at the hands of Holger Ponce had wounded his pride and the brutal result of his revenge matched his philosophy of 'an eye for an eye.' No one could accuse him of anything other than rushing over to show an old friend a shocking news article. He beamed at the driver and strode across the airport to catch a chartered flight being too impatient to wait for the scheduled one at midday. The driver noticed him smiling in his rear-view mirror and imagined his boss was going to meet a new girlfriend.

'Have a good trip, sir.'

'I will now, thank you.'

***

By the time he got to the hospital, Hernan Sanchez was desperate to find Gloria. Whilst he knew that she was okay and had only fractured an arm, she was still his only child and much beloved. The hospital reception directed him to a wing on the second floor, dedicated to private patients. As he passed the nurses station, one of them asked him who he was.

'My name is Hernan Sanchez. I am here to see my daughter Gloria. They told me downstairs that she is in room two zero six.'

'Yes, that is correct, sir.'

'May I visit her?'

'You go on ahead, Mr Sanchez. Oh, congratulations by the way,.'

Congratulations? What was the woman on about? Had she mistaken him for someone else? He found the room and knocked on the door.

'Come in.'

'Sweetheart, it's me at last.'

'Papi! It's so great that you came.'

'How's the arm, flower?'

'The arm?' She looked confused for a moment. 'Oh yes, fine, fine. Didn't the doctors tell you?'

'Tell me what? Oh God! Is there something else wrong with you?'

'Not wrong, Papi. You'd better sit down.'

Sanchez pulled a chair up to his daughter's bed and held her hand praying silently. Please, don't be cancer again. I wouldn't survive a second loss.

'So? Tell me.'

'Don't look so worried, it's good news. I'm pregnant. You will be a grandfather soon.' She trailed off. The look of astonishment on Hernan's face rippled back and forwards for several seconds before he spoke.

'You're what? How? I thought you couldn't have children. The doctors…'

'They were wrong. I was vomiting a lot on this trip and I mentioned it to the medical staff here. They did some tests and, well, I'm going to have a baby.'

'Who's the father?'

'Alfredo.'

'I'll murder the swine.'

'You may not get the chance.'

'I was only joking, I forgot they were still prisoners. Forgive me, my angel. I am the happiest man on earth right now.'

'Forgiven. You couldn't be happier than me. It's like a miracle.'

'Do you have any news about the others? Segundo told me he was going straight back to get them.'

'No, he only left last night. He will rescue them alone.'

'He's not the only weapon we have. I have some great news of my own. The Miami Herald published Ramon's research in an article condemning the Sierramar government's collaboration with the Nazis and Reuters is distributing it worldwide today. Every newspaper in Sierramar will have the revelations tomorrow and the news will spread like wildfire.'

'That's fantastic news. Hopefully, when it gets to San Blas, the Nazis will flee the country and let Alfredo and Sam go free.'

'I can't imagine why the Nazis would bother to hold them anymore, now that we have discovered their whereabouts.'

'It's a mystery. I can't help feeling there's more to this than meets the eye.'

CHAPTER XXVII

Segundo woke up when it was still dark and left the hotel in the dim street lighting to walk to the main square in Lago Verde. A cold wind pierced his jacket. The place was deserted but a kiosk at the bus stop was selling bus tickets and breakfast. He chased some sticky pastries down with a hot sweet coffee while he waited for the first bus to San Blas. The dawn was breaking, but the clouds were dark grey with rain. The streets were empty, except for a tourist couple from the port of Guayama, who were sitting together at the bus stop, half asleep. The lack of passengers going to work surprised Segundo.

'Where is everyone?' he asked the bus driver. 'What time do they start work in San Blas?'

'Are you joking? Those German racists won't let anyone from Sierramar work at their village. They say it would ruin the concept.'

'What concept?'

'It's supposed to be like a real German village, with authentic food and housing, and authentic villagers. I don't think there are many mestizos in Germany.'

'You're probably right.'

Segundo realised that he would stick out like a sore thumb if he got off the bus at San Blas. He bought a ticket and sat at the front so he could talk to the driver.

'Can you tell me how far you go?'

'I go to the other side of San Blas where the road ends, and then I come back through the town again on my way out.'

'Is there a forest there? And a round hill?'

'Yes, that's the place. How do you know?'

'Oh, my cousin is cutting some wood out there. He asked me to meet him.'

'I'd be careful if I were you. I often see some of those German bastards out there with guns. What they are shooting? Sheep?'

'You know the Germans. They're like Americans and want to kill everything that moves.'

They both laughed.

No one else arrived to catch the bus and soon they were trundling along the narrow road between the high peat banking on either side. Several startled rabbits ran ahead of the bus darting to-and-fro until they could shoot off into an opening. Weak sunshine leaked through the dark clouds as the bus arrived at San Blas. The streets were empty but Segundo crouched down in the sunken entrance steps of the vehicle to be invisible from the pavement. The driver raised an eyebrow and wagged his finger.

'Are you poaching?'

'You won't tell?'

'Of course not. Anyone who steals from that lot has my blessing.'

They continued through town and out the other side. A forest loomed into view, black and threatening, the damp trees with their dripping branches cutting out the light. The road stopped abruptly at the edge of the trees, lacking the courage to continue. The bus driver opened the door and dropped Segundo at the end of the road.

'Are you sure this is the right place? It seems spooky to me.'

'This is it. Thanks a lot.'

The bus driver turned back to San Blas, waving in his mirror at Segundo until he was out of sight. There were several vehicles parked under the trees at the side of the road but no sign of any occupants. Segundo could not see any reason for them to be there so he slipped into the woods and found a hollow from which he could watch the cars and the hill. He took a piece of plastic out of his pocket and placed it flat on the earth and lay on top of it. Despite the covering, it was freezing, and he shivered to warm himself up. He camouflaged himself with leaves and settled down to wait.

***

Sam woke up with sore breasts. They felt hot and swollen and uncomfortable. She assumed that it was a symptom of her now unwanted pregnancy. No doubt she would start vomiting any day now. Her mood couldn't get any worse although blaming it on her pregnancy seemed a little naïve. The irony of the situation she was in made her almost hysterical. The Nazis were planning on implanting her with an unwanted baby, when she was already carrying one. How did this happen? Contraception had always been a priority for her.

She couldn't understand why she was so different to the other women she knew. Even Gloria, the adventurer, the non-conformist, was desperate for the child she couldn't have. Sam couldn't understand why having a baby was so alien to her, when most women of her age were like ticking timebombs. Now she would be the mother of Hitler? There was a satirical show in there somewhere. On another occasion Alfredo would have enjoyed the joke but by the look of him, now was not the time.

The door rattled and Boris Klein entered with Kurt Becker. Sam stepped backwards and Alfredo put a protective arm around her shoulder.

'We need a blood sample,' said Becker.

'You must be joking,' said Sam.

'We can do this the hard way or the easy way,' said Klein.

Sam considered her options. Segundo must be on his way by now. If she could stall them for a day, there was the chance of a rescue. There was no point in getting injured. She might need to run away.

'Okay,' she said, 'don't take too much. I need it.'

She rolled up her sleeve. Klein grabbed her at the same time brushing his hand over her breast. She knew it was deliberate and a cold fear swept up her back.

'Don't touch me,' she hissed, 'or you'll regret it.'

'Ha, the British bitch has spunk at least,' he said.

'Stop messing around, Boris. Sit down while I take the sample.' Kurt Becker pushed Boris back towards the door. Sam calmed down and sat on the bed, proffering her arm. Alfredo, who had been silent, sat down beside her and held her hand.

'Hang in there. You're not alone.'

'You soon will be,' said Boris, 'alone and on your way to Argentina. They'll never find you there.'

'Shut up!' said Becker, and he pushed Boris out into the passageway, his irritation showing. He shut the door behind him so Sam and Alfredo couldn't hear what he was saying. 'Why don't you go into town and check with the hotel for any news?' he told him. 'We need to do the procedure as soon as possible and get out of here before our options reduce.'

'What about Dr Vargas?'

'We'll leave him here. You can kill him tomorrow. He keeps Sam calm which is vital right now.'

'Great. I can't wait to rid us of that superior bastard.'

'And for God's sake, stop baiting Sam. She doesn't look defenceless to me. I don't see any fear in those eyes, only fury. I'd watch your balls if I were you.'

***

Segundo was cold to the bone after several hours spent hiding in his hollow in the woods. His feet felt like concrete bricks. Suddenly, he heard what sounded like a lock being opened. He watched in amazement as a door opened in the grass on the side of the hill. It was hard to see the outline in broad daylight, even when he knew it was there. A large man with grey hair and a goatee stepped outside, shielding his eyes. He was followed by a man wearing an old uniform, which looked like it had seen better days, who was carrying a pistol. They walked over to a pickup truck talking in loud voices. Segundo still struggled to make out what they were saying.

'… tomorrow, I think. Be ready to leave then.'

'Okay, Mr Klein. Shall I come with you?'

'No, stay here, Dr Becker may need you.'

The bearded man got into the pickup and drove off, and the guard wandered back inside. Segundo waited until he had shut the door, and then he crept through the trees until he could see the doorway better. A plan was forming in his head but he needed confirmation that Sam and Alfredo were being held in the hill. He circled around behind it and discovered a large tank of diesel hidden under the cover of some leafy bushes. As he got closer to it, the chugging of a large generator which was dug into the hillside for soundproofing, became clear.

The only other outward sign of its existence was the exhaust pumping smoke into the air. He crept closer and crawled up to the top of the hill where he found several shafts dug vertically into the hill. The Nazis had lined these with mirrors. He lay on his stomach and tried to put his head at the correct angle to see down into the holes. A shadow moved across his vision. Alfredo! He had found them. Sam had been right.

Grudgingly, he gave her credit for spotting the hill on the aerial photographs. He would not have known where to start. It would have been nice to alert them to his presence, but he worried that someone else might spot him. He continued to reconnoitre the hill, sliding through the grass like a python. Down another of the holes, he could see a laboratory with an old man fiddling with some test tubes. He couldn't believe his luck. They had staffed the Nazi headquarters with two old men and a guard who spent most of the time asleep. He decided to pick them off one by one and crept back down to his hiding place.

**

Boris Klein drove into town with his usual disregard for safety, scattering chickens and sending up curtains of muddy water from the puddles lining the road. He got to Schmidt's hotel and put his pickup in the carpark. He came through the back door in the dining room, saluting the picture of the Führer which had been replaced over the fireplace. Franz Schmidt was reading a scurrilous local newspaper and admiring the scantily clad women that adorned its pages. Boris looked over his shoulder and sniffed.

'You can't fancy those Indians?' he said, 'you've been here too long.'

'I guess. A woman's a woman as far as I'm concerned.'

'As long as you aren't planning on breeding with them. I'm sorry about your nephew. He was a brave man, and he died for the Fatherland. How is your brother coping?'

Schmidt grunted. 'How do you think? What do you want anyway? How are things with Dr Becker?'

'We've had a little local difficulty, but we have sorted it out.' Klein had no intention of telling the town's biggest gossip what was happening. 'Becker and I will take the project to Argentina to prevent further problems.'

'That sounds serious.'

The telephone rang. Both men stared at it without answering but it didn't stop. Schmidt shrugged and grabbed it.

'Yes, San Blas Hotel at your service. Yes, he's here now as a matter of fact. Please hold.'

He put his hand over the receiver. 'And talking of Indians, it's Kleber.'

'Who?'

'Kleber, the Minister's assistant.'

'Oh, him.' Klein grabbed the receiver and shoved it to his ear. 'Yes?'

'Mr Klein, it's Kleber.' His voice sounded funny, like it was breaking. It was an octave higher with emotion.

'Yes boy, what's up?'

'It's Minister Ponce, he's had a stroke.'

'Christ, is he going to be okay?'

'They don't have the prognosis yet. They took him to hospital this morning.'

'That's terrible news. I need you to wait at the hospital and keep us updated. Can you ring again and leave a message here at the hotel when you find out how he is?'

'Yes, but that's not all. I think it was the other news that gave him the stroke.' He hesitated. Klein could hear him fidgeting.

'What other news? Get on with it. What could be worse?'

'Hernan Sanchez visited Minister Ponce this morning and gave him a copy of a news report that Reuters has sent to the agencies in Sierramar. The Miami Herald has done a lead article about a Nazi group present in the country. It mentions you, and Dr Becker. It even mentions San Blas. Every newspaper will have it on the front-page tomorrow morning.'

Klein turned white with fury, alarming Schmidt who stepped back behind the counter.

'What a fucking train wreck! How did they get this information?'

Kleber stuttered.

'I have the press release from Reuters right here. It says that they based the report on the research of Dr Ramon Vega and there is a photograph of him. He's in Miami promoting it.'

'I thought that bastard died in the fire. You told me the police found two bodies.'

'They did, Mr Klein, but Dr Vega wasn't one of them. It says here that he escaped the fire and that it was a case of mistaken identity.'

'Jesus! You idiot. We are fucked.' He dropped the receiver as if it were a poisonous spider. It was happening too fast. They had to get out of there before the news spread any further.

'Are you feeling okay, Boris?' asked Schmidt, 'you have gone ashen.'

'It's time to get out,' he said. 'We need to leave for Argentina. We are no longer safe here. Tell your brother, and the others. Pack up and leave tonight or it will be too late.'

***

Back at the laboratory, Kurt Becker was feeling a little more hopeful. He had tested Sam's blood and been thrilled to find that Sam's hormone levels showed that she was ovulating. It couldn't have been the injection that she had received because it hadn't had time to take effect yet. Her womb would be receptive to their implant. It had to be a lucky coincidence, and they needed one. Time was closing in and he had to implant the eggs that evening to be confident they had time to settle on the womb and embed before they left for Argentina.

The journey would not be easy. They would have to keep her comatose to prevent her trying to escape. He had seen the fire in her eyes when Boris had touched her breast. She was a typical British person. They seemed so meek and reserved but God help you if you provoked them to a fight. Their ability to defeat the Luftwaffe despite the overwhelming odds against them had astounded him. Until they realised that British scientists had developed radar, there was total incomprehension in the German ranks about how the British air force was always in the right place at the right time to shoot down their bombers.

And how on earth had Sam found them in San Blas? Alfredo had never mentioned that anyone else knew where they were going and he never appeared to think they might rescue him. His amazement when Sam turned up was not faked.

It was time to check on the eggs. It would be touch and go to get them implanted in time even if they were ready. He felt a deep resentment that his years of research were for nothing and that circumstances had forced him into a single throw of the dice. No one appreciated the fine line between success and failure like he did. Mostly because he had been economical with the truth. He had exaggerated his successes with the cloning of sheep, hoping that his results would catch up with the reports before anyone noticed. Expectations were so high. The original team were getting old and their offspring were not as keen on a Fourth Reich, being more interested in pop music and sex. Many of the younger generation had drifted away from San Blas to go to university in Calderon and they had not come back. Only less intelligent young men like Hans, with no interest in education, got a thrill from the stories about the power and superiority of the Nazis.

'If we're so superior, how come we got beaten by the inferior races?' said one of Kurt's daughters, earning herself a slap.

They would learn. When they saw Hitler in his prime again, they would understand and come back to the fold.

To distract himself, he took the eggs that he had manufactured the day before out of the cabinet, removing the electric wires which were supplying a light current through the dish where they were stored. He removed a concave slide from the same cabinet, he dropped some clean saline into the depression on the glass. Then he squeezed on the bulb of a pipette and sucked one egg from the solution. He transferred it into the depression, expelling it into the saline pool. Then he slid a thin glass protective cap over it and pushed it under the microscope. He held his breath and put his eye to the lens.

***

Sam rubbed her arm where they had extracted the sample.

'Why do you think they needed the blood?'

'It must be something to do with hormones,' said Alfredo.

'Can they tell from the results that I'm already pregnant?'

'I don't know.'

'It's probably too early to show. I don't feel pregnant and I haven't been sick or developed a craving for pickles yet.'

'I'm so sorry about this. It's my fault. I should've guessed Saul wasn't telling me the whole truth.'

'Don't be silly. How is this your fault? Anyway, this cloning business was a complete surprise. He was looking for revenge for his family. There was no way of guessing what they had planned.'

'But he had a gun. I saw it and I still didn't realise the danger we were in.'

'Jesus, Alfredo, ninety-nine percent of the male population of Sierramar have a gun. They're not planning to take over the world, are they?'

'No, I guess not, but I wasn't expecting you to get involved.'

'That was my choice. We'll be fine. Hang in there. Segundo will be on his way by now.'

The sound of a horn being blown drifted down the shaft.

'Hey! Did you hear that? There's something happening outside.'

'Maybe Segundo is here to rescue us.'

'I hope so, I don't think we have much longer.'

***

Klein screeched to a halt outside the laboratory and put his hand on the horn of the truck. The sound echoed across the forest. In his leaf-covered hollow, Segundo jumped with fright, his heart pounding as the adrenaline flooded his system. He spun around in his hiding place so that he could see the truck. The man with the beard was still inside, banging the dashboard with his fist. Segundo risked moving nearer to eavesdrop. He flattened himself and slithered closer to the edge of the glade and hid behind a large tree. The door in the hillside flew open and Kurt Becker came out gesticulating. He approached the truck and approached the driver's side, his face screwed up with frustration.

'For God's sake, Boris. What the hell is wrong with you? Why don't you sell tickets?'

'The bastard published his report.'

'Which bastard? Didn't we burn the report? It was in the backseat pocket of Dr Vargas' car and it got incinerated when we got rid of the vehicle. Remember?'

'Ramon Vega. He's alive. Apparently, Kleber set fire to Vega's girlfriend instead of him.'

'What do you mean?'

'Vega was having an affair. The body in his bed was his girlfriend, but they kept it quiet because she was married and Vega had disappeared.'

'But Kleber told us that there was only one copy of the report.'

'Apparently not. Vega has published it in Miami and it will be all over the news here tomorrow. They have screwed us.'

Becker sighed. The tired sigh of a defeated man.

'What do you propose, Boris?'

'You must inseminate the bitch tonight and we'll make a break for it at dawn. Is that enough time for the procedure to take?'

'If we keep her asleep and put her flat on a mattress in the back of the pickup, the egg may take. It's a big risk.'

'It's a bigger risk sitting around here until they come and get us.'

'Okay, what about Vargas?'

'We must dispose of him. I'll help you anaesthetise the gringa and then I'll take him outside and shoot him.'

'I need to get ready. Give me a couple of hours.'

Becker returned inside, slamming the door behind him. Klein stayed outside, lighting a cigarette and leaning against the warm bonnet of the truck. The smell of the cigarette reached Segundo who sucked it in, wishing he had one, too. Segundo was not an educated man, and he did not understand why the men were talking about inseminating a bitch when they had to get away from San Blas. However, they had said that they would dispose of Alfredo so he had to be ready for action. He crept back to his hideaway and removed his gun from its plastic bag.

***

Quivering with fury, Kurt Becker entered the laboratory. The revelation about the report had shaken him to the core. When Kleber had burnt down Roman Vega's house, they thought that they had plugged the leak caused by his research. The older generation in Sierramar who had glossed over the Nazi presence, were now ashamed of their collaboration with the Nazi regime. It was not in their interest to point the finger when there were government ministers complicit in hiding fugitive officers in plain sight.

But now, the truth was out, and their refuge had become a trap. There was only one road out and if they didn't use it before the press published the newspapers, they would never escape. He sat down and put his head in his hands, massaging his temples and trying to calm down. It wasn't as if the report was the only problem. He hadn't told Boris about the eggs.

He had put the first egg under the microscope with his hopes still high but they soon turned to despair. The contents were amorphous, a grey slime with no form or partition. He threw it away, washing it off the slide with a stream of saline into the plastic bin beside the counter. Using the pipette, he selected another egg and placed it in a pool of saline in the concave slide. He slid it onto the platform and peered down the lenses. The same result. His efforts were now those of a desperate man. One by one he examined the eggs under the microscope only to find that they were full of the same grey pulp. There was not a single viable egg. This was terrible but even worse was the fact that he was not the slightest bit surprised by this result. They had kept the finger frozen for forty years in freezers prone to electricity cuts. There were a couple of occasions when he suspected that the emergency generator did not immediately take over, but, so desperate was he to maintain his position in the group and to prove his theories that he ignored the facts staring him in the face.

Boris and the Schmidt family had the intellectual

rigour of footballs. They worshiped the ground he walked on and never questioned his judgment on anything. He had worked for a dream that would never become a reality. As a group, they had dedicated their whole lives to an idea that had as much chance of working as a chocolate teapot. Had he always known it was doomed to failure? Probably. But he wanted it to be true. He loved the order of the Reich and the importance of science and the development of the master race. Now it had become pointless, and he had reached the end of the road. He sat down on the chair in the laboratory and cried like a little child.

CHAPTER XXVIII

Kurt Becker had pulled himself together. He had a plan. Not much of a plan, and he knew that it was unlikely to be a success in the long run, but a plan that might get him to Argentina. He could run away once he got there and start a new life with one of those Latin women who looked like horses with their bony faces and long hair. He needed to fantasise about one of them right now.

He had locked the door to the laboratory, and he was sitting on the chair with his trousers around his legs. In his hand, he held his flaccid penis dangling over a plastic pot. He shut his eyes and imagined they surrounded him, whinnying in Spanish. Touching him and stroking him and kissing his back. He could feel the hairs on his arm stand on end and his penis sprung to life as he disappeared into a herd of horsey women rubbing themselves against him. He masturbated vigorously, carried away in a sea of caresses. There it was, on its way, into the pot. He let out a shout.

There was a knock on the door.

'You ready, Kurt? We have little time.'

He pulled up his trousers and tightened his belt and regained his grip on reality.

'Yes, sorry, I dropped something. I'll be five minutes.'

He became a man of action, cleaning up the redundant eggs and throwing away the evidence of his failure. Opening the fridge, he found that the remnants of the finger, with its macabre nail, were still where he had left them. He searched for the metal tube in which they had stored it for the last forty years and cleaned the inside with a strong acid and sterilisers. Then he filled it to about half way with formaldehyde. With great reverence, he picked the finger up with a pair of forceps and dropped it into the liquid which rose to up the tube. He topped it up with formaldehyde and screwed on the lid.

He slipped the tube into his pocket and continued to ready the lab for the insemination feeling strangely content. Sam was ovulating already, so it wasn't a stretch to imagine what would happen if they added if some fresh sperm to the equation. There was an even chance that the child would be a boy. By the time he grew to adulthood as a blond, six-footer instead of a dark, short man, questions would be asked, but Becker would be long gone.

He added the stirrups to the operating table and covered it with a clean towel. The pot of sperm was on the side ready for use. There was no point slowing down the spermatozoa by putting it in the fridge. They lived for forty-eight hours inside the human womb. He opened the door.

'Boris?'

'Yes, Kurt.'

'We are ready.'

***

Sam counted down the hours. Every minute that passed took them closer to safety but also increased the immediate danger that Klein and Becker posed. They could come for her at any moment. Boris Klein, and what he might do to her, was a terrifying prospect. She wanted to make a break for it but Alfredo had suffered a collapse and was whimpering under his blanket. She wondered if it might be delirium tremors but it was as likely to be terror.

'Alfredo, are you okay? We need to make a plan,' she said.

'They will shoot me soon.'

'Don't be silly. Why would they do that?'

'Because they don't need me anymore. They only kept me in case they needed more fresh fingers. Now that they are planning to leave, they only need you.'

'They'll kill me, too, when they discover that I'm already pregnant.'

'Oh God, I hadn't thought of that. I don't want to die. I want to marry Gloria.'

Sam, who on a bad day considered that marrying Gloria was a fate worse than death, said 'And you will. Segundo has time to rescue us. Hang in there.'

But her optimism was fake. How would Segundo find the hill? He had thrown the aerial photograph back at her without looking at it. They would die. There was no way out of their cell. The shaft in the ceiling was far too high to reach. Even if she put the chair on the table. And the door was metal with a massive lock. No wonder Alfredo had given up. Come on Sam, think. And then she saw it. The bed. Alfredo's bed was more of a camp bed but hers had a frame. It was rusty but sturdy. What if they put it on its end?

'Alfredo! Help me.'

Sam dragged the bed into the middle of the room. It

was heavy and squealed as she dragged it.

'Help me lift the end.'

'What's the use?'

'Don't you see? If we put the bed end up, we can reach the shaft. Then we can haul ourselves out.'

Alfredo peered upwards. He smiled.

'Sam, you are a genius.'

'Come on, then.'

They lifted the bed and levered it onto its end. Then Alfredo pushed the table alongside it.

'You go first,' said Sam. 'You can pull me up from outside if I can't manage.'

Alfredo stepped from the chair onto the table and up onto the top of the frame while Sam held it steady. His head and shoulders disappeared into the shaft.

'I can see the sky,' he said. 'Give me a minute.'

'Hurry. They might come at any time.'

Alfredo pushed his arms up into the shaft and jammed his elbows on top of the wooden frame holding it open. He grunted as he pulled himself up far enough to get one of his knees wedged into the bottom strut. He had to scramble to avoid slipping back down, he forced himself higher up the shaft and both his legs rose into it. There was a scuffling sound and then silence.

'Alfredo?'

'I'm out. Come on, your turn. Quickly.'

The door rattled as Klein inserted the key in the lock. Sam got herself balanced on top of the end of the bed and reached upwards, desperately feeling for a hand hold. Someone grabbed her legs.

'Get down from there.'

She was trapped. Sam lowered herself down onto the floor.

'Where is Dr Vargas?' said Becker.

'I don't know. He left,' said Sam.

'Boris, get Dr Vargas. He can't have gone far.'

At that moment the guard appeared, pushing Alfredo ahead of him with a gun, back into their cell.

'I'm sorry, Sam. I guess I'm a dead man.'

'No, I won't let them. They can't shoot you for no reason.'

'Save yourself. Don't do anything stupid. Cooperate with them for now. You'll get your chance to escape.'

'Don't kid yourself, you have no chance of getting away,' said Klein.

'It's time,' said Becker, 'I am sorry, Alfredo. The sands have run out. It won't hurt, you know. Don't struggle and it'll be over in a second.'

'Come with me Dr Vargas. We're going for a nice walk in the woods.'

Klein grabbed Alfredo's arm and pulled him towards the door. Alfredo reached over to Sam. He hugged her close and whispered to her. 'Tell Gloria I love her.'

Klein pushed him out into the corridor. 'Come on. We haven't got all day.'

CHAPTER XXIX

Boris Klein had not held a man at his mercy like this for many years. He smiled in anticipation and caressed the pistol in his hand. He shoved Alfredo in the back and pushed him out of the entrance towards the forest.

Alfredo was frantic. All he could think about was Gloria and the purposeless of his life until he'd met her. He had finally found a reason to live just when he was about to die. The irony made him sigh. One of his last breaths. He didn't want his last thought to be regret. There was only one thing to do. He was going to make a run for it. Better to be shot trying to escape than on his knees. He looked for the opportunity to make a break for it. They moved deeper into the trees. It was almost dark and the wet branches brushed his face.

'Stop here.'

He stopped. It was now or never. He tried to run but lead filled his legs.

'Kneel.'

His legs buckled. It was as if his muscles had gone on strike. He fell to his knees as his shoe got caught in the root of a tree. The birds stopped singing. He heard the safety catch being taken off.

'How did you find us?' asked Klein.

'It was a combination of things. Ramon Vega's report started us on the trail and then we got confirmation from the widow of Rolf Kaufmann. She showed us photographs of your group in Nazi uniforms.'

'Silly old bat. Her husband was a bit of a monster. He liked little girls.'

'And you don't?'

'That's your last joke, Dr Vargas. I'll give it to you free. Do you want a minute to pray?'

'I don't believe in God.'

Boris Klein steadied himself on the mossy ground. He lowered the pistol to the nape of Alfredo's neck. Alfredo shut his eyes at the touch and tried to picture Gloria. It was so unfair. The damp crept into the knees of his trousers and he spotted a beetle pulling a moth into a hole. Time stood still.

***

Sam heard Alfredo shuffling towards the exit. 'Please,' she said to Becker, 'you don't have to kill him. He can't hurt you in Argentina.'

'I'm sorry. He knows too much.'

Sam sobbed in grief and frustration. She sank to her knees on the floor. They would not make it. Last minute rescues were for the movies. Becker looked down at her in sympathy.

'Can you get up and come with me or do you want to wait for Boris? This won't hurt. The procedure is a little uncomfortable.'

'I would prefer it if I never saw Boris again,' said Sam with a bravado she did not feel. Then she remembered.

'Can I get some underwear out of my bag?'

'Okay,'

She grabbed her rucksack and searched around at the bottom of the bag and her fingers closed around the plastic Taser. She slipped it into her trouser pocket and followed Dr Becker into the laboratory. It was too warm in there, making her nauseous. The white walls were flecked with dirt and blood.

'Can you lock the door, please? Klein mustn't watch this. I don't want that man looking at me naked.'

'Fair   enough.   I   wouldn't   either.' Dr Becker locked the door.

'Sit down for a minute while I check that we are ready to go.'

Sam tried again, pleading.

'Please, can't you stop him? Stop Boris? Don't let him shoot Alfredo.'

'I can't stop Boris. No one can control that man. He's an animal.'

'Alfredo is my friend.'

Dr Becker looked at her with his cold blue eyes but she saw no pity there.

'There is nothing I can do. You are lucky to be alive. If we didn't need you, you'd be dead, too. Now, take off the clothes below your waist and get up on the operating table.'

Sam sat down and took off her shoes and socks. She hung her jeans over the back of the chair and slipped out of her knickers. Time stood still. She couldn't help it, she was listening for the shot. Run Alfredo, run, give yourself a chance. Please. And, there it was, a single shot. It seemed to reverberate around the room. She wailed and put her hands over her ears as if it would shout out the truth of the sound.

'Alfredo. No!'

'I'm sorry, Sam. There was no choice.'

'There was plenty of choice. You should've left him tied up for someone to find later. You're a murderer.'

'So many deaths. What's one more to add to the list?'

'And me? Am I next? The mother of Hitler? It would be like shooting the Virgin Mary?' she said.

'Calm down or I must put you to sleep for the procedure.'

He moved her clothes off the chair and onto the counter behind him. Sam stood there rigid with fury and impotent rage. Trying to think logically, she considered the options. Without knowing it, he had moved the unit out of her reach. The man was about to discover that she was pregnant and that would mean one thing. He would murder her, and if he didn't, Klein would or worse, he would rape her first. She had seen the way he looked at her. Becker would probably give her an overdose of the anaesthetic when he discovered her secret. She would never wake up. That was appealing. She found it hard to believe these were her last moments on earth. It was so mundane somehow. 'I'm afraid. I can't take any more today. Can you please make me sleep?'

'Okay, if that's what you want. I'll give you some air and gas. Some light sedation should be sufficient.'

He pulled an ancient trolley with a squeaky wheel up to the operating table and turned some valves on a couple of tanks.

'I need you to lie down now and put your feet in the stirrups. That's right. Shift your bottom along towards me. There we go.'

He might have been prepping her for a smear test. 'Are you ready? Okay then, take a deep breath.'

***

There was a loud bang and Alfredo fell forward into the leaves as his legs gave way. He waited for bright lights or tunnels to appear. To his disappointment, he was right about the absence of heaven. Darkness dominated. Why were there leaves in his mouth? He spat them out Had Boris missed? Was he still alive or was this his last sensation on earth?

'Dr Vargas, are you alive?'

He knew that voice.

Segundo? 'Yes, I think so.' He raised himself up on his hands, with their blood-splattered palms. Disgusted, he wiped them on the leaves making them bloodier. His legs wouldn't move. Was he injured? And then he realised that Boris Klein was lying on top of them, half of his head missing. He grunted as he pulled his legs free of the bloody corpse and stood up to face his saviour, who was covered in leaves and twigs, like a forest sprite.

'That was close. I didn't see you both until you almost trod on me as you walked past.'

'I thought I was a goner. Thank goodness you're here. We have to rescue Sam.'

'I have to rescue Sam. Wait outside.'

***

Dr Becker removed Sam's legs from the stirrups and pulled her up the operating table, putting her on her side for safety. He put her clothes beside her in the nook between her thighs and stomach so that she would get dressed without getting off the trolley. He looked at his watch. She should come around any minute. He would need Boris' help to get her into the truck and tied down. Where was he anyway? The shot had echoed around the laboratory at least ten minutes before. Perhaps he was hiding the body? Becker fussed around the laboratory, cleaning away the evidence of their project and sealing it in a large black rubbish bag. They would have to take this with them and dispose of it down the cliffs outside Lago Verde.

Sam moaned and thrashed around. He went to her side and held her down so she would not roll off, taking advantage of her comatose state to admire her from close up. It's a pity she was so unapproachable. She was an attractive woman in the prime of her life. No wonder Boris was salivating around her. If he had been younger, she would have been tempted him too. He stroked her leg, lingering on her soft skin and thinking about those Argentinian women waiting for him. His hand explored her body in a leisurely way.

Suddenly, she sat up. Before he had time to react, she had removed his hand and thrust something into his chest. A jolt of pain radiated over his body. He flew backwards onto the floor. Had he experienced a heart attack? Sam was lying down again still holding an odd black unit in her hand. She was laughing. Before he got up, there was a loud bang and the door of the laboratory flew open.

'Are you okay, Sam?' said Alfredo.

'You're alive?' said Becker, staggering to his feet.

'That's twice you've been dead this week,' said Sam, who was still lying on the trolley. 'I hope you won't make a habit of this.'

'I like to make an entrance.'

'Step away from her now.' Segundo had moved forward into the laboratory. He was pointing a pistol at Becker's head.

Becker didn't recognise him but the threat in the voice was real.

'I don't think I will.'

'Come on now. It's over,' said Alfredo.

'Where's Boris?' said Becker.

'Mr Klein will not be joining us,' said Segundo.

'Jesus, you killed him?'

'It was kill or be killed I'm afraid.'

'Where is the security guard?'

'He's having a nap. Move away from the trolley. Or I'll be forced to shoot you, too.'

'Oh, that won't be necessary. I'm leaving.'

He reached into his pocket and took out a little silver box which he opened by sliding the lid off. There was a capsule rolling around in the box. He smiled and saluted at them.

Before Alfredo or Segundo could move, Becker had thrown it into his mouth and bitten down on it. His eyes rolled back in his head and he grabbed the fridge, gasping. Foam formed at the corners of his mouth. There was the smell of almonds in the air.

'Shit, cyanide, he's a goner,' said Alfredo. 'Don't go near him, that stuff's lethal.'

Becker fell to the floor without lifting his arms to cushion his fall. There was a sickening crunch as his face met the tiles. Blood trickled along the white surface and into the drain. They didn't need to touch him to know that he was dead. Sam groaned and Alfredo rushed over to hold her hand.

'Are you okay?'

'You're alive? Why? I don't understand what happened.'

'Neither do I. Are you still pregnant?' said Alfredo.

'Oh God. I'm going to be the mother of Hitler. Help me down. I must go to the shower right now.'

Alfredo helped her swing her legs to the floor. She had wrapped herself in a surgical sheet and looked quasi-biblical. The men stared at her in the flimsy covering. Sam was built like a Valkyrie and being wrapped in a sheet emphasised her athletic body.

'What are you looking at?' she hissed, grabbing a couple of towels from the side. She shoved her feet into her shoes and pushed passed Segundo, heading for the shower.

'What did she mean? Mother of Hitler? What on earth is going on here?' he said.

'It's a long story.'

'These fucking Germans are weird.'

'Nazis, not Germans.'

'Same difference. I need some fresh air. This place is claustrophobic.'

'All Nazis are not German, and all Germans are not Nazis. Come outside and let Sam have some privacy, and I'll explain a few things to you.'

***

Sam lay on the floor of the toilet washing herself out with soap and water using a plastic water bottle. The floor was not clean, and the cement was scratchy and uneven but it didn't put her off. She wasn't taking any chances and had her legs up on the wall so that the water penetrated to her cervix. It was undignified but compared to the alternative, an easy choice.

She watched the soapy water flowing across the tiles and into the drain. There was some weird satisfaction in watching Hitler washed into the septic tank to join the rest of the sewage.

She was still groggy and there were things she didn't understand. If she was pregnant, how come she was alive? And why didn't she have any symptoms? She had not put on any weight and the only person who was vomiting was Gloria. It was weird. She tried to stand up, but she wasn't ready so she stayed sitting on the floor under the jet until the hot water turned cold.

CHAPTER XXX

A plate of hospital food dried in the sunlight flooding into Gloria's room. She was wearing a pair of her mother's pyjamas, sitting propped up by pillows covered by an old blanket. A big bunch of stargazer lilies were shedding perfume and pollen in equal measure, staining the off-white doily on the bedside cupboard. Hernan Sanchez sat on the edge of Gloria's bed. His manner suggested that he wanted to say something but couldn't find a way.

'Okay, what's wrong? I can see you want to tell me,' said Gloria.

'There is something you should know before you read about it in the newspapers.'

'What is it, Papi? You're worrying me.'

He took her hand and looked into her face.

'I'm ashamed to say I was involved with the Nazis as a young man.'

'You? How? I don't understand.'

'I was working with Holger Ponce before he was Minister for Public Works.'

'I don't like that man. He's so creepy, and he always

tries to touch me.'

'He won't ever try that again. He had a stroke this morning. I doubt he'll survive, to tell you the truth. Anyway, he wasn't nice back then either, but I was from a poor family, and being linked with him was a huge advantage for me. He organised minor contracts for public works for me and then we split the profits.'

'I always knew there was something not-quite-right about the amount of work you got.'

'Well, that's how most people in Sierramar got government contracts in the past. It's getting more regulated now. Anyway, he introduced me to some Germans who were building a village near Lago Verde and needed a road. I wasn't stupid, I realised early on that they were fugitives, but I took the contract because I needed it.'

'But they were Nazis, I don't understand why you helped them.'

'I was young and foolish. A lot of us admired the German war machine and fascist ideals. It was exciting to be involved with notorious criminals.'

'And getting government contracts at such a young age.'

'It's ironic because I didn't make any money from building the road as the mayor of Lago Verde and Holger Ponce fleeced me.'

'And afterwards?'

'Afterwards I started hearing about the concentration camps and other atrocities perpetrated by the Nazis in Europe and I refused to do any more work for them. I wanted to report them but Holger Ponce told me that I would never work again if I mentioned it. So, I've kept my mouth shut.'

'Is that why you sent the report to Ramon Vega?'

'Yes, I thought it was time to earn your respect.

You're so brave. Your mother would be proud.'

'Thank you, Papi. I understand it was hard for you to tell me that.'

'You don't hate me?'

'Don't be silly. The baby needs a grandfather.'

***

After Sam had finished her shower, she walked outside to sit with Alfredo. Segundo came back into the laboratory to set a scene for the police. He put his gun into Kurt Becker's hand and wrapped his fingers around the trigger. Then he used a laboratory glove to pick it up and placed it on the seat. He removed Becker's shoes and took them outside to where Boris Klein's body lay. He used them to kick the leaves where Alfredo had lain, assuring they got splashes of blood on them, and then he took the shoes inside and put them back on Becker's feet. When he had finished, he found Sam and Alfredo sitting on a tree trunk in the sun.

'We need to wipe down the site for your prints,' said Segundo. 'Can you help me?'

They put the bed back against the wall and wiped down the furniture and the door clean of prints. Sam tried to remember what she had touched in the laboratory besides the trolley. She shook out the covers to check that she had left nothing behind and the snakebite unit fell out onto the floor.

'What's that?' said Segundo, 'it looks sinister.'

'It saved my life,' said Sam. 'It's a stun gun. Do you want it?'

'Yes, please.'

'It's yours. I don't think I want to be reminded of what happened today.'

The security guard who had come around from

being hit on the head, was happy to corroborate the story that Becker and Klein had fought, and that Becker had killed Klein and committed suicide. In return for his freedom, he told the police later that there was no one else in the laboratory. Segundo was not a man to be crossed, and the guard had no wish to go to prison for helping the Nazis.

Sam returned outside after a while and sat on the log while the others cleaned up. Confusion overwhelmed her. Relieved, but sad too. The whole Nazi thing was still a mystery to her. Why anyone would want to clone a mad dictator was something she would never understand. They had waded into something so far outside the norm that it felt like a nightmare and not like a real event that took place. At least they were alive, except for poor Saul. Alfredo had promised to get his body sent back to New York for an honourable burial. Segundo had arrived in the nick of time and it had saved her from a short life as a surrogate mother for Hitler.

Where did that leave her with Simon? She was missing him despite herself. He had asked her to move in with him. How many times had she fantasised about that? And she had ruined it by blurting out the pregnancy thing. It felt like her fault. The course of true love was never smooth. She had picked a man who was giving her a bumpy ride, but it didn't feel over, not yet. In her heart she knew it was over but she just couldn't accept the truth.

When they finished at the laboratory, they got into Boris Klein's pickup and drove it to Lago Verde where they picked up Gloria's car. Segundo had left it in the hotel car park and he tipped the hotel manager with a large note and a warning to forget about his visit.

On their way out of town, they had to reverse into

the ditch several times to let vehicles pass, as the media circus was coming to San Blas in a convoy of flashy vans with satellite dishes on top. Segundo drove them as far as the main road where he descended from the vehicle.

'I'm going back to Calderon now,' he said. 'You take the car south to the hospital at Valle de las Incas. Don Sanchez is there with Gloria.'

'Thank you, Segundo, we owe you our lives.'

'Miss Sam, I could never have found the place if it wasn't for your work on the aerial photographs. I'm sorry I was so dismissive. Alfredo would be dead without you.'

They shook hands and Segundo waited at the stop for the regional buses.

'Shall I drive?' said Sam, 'The driver gets to choose the cassette.'

'Go on then. Are you feeling good enough to drive?' said Alfredo

'If you were a girl, I could tell you how I feel,' said Sam

'Right. Don't tell then. I don't think I want to know.'

'Let's have some *AC-DC*.'

***

They got to the hospital in the early evening. Visiting time was over but the staff allowed themselves to be persuaded to accept a generous donation to the office party fund and waived the rules. Hernan Sanchez, to whom the rules did not apply, saw them walking down the passage and came towards them. He embraced Sam and had an awkward handshake with Alfredo. Sam tried to go into Gloria's room but Hernan stopped her.

'I think Alfredo should go in first,' he said winking.

Sam was amazed and confused in equal measure.

'Okay sir, thank you,' said Alfredo, who had already started down the corridor.

He got to the door and opened it. The door swung shut behind him, leaving him standing there, gazing at Gloria was sitting up in bed with her eyes shining.

'Darling,' she said, 'You're not hurt?'

'You silly goose, aren't you the one who's in hospital?'

He rushed forward and took her in his arms.

'Oh God, I thought I'd never be able to do this again. You can't escape from me now. I'm going to marry you.'

'And who said I was going to accept?'

'Aren't you?'

'Well, since I'm carrying your baby, it might prevent my father from having you shot.'

'Baby? What do you mean? I thought, you said, didn't you, what? How? Are you sure?'

'They say it's four months gone already. I thought I was getting a little plump. I never imagined I was pregnant.'

'But isn't Sam pregnant? Has the world gone mad? What's going on?'

'I don't know. What do you think?'

'I think I'm the happiest man in the world.'

'You must compete with my father in that case.'

'Could we call it a tie?'

Sam, who had caught the last comment asked 'Call what a tie?'

'Sam, you're safe, thank goodness. Are you okay?'

'Yes, I'm fine. I'll tell you the gory details later. How about you?'

'I'm pregnant.'

'You're what?'

'Pregnant. They've done the tests. I'm going to be a mother.'

'Oh my God, that's why you were vomiting. What fantastic news! When are you due? We are going to have babies.'

'Sam, are you sure you're pregnant?' Sam's excitement evaporated, and she blanched.

'I'm such an idiot,' she said. 'I remember now. The stick thing from the pregnancy testing kit landed in a pool of liquid under the toilet. The liquid must have contained hormones from your pee which gave me a positive test. I'm not pregnant. So that's why Becker didn't kill me.'

'You must explain that comment later. I'm a little tired for so much excitement today.' 'I have booked a private flight back to Calderon tomorrow,' said Hernan Sanchez. 'I'll get one of my drivers to collect Gloria's car.'

***

Back in San Blas, there was a solemn meeting of the residents, chaired by the Schmidt brothers dressed in black suits and white shirts with fat black ties. The atmosphere in the hall was an interwoven mix of worried muttering and thick cigarette smoke percolating the air. There was blond hair turning grey on heads bowed with age, and many chairs had walking sticks balanced against them or hooked on the back. Franz Schmidt stood up to speak. He grasped the lectern like a drowning man gripping a lifebuoy, his knuckles white.

'By now, most of you will know Boris Klein and Kurt Becker have been found dead in the woods outside of town. We may never know what happened to them although it is rumoured to be connected with the death of my son, Hans. The police have designated it a murder-suicide and we don't want to arouse their suspicions. It would not be wise to pursue it,' he said.

'What will happen to our town?' shouted someone.

'There is no reason to believe we are finished. What is certain is that our community is wounded and will never be the same. I understand some of you plan to move to Argentina but I'll be staying here in San Blas, and I hope many of you will also stay here with me. The war is over. This is my home. I want to live my last years in peace. I have met a woman from Lago Verde and I intend to marry her.'

There was some loud murmuring which he quelled by raising his hand.

'Some of you will object to her ethnicity but I don't care anymore. I think it is time that we woke up and joined the twentieth century. We need more workers to make a success of the village and I propose to go to the mayor of Lago Verde and organise some interviews. Is there anyone who objects?'

No one spoke.

'Okay, I'm going to take that as a yes. We'll have a service on Sunday for Boris and Kurt and I would be grateful if the memorabilia could be discrete as the police may still be here spying on us.'

'Thank you and for the last time, Heil Hitler.'

***

Sam was overwhelmed. She needed a minute to herself, so she left them in Gloria's room and sat in the stairwell. So, she wasn't pregnant. She wasn't clear how she felt except relieved. Thank God. She expelled the air she felt like she had been holding in her lungs for weeks and laughed. That was close. If she ever made up with Simon, she was going to make him wear a condom as well as her taking the pill. No more heart-stopping panics for her.

And would she take him back? She wasn't sure. It wasn't his fault that he panicked when she rang him out of the blue. He would probably be waiting at the airport with flowers, and she did enjoy their reconciliations. She would make him beg, though.

***

The reaction to the article in the Miami Herald was instantaneous. Ramon Vega was famous. They invited him to speak on the important talk shows in America. Larry King Live and CNN news invited him for interviews and they feted him from pillar to post. Women were falling over themselves to help him get over the trauma of his near incineration. He took full advantage of the therapy that they offered, reasoning that one should never look a gift horse in the mouth.

It was exhausting being in the public eye. He flew first class and stayed in the best suites. Money poured into his bank account. Publishing houses begged him to write a book, or several. Nazis were, as Guido Luna had remarked, irresistible copy for journalists. Ramon had always imagined that this was what he wanted but when a woman bribed her way into his hotel room and was lying naked on his bed covered in sushi, he realised that too much of anything is boring. He did eat the sushi, which was lukewarm, and ravish the woman, who was not, but he came to the realisation that he wanted to go home. He rang Alfredo.

'Hello, old friend.'

'Hello, you reprobate. Aren't you supposed to be dead?'

'Reports of my demise were greatly exaggerated.'

'I hear that you're famous.'

'A bit.'

'Where are you now?'

'I'm at the airport.'

'Which airport?'

'Miami. I'm coming home and I thought you might put me up for a while as some bastard burnt my house down.'

'You can live in Gloria's flat for the time being. She's moving in here with me.'

'Wow! Congratulations. Any reason for the hurry?'

'I'm going to be a father.'

'Brilliant! What does Senor Sanchez think?'

'He thinks we'd better get married straight away. And I agree, not that I was given a choice.'

'You're getting hitched? Do I know the best man?'

'I believe he's on his way from Miami. By the way, what time do you arrive?'

***

When she got back to Calderon, there was only one thing on Sam's mind. She rang Hannah.

'Hello, it's me.'

'Oh, hi, Sam. How are you doing? How's Sierramar?'

'Is there someone with you?'

'No, that's the television. I'll turn it down.'

'Since when is the television in your bedroom?'

'I meant the radio. How are you anyway? Any news?'

'I'm not pregnant if that's what you are asking.'

'Oh, thank goodness! You must be relieved.'

'Well, yes, I guess so. The mind plays funny tricks on you. I had my period at last.'

'How is Gloria?'

'Oh, she's pregnant and she's getting married.'

'What? I remember you telling me that she couldn't have children. How did that happen?'

'The doctors don't understand. They say it's a miracle.'

'Who on earth would marry Gloria?'

'Alfredo. He's blissfully happy.'

'You mean drunk, don't you? Wasn't he missing?'

'Not any longer. We found him and he asked Gloria to marry him.'

'Your friends are completely bonkers. Don't stay too long or you will end up like them.'

'The wedding is next week. I'm planning on coming home when they leave on their honeymoon.'

'Oh, great, that will be wonderful.'

'Hey, don't sound so enthusiastic then.'

'No, sorry, I was distracted. That is great news. I'll ring Mum and Dad and tell them.'

'Okay, I gotta go. See you soon.'

'Bye.'

Hannah rolled over in bed to face Simon, who had heard every word and was ashen -faced.

'Oh God, she's coming home.'

Thank you for reading my book. If you enjoyed it, won't you please take a moment to leave me a review at your favourite retailer?

Thank you

The next book in the Series is **The Star of Simbako.**

All books are available in paperback from your favourite retailer

Other Books in the Sam Harris Series

Fool's Gold - Book 1

It's 1987. Newly qualified geologist Sam Harris is a woman in a man's world - overlooked, underpaid but resilient and passionate. Desperate for her first job, and nursing a broken heart, she accepts an offer from a notorious entrepreneur Mike Morton, to search for gold deposits in the remote rainforests of Sierramar. With the help of nutty local heiress, Gloria Sanchez, she soon settles into life in Calderon, the capital. But when she accidentally uncovers a long-lost clue to a treasure buried deep within the jungle, her journey really begins.

Teaming up with geologist Wilson Ortega, historian Alfredo Vargas and the mysterious Don Moises, they venture through the jungle, where she lurches between excitement and insecurity. Yet there is a far graver threat looming; Mike and Gloria discover that one of the members of the expedition is plotting to seize the fortune for himself and is willing to do anything to get it. Can Sam survive and find the treasure or will her first adventure be her last?

The first book in the Sam Harris Series sets the scene for the career of an unwilling heroine, whose bravery and resourcefulness are needed to navigate a series of adventures set in remote sites in Africa and South America. Based on the real-life adventures of the author, the settings and characters are given an authenticity that will connect with readers who enjoy adventure fiction and mysteries set in remote settings with realistic scenarios.

Set in the late 1980s themes such as women working in formerly male domains, and what constitutes a normal existence, are examined and developed in the context of Sam's constant ability to find herself in the middle of an adventure or mystery. Sam's home life provides a contrast to her adventures and feeds her need to escape. Her attachment to an unsuitable boyfriend is the thread running through her romantic life, and her attempts to break free of it provide another side to her character.

The Star of Simbako - Book 3

A fabled diamond, a jealous voodoo priestess, disturbing cultural practices. What could possibly go wrong? The third book in the Sam Harris Series sees Sam Harris on her first contract to West Africa to Simbako, a land of tribal kingdoms and voodoo.

It's 1990. Nursing a broken heart, Sam Harris goes to Simbako to work in the diamond fields of Fona. She is soon involved with a cast of characters who are starring in their own soap opera, a dangerous mix of superstition, cultural practices and ignorance (mostly her own). Add a love triangle and a jealous woman who wants her dead and Sam is in trouble again. Where is the Star of Simbako? Is Sam going to survive the chaos?

This book is based on visits made to the Paramount Chiefdoms of West Africa. Despite being nominally Christian communities, Voodoo practices are still part of daily life out there. This often leads to conflicts of interest. Combine this with the horrific ritual of FGM and it makes for a potent cocktail of conflicting loyalties. Sam is pulled into this life by her friend, Adanna, and soon finds herself involved in goings on that she doesn't understand.

The Pink Elephants - Book 4

It's 1993, Sam gets a call in the middle of the night that takes her to the Masaibu project in Lumbono, Africa. The project is collapsing under the weight of corruption and chicanery engendered by management, both in country and back on the main company board. Sam has to navigate murky waters to get it back on course, not helped by interference from people who want her to fail. When poachers invade the elephant sanctuary next door, her problems multiply. Can Sam protect the elephants and save the project or will she have to choose?

The fourth book in the Sam Harris Series presents Sam with her sternest test yet as she goes to Africa to fix a failing project. The day-to-day problems encountered by Sam in her work are typical of any project manager in the Congo which has been rent apart by warring factions, leaving the local population frightened and rootless. Elephants with pink tusks do exist, but not in the area where the project is based.

The Bonita Protocol - Book 5

It's 1996 and Geologist Sam Harris has been around the block, but she's prone to nostalgia, so she snatches the chance to work in Sierramar, her old stomping ground. But she never expected to be working for a company that is breaking all the rules. When the analysis results from drill samples are suspiciously high, Sam makes a decision that puts her life in peril. Can she blow the lid on the conspiracy before they shut her up for good?

I worked in a very similar project in the early days of my career and the experience is as vivid today as it was to a newly-minted geologist in those days. I have based the stock exchange happenings on the Bre-X scandal which was from a different era but also a key event in my exploration career as work dried up for years afterwards

Digging Deeper - Book 6

A feisty geologist working in the diamond fields of West Africa is kidnapped by rebels. Can she survive the ordeal or will this adventure be her last? It's 1998. Geologist Sam Harris is desperate for money so she takes a job in a tinpot mining company working in war-torn Tamazia. But she never expected to be kidnapped by blood thirsty rebels.

Working in Gemsite was never going to be easy with its culture of misogyny and corruption. Her boss, the notorious Adrian Black is engaged in a game of cat and mouse with the government over taxation. Just when Sam makes a breakthrough, the camp is overrun by rebels and Sam is taken captive.

Will anyone bother to rescue her, and will she still be alive if they do?

You can order these books in paperback at your favourite retailer or on the PJ Skinner Website. Please go to the PJSKINNER website for links.

Connect with the Author

If you would like updates on the latest in the Sam Harris Series or to contact the author with your questions, please go to the following links:

Website: www.pjskinner.com

Facebook: https://www.facebook.com/PJSkinnerAuthor

Twitter: https://twitter.com/PJSkinnerAuthor

About the Author

PJ Skinner is the author of the Sam Harris Series of adventure mystery novels. A geologist who has spent thirty years roaming the planet and collecting tall tales and real-life experiences, she now writes fact-based novels from the relative safety of London. She still travels worldwide collecting material for the series and having her own adventures.

The author is working on the fifth book in the Sam Harris Series, The Bonita Protocol, about gold exploration in South America, which will be published on 1st of July 2019. She is also researching two other new books, one of which, Rebel Green, is being written with the help of a childhood spent in Ireland.

The Sam Harris Series will appeal to lovers of adventure and mystery. It has a unique viewpoint provided by Sam, a female interloper in a male world, as she struggles with alien cultures and failed relationships.

Printed in Great Britain
by Amazon